"What are you doing?"

Lily's palms flattened against his chest. Garrett felt his skin heat under her touch. She'd been the last woman to touch him, that night in the gazebo, and his body remembered the sensation of her hands now. His fingers crept into her soft, smooth hair.

"Thinking about kissing you."

"Just thinking about it?" The admission in that statement cost her; he could tell by the way her shoulders stiffened and her neck went tight. So there was heat under the ice. It was foolish to act on this attraction between them, but right now there was no listening to sense.

Garrett cupped the back of her head in his palm. "Should I be thinking about it?" He tipped his head just right, moved in until her sweet breath touched his lips. "Or acting on it?"

Dear Reader,

As a career emergency medical technician of fourteen years, who is also married to a firefighter, I can tell you that I've had some scary moments on the job. Day after day of helping people through some of their worst life moments gets pretty stressful, and in a way, can make you very afraid of the world around you. In fact, a couple years ago, I reached my tipping point and started to become unusually anxious and afraid of everyday things, like driving to the grocery store, or catching a horrible disease. I was afraid of letting my children out of my sight, because I was so certain that something bad was going to happen.

This type of fear-related stress is not uncommon for emergency workers and firefighters. Hence, in *The Firefighter's Appeal,* our hero, Garrett, is dealing with the very real fear of something bad happening to those he loves.

Luckily, with a bit of rest, relaxation and time away from the job, this problem can be overcome, and for most of us, it is. It's always good to remember the good things in life to balance out the scary parts. The best cure of all? The love of friends and family to pull you through.

I hope you enjoy *The Firefighter's Appeal.*

Elizabeth Otto

ELIZABETH OTTO

—

The Firefighter's Appeal

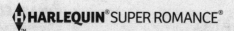

HARLEQUIN® SUPER ROMANCE®

Recycling programs
for this product may
not exist in your area.

ISBN-13: 978-0-373-60867-6

THE FIREFIGHTER'S APPEAL

Printed in U.S.A.

www.Harlequin.com

ABOUT THE AUTHOR

Elizabeth Otto grew up in a Wisconsin town the size of a postage stamp where riding your horse to the grocery store and skinny-dipping after school were perfectly acceptable. No surprise that she writes about small communities and country boys. She's the author of paranormal and hot, emotional, contemporary romance, and has no guilt over frequently making her readers cry. When not writing, she works full-time as an emergency medical technician for a rural ambulance service. Elizabeth lives with her very own country boy and their three children in, shockingly, a small Midwestern town.

To those who run in when everyone else runs out.

To my critique partners and besties who never let me give up and cheer me every step of the way. And to my real life firefighter for the inspiration, and looking good in turnouts.

CHAPTER ONE

"How did you talk me into wearing this?" Lily Ashden pulled at the itchy straps that held her coconut bra in place. Combined with the grass skirt she wore over khaki shorts and the plastic lei around her neck, she was about as novelty Hawaiian as a girl could get. The outfit was considerably skimpier than Lily was accustomed to, and she still wasn't sure how her friend Macy had conned her into it.

Macy snorted. "Please. It matches your tattoo, so stop complaining." Macy leaned over the table, grabbed Lily's right hand and dumped bingo chips into it. "Just put your chip on B 14 and stick your coconuts out. How else do you expect to get men to buy us drinks?"

Lily rolled her eyes with a grin and willed away some of the tension in her shoulders. She'd been a little off since stepping foot in the bar a couple of hours ago. The Throwing Aces was the hottest sports bar in the bustling town of Danbury, Kansas, and though she'd never been in there before, Lily had heard it drew a huge crowd on any given evening. Tonight the bar was hosting a luau-themed fire department–sponsored fundraiser and the place was bursting at the seams with no shortage of good-looking men.

She'd been considering tiptoeing into the dating scene for a while now. What better place than a sports bar with a hot, young crowd? If there was one good thing about the outfit, it was that it drew some attention. She'd seen men glance her way more than once. Still, Lily felt out of her element, but that was to be expected. The past year had been rough. Lily realized that this was a good time to get back to the land of the living. She just hadn't been ready before now.

The bingo announcer yelled out another number. Macy wiggled excitedly on her stool and placed her chip, her corkscrew cinnamon curls doing a bounce and flop around her face. They'd been besties since grade school, and Lily had fully expected Macy to guilt-trip her into coming along tonight. And sure enough, one sob story— "The fire department is raising money for one of my kindergarten students whose dad was in an accident. You're my *best* friend. If you say no, I'll understand, but…"—had done the trick. That and the batting eyelashes and pouty smile that had earned Macy the Kansas Corn Princess crown five years in a row when they were kids.

How could Lily say no to raising money for a worthy cause?

"These coconuts do make my boobs look good." Lily hoped the lightheartedness spreading inside her would stick. The outfit did go well with her full-sleeve tattoo of orange hibiscus flowers and green vines. She rarely had the opportunity to show off her artwork, and it was kind of nice. In a small way, the outfit and being surrounded by men reminded Lily that she was young and feminine and had a lot of living ahead of her yet. Second chances at life and all that. She'd been given one, and she didn't intend to waste it anymore.

A couple of men wearing T-shirts with the Danbury Fire Department logo on the back brushed by. Lily glanced at them, her gaze latching on to the DFD logo. Her heart gave a hard flip, the same way it had the other times she'd seen the logo tonight. The men stopped by a table where two blonde women sat. One of the women gestured to the tallest man's shirt, her smile wide and toothy. He nodded, said a few words, and she responded by giving an appreciative raise of her eyebrows and grabbing his biceps with a squeeze and a giggle.

Hero worship. It wasn't the first time Lily had seen it in action tonight. Firemen drew women like a handbag sale at Nordstrom, and the women in the room didn't seem shy about fawning over the proud wearers of those DFD shirts. Even Macy had fallen victim, flirting and giggling her way through the crowd on the way to the bar and back a couple of times. Lily turned away from the foursome. She didn't get out much, but this was a cozy town. People talked, and they weren't shy about slinging gossip about the local fire department. Mixed in with gratitude for the work the department did were the hushed rumors of several of the firemen's playboy ways. All it took was a trip to the grocery store to hear the latest. It was like Danbury's own live soap opera. Macy had been quick to fill her in when they'd arrived at the bar, sharing the latest gossip about a fireman who'd left his wife of twenty years for one of the teachers at the elementary school.

Heroes with huge egos, it seemed. All this hero worship seemed misplaced and wasted, Lily thought bitterly. She took a hasty drink of water, surprised by that sudden thought, though it made sense. She'd considered how she might feel coming to the bar, knowing the fire department would be there. But she'd reminded herself that this fire department wasn't the same one who'd attended the fire that had changed her life a year ago. No, this wasn't the department that had stood by and done nothing as innocent people burned to death.

Oh, God, she wasn't thinking about that now.

She was here to have fun—she *was* having fun—
and the past was going to stay in the past, at least
for the night. She'd vowed to be present in her
own life, to enjoy life in the moment, and that
was what she was going to do.

"He's looking at you again." Macy's low voice
puffed in Lily's ear.

Lily set down the water as her angst faded.
"Again?" She dared a quick look at the bar across
the room. The lighting was dim, but there was
no doubt the bartender who'd been glancing her
way all night was stellar in the looks department.
At first she'd thought he was just people watching, but his gaze strayed to her too frequently and
held too long. Maybe he thought he knew her.
Maybe it wasn't coincidence—*maybe*. It had been
eleven months since her engagement had ended.
Lily thought she was ready to dive back in, find
a man and have some fun. She hadn't actually
tested that theory yet, so she couldn't be sure. But
the bartender was tempting her to give it a shot.

Lily ran her right hand down the back of her
hair. She hadn't been with anyone since Rob had
packed up and walked out. She didn't miss him
that much, but she was still hurt that he'd left
the way he had—while she'd been at a therapy
appointment and without a word of explanation.
Hearing from his family that he'd gone to Mississippi with another woman soon after was a kick

in the gut. That and the loss of years she'd spent on a man who had promised he'd loved her, was committed, said he wanted a family. The uncertainty over why he'd walked out still burned; it bugged her that she'd never had closure. But she was doing fine on her own. Although it might be nice to have someone around now and then. This loneliness had been nagging her more and more lately. It was definitely time for a change.

Lily risked a sideways glance. Even from this distance and in the dim light, it was obvious Mr. Hot Bartender was built, with muscles easily visible beneath his shirt. His biceps turned into bulging hills when he grabbed a glass and brought it close to his body. His hair looked dark blond under the lights, and, if she had to guess, that rugged face probably sported blue eyes. No wonder there'd been a lineup of women at his end of the bar. He made looking flattered an art form, flashing a killer smile and dipping his head when a woman leaned in close or touched his arm. You'd need a thick coat of armor to push your way through that crowd.

Lily hitched a brow as she watched him—*looks like Thor and probably throws a mean cocktail*—and wished she could see his face more clearly. An ember of interest started to smolder. Her nights might get a whole lot less lonely if she had a man like that around. As if she'd have the nerve to approach him. Cheesy pickup lines began to play in her head. *Did they teach you to mix drinks in Adonis school, or are you naturally talented?* She laughed at herself and turned back to the bingo game. Yeah, she was a little rusty.

The band started up again, taking over from the crappy music on the jukebox, and burst out a song about a man who loved his red Solo Cup. Macy and half the people in the bar, who were really just rednecks stuffed into Hawaiian outfits and fire department shirts, jumped from their seats and gave a cheer. Lily remained in her seat, watching the crowd. Truthfully, it was nice to get out of the house and forget about the pile of city permits and construction bids she had waiting on her desk. Her social life consisted of arguing with her business partner and father, Doug, during the day, and talking to her cat, Adam, at night.

Pretty pathetic for a twenty-seven-year-old.

Macy sat back down. She made eyes at Lily, cleared her throat and nodded toward the bar. The hot bartender was giving her another glance. He didn't look away when she looked at him— seemed to almost be daring her with his eyes. She made out his crooked smile—sexy and sassy— aimed right at her, before he turned to talk to a customer.

"He's pretty good-looking, huh?" Macy smiled

knowingly and ran a hand down the back of Lily's hair.

"Not bad." Lily shrugged.

"Man, your hair rocks. It's so smooth and *black*." Macy continued to pet her.

Lily blew a stream of air over her fringe bangs. She'd just had them cut long enough to touch the tips of her eyelashes, and the blue-black color had been too awesome to resist. It went well with the crimson lip gloss she'd slicked on earlier. Nothing went with bitching black hair like red lipstick.

"If you keep petting me, he's going to think we're a couple." Her eyes slid to the bar. Anxiety and sweet anticipation tickled her insides.

Macy smacked her lips. "If he's like most men, and I'd bet money he is, he wouldn't mind one bit." She nudged Lily with her shoulder. "You've been eyeballing him since you got here."

The bingo announcer called out another number. Lily's face went hot. She sighed and picked at her fingernail. She wasn't sure if she was trying to put Macy off or drum up the courage to catch the bartender's eyes. "Kind of hard not to."

Macy leaned on her elbows over the small round table until her nose touched the tip of Lily's. "And?"

Lily placed one finger on the tip of Macy's nose and pushed gently until her friend backed up. "And what?" Macy's eyebrows rose excitedly.

4

Lily shook her head. "And, no. I'm not going over there. Too much, too soon."

The protest sounded lame even to her own ears. Was there a store where she could buy extra nerves to maybe—*maybe*—walk up to him? Lily knew her retro pinup style and tattoos gave most people the impression that she was a badass, but underneath the ink and lipstick, she was reserved. Cool, even, mostly to her disadvantage.

The stress she'd been under these past months didn't help; in fact, they'd kept her from finding any real joy in life, or any reason to actively participate in it. No wonder she felt antsy and ready for something fun and amazing to happen. No wonder she also wanted to run out of the bar and head straight home. Part of her suddenly wished she and Macy were in another bar, one that wasn't filled with reminders of why she'd been under so much stress and grief in the first place.

The announcer's voice boomed through the mic. "B 12."

Lily grabbed a chip; Macy smirked. "Look at him again. How can you say too much, too soon?"

He was facing the bar, giving Lily a perfect view of all six-plus feet of him looking fine in a dark T-shirt with Throwing Aces in white lettering across the front. The way the fabric stretched just a bit over his tight middle and settled into the dips and rise of his pecs whenever he turned or twisted was a gift to every woman in the room. Excitement shot low in her belly. Lily frowned at her body's sudden reaction. That hadn't happened in a while.

"Of all the women here tonight, he's been eye locked on you, and you're overthinking again. Remember what you said? Be present." Macy gave a lazy eye roll and slumped her shoulders in dramatic exasperation. Her curls made a Shirley Temple bounce as she leaned back on her stool. "I have three words for you, Lily. *Crazy. Cat. Lady.* That's what you're turning into."

Lily's lips parted. She tried a little lightness, hoping to tame Macy's enthusiasm before it turned into an atom bomb, as usual. "Adam is not a cat. He's people."

Macy managed to raise a brow and scowl at the same time. "Your Adam Levine fangirling is not a suitable replacement for a real man, Lily. Crazy cat ladies usually *don't* have a man around, which is why they name their cats after celebrity men they'll never have."

Lily laughed. "I have one cat!"

Macy shrugged one petite shoulder and thrust out her lower lip as she fiddled with her bingo board. "That's how it starts, Lily. That's how it starts."

Lily was about to throw in a snarky retort

when someone bumped into her shoulder. She looked over as a tall man in a DFD T-shirt made a quick apology as he walked away. Lily shuddered. The man maneuvered through the crowd until he was out of sight. *Firemen.* The last time Lily had been surrounded by this many firemen, she'd been lying on the ground with soot burning her lungs and throat.

"Hey, you missed the number." Macy leaned over and slid a chip onto Lily's board, but Lily wasn't paying attention. She eyed another fireman. Same shirt. Same memory. Anxiety clenched her gut with a painful grip. Dang, this wasn't supposed to happen. There was no reason for this to be happening. She'd gone to therapy, and even though she refused to go into detail about that night, Lily had made progress. Just the fact that she'd finally left her house to go somewhere other than work or the grocery store was huge.

Macy's voice dipped low. "I'm sorry, Lil. I shouldn't have asked you to come to this tonight. I just thought…maybe some of the wind had run out of that storm, you know?"

Lily's stomach went into free fall. This was the last thing she wanted to talk about. She was doing well—was reining in her anxiety like a champ, thank you.

"I mean," Macy continued just audibly above

the racket, "this fire department wasn't even the one who…you know…that night."

Lily knew that, but it didn't take the bitterness away. It didn't matter what fire department had been present the night her sister had burned to death and Lily had been nearly killed. Firefighters were firefighters—they all represented the crew that failed her so spectacularly. Combined with how unabashedly members of the Danbury crew flaunted their womanizing, it was hard for her to see firemen in the positive light everyone else seemed to. Knowing Macy, her friend would leave the moment Lily asked her to. But Macy was having a good time, and Lily didn't want to ruin that. Macy was the only person who stood by her through thick and thin, and Lily owed her. Besides, this was silly. *She could do this.* They were men…just men. A guy didn't have to be a fireman to be a womanizer—Rob had proved that. There had to be at least a few good ones around this town.

Lily smiled, and her lips parted to give a reassuring reply when something hit Macy in the back of the head. A roar of excited laughter went through the room. Lily's gaze snapped back to the bar, saw the barrel of a T-shirt cannon pointed her way. All three bartenders had them and, instead of shirts, they were shooting small packages around the room. People started to jump up to catch the prizes, making mad dashes across the floor and over tables to grab handfuls. Lily frowned. What the hell was in those packages?

The hot bartender aimed one her way, a big smile crossing his face as a packet hit her in the side of the head before plopping onto the bingo board. Lily cupped her head in astonishment, her eyes falling to the item that had hit her. Candy.

Macy snorted. "Damn, Lily. That was either a challenge or an invitation. Probably both, you lucky bitch."

Lily palmed the package, then shrieked when another pinged painlessly off the top of her head. She looked; the bartender was staring at her, the I-dare-you smile too much to resist. The crowd of women by the bar had thinned, giving her an easy path. Could she do it? Even if she made a fool of herself—which was pretty much a given—it wasn't like she'd be back at this bar. She'd never see him again.

Lily pushed away from the table. Before the fire, she'd just started becoming more social and outgoing. An introvert by nature, she found it terrifying and often exhausting to plop herself in social situations, but she'd been trying. Macy was always a ray of light and energy, everything Lily wasn't, and Lily had craved some of that for herself.

So she'd been forcing herself go to friends'

houses for dinner parties or to the movies by herself. Instead of rushing through shopping trips as quickly as possible, she'd made herself slow down and browse—take some time to enjoy her surroundings. And it had been working until the fire. Afterward, she'd holed up in her own little world again, blocking out everyone but her father, brother and Macy.

She really missed those little peeks of the extrovert she'd experienced before. Risk or not, she owed it to herself to try to find her backbone again. The bartender turned away from the crowd, giving Lily a boost in the nerves department. He wouldn't see her walk up to him, making it a little easier to approach—or make a detour and go back to the table if she chickened out. She stood before she could talk herself out of it.

"I'll play your board while you're—whatever. Okay," Macy shouted as Lily walked away. Lily smoothed her hair as she pushed through the crowd. Three steps in, she had to fight the urge to run back to her secluded table in the corner. Lifting her chin, Lily made it to the bar, but a row of people waiting for drinks separated her from the cocky smile she wanted to see up close. She moved down until she found an opening and squeezed up to the bar. The bartenders bustled around. The air cannons had been put away in exchange for bottles of booze.

"Can I help you?" A tall, lean man with glossy dark hair grabbed a glass from the overhead rack. His eyes flashed with good humor and a dimple appeared in his left cheek when he smiled. She glanced around him, latching on to the man she'd come to see.

"Ah," the bartender said with an amused smile. "Hey, September! You have company."

September? Lily mulled that over, observing the decor behind the bar in an attempt to settle her nerves. Old license plates, sports memorabilia and beer signs were artfully arranged in between chalkboards full of menu items and fantasy football scores. A glass display case sitting on a shelf caught her attention. It took her a moment to realize a firefighting helmet sat inside. She cocked her head, noticing how the front of the helmet looked normal but the back was a lump of what looked like melted plastic. Must be a prop of some kind, because fire helmets weren't supposed to melt, right? The men were covered head to toe in gear that could withstand flame and heat—gear that allowed them inside the chaos to rescue the people trapped inside.

Lily clenched her jaw. *Damn. It.*

Suddenly, cold liquid spilled over the curve of her lower back as someone rammed into her.

Lily yelped and spun to see a very drunk man stumbling away with an empty plastic cup. Her arms went wide, chills racing down her spine and curving around her hip bones.

"Here," a deep voice called to her. Lily turned around and glimpsed a fluffy white towel sliding across the mahogany bar top toward her. Her eyes tracked up from a broad chest to the face she'd wanted to see up close. Narrow blue eyes, framed by eyelashes so dark they made the blue brilliant. They were the kind of eyes that would glow seductively in a black-and-white photo, grab you by the ovaries and never let go. Square jaw, round chin…lips full enough to be soft, with a firm outline that promised they could also bruise.

Lily took the towel with a shaking hand. He was definitely as good-looking as she'd suspected. Her heart pumped. Smiling was probably a good idea. Lily gave a little grin—at least she hoped that was what it looked like because her cheeks were tight and hot.

"Thanks," she managed to say, wiping the liquid off her back. Unsure what to say next, Lily dropped her gaze to the bingo board lying on the bar. Talking would probably be good, too. "Four corners—you won…" When was the last time her face had been this hot? Her scalp tingled; her gut tightened. Bingo talk was good, right, when her brain was otherwise at a loss?

The bartender chuckled softly, a deep sound that was somehow soothing. "Yeah." He nodded to the board. "What do you think we should win?" *We?* His blue eyes were twinkling, and the way he leaned one elbow on the bar, his chest turned toward her, made it clear that he was flirting.

Lily propped her right arm on the bar. "Well, considering I had to wear this getup, a trip somewhere warm and exotic would be nice." She let out a tiny relieved breath. This talking thing wasn't so hard.

He set both forearms on the bar and gave her a quirky, self-confident smile that threatened to set her panties on fire. "Considering I was born and raised in Hawaii, I can't argue with that." He winked and backed off, leaving her mouth dry and her chest breathless. Before she could think of an appropriate response, he cocked his head.

"Beer?" His mouth opened to let the word out…closed again—the tip of his tongue peeking out to wet the lower lip. Lily's heart rate jacked up. He leaned closer. The stubble over his jaw and down the sexy column of his throat made her itch to touch it. She swallowed hard, realized he'd spoken.

"No. No, I don't drink." She leaned back an extra inch from the bar. "Water, please." He was already reaching under the bar and then produced a cold water bottle, cracked the top and set the bottle in front of her. Lily hesitated before taking it, pretty sure she was going to have to dump it over her head to cool herself down. Irritated by how flustered she was, Lily took a drink. The water was shocking to her parched throat. The bartender took a swig from a beer bottle and set it down, then extended a hand. Lily hesitated before shaking it.

"Garrett."

"Lily."

He gave a brief nod and turned to fill a glass for a waiting patron. A man in a fire department T-shirt slipped behind the bar, looked at Lily and put a finger to his lips as if to silence her. He opened a small refrigerator behind Garrett and took out two beers. Garrett spun around just as the man pulled the beers to his chest like a football and scurried out, dancing through the crowd.

Garrett cupped his hands around his mouth. "That calls for revenge, Mikey!" He turned back to her, his grin scrunching the outside corners of his eyes. His smile wrenched the breath out of her like a cold wind. The tension in her body let go. He was really too good-looking to be out in public.

A waft of perfume rippled by Lily as two blondes with pink-painted smiles shimmied up to the bar, eyes zoned in on Garrett. He gave them a nod, waved another bartender over to assist them as he leaned against the bar in front of Lily again. A flood of warmth pooled in her chest and spread down her arms. She couldn't remember the last time she'd had a man's full attention on her and it was terrifying…and kind of wonderful.

She leaned against the bar. "So why did you hit me in the head?"

His eyebrows raised and his smug expression deepened. "Did I? I'm sorry."

Her eyes fell to the thick, strong lines of his neck, and she could feel her nipples perk up inside the bra. Lily resisted the urge to cross her arms over her chest. Thank goodness the bra was hard, so he couldn't see how her body was reacting. She huffed with a grin. "No, you're not."

Garrett leaned a little closer toward her. "Okay, Lily. Truth?"

One corner of her mouth tugged up. "Yeah, truth."

Garrett reached out and touched her shoulder. Before she could object, his fingers wrapped around her upper arm and drew her closer over the bar. Shivers of pleasure dotted her skin, followed by hot streaks when his fingers ran down the length of her tattoo.

"I wanted to see your ink. Since I can't leave here, I figured I'd get you to come to me."

She shrugged off the lightness that admission

gave her. The sensation of his warm fingers trailing along the big white-and-orange flowers on her shoulder and down to her wrist caused a fog machine to open up in her head. Slowly, his index finger outlined the arch and curve of the hunter-green leaves and lighter kelly-green vines that swirled throughout the artwork.

Lily drank in his appreciative expression as she cataloged the handsome lines of his round chin and the firm, masculine outline of his soft, full lips. She found herself leaning into the press of his hand, just as his fingers trailed away. Little wonder she was tingling from head to toe—it was the first time she'd been touched by a man in almost a year.

And her ex had nothing on Garrett.

"Beautiful work."

She took a drink, immediately missing the feel of his hand on her, but hating how weak her legs were just then. With one touch, he'd thrown her into a fun house with a crooked floor.

"Thank you. Do you have any?"

A shout came from the other end of the bar; Garrett grabbed a bottle from the fridge behind him and tossed it to someone Lily couldn't see. He turned back to her with a shake of his head. "Nah. I, uh…well, it's probably a strike to my manhood to admit, but I have a *thing* about needles."

She snickered despite herself. "You're what? Six-two—"

"Six one and a half, thank you." He took a swig from his beer around a chuckle. "I know, I know. Someone like me, scared of needles. It's sacrilegious." His voice was deep with a resonance that shivered through every nerve in her body. "Since we're being truthful here, you should also know that I'm…" He looked around as if to see if anyone would overhear before locking his gaze on hers. "I'm also deathly afraid of spiders."

She feigned horror. "No!"

He wagged his eyebrows, a move that was equally boyish and sexy, drawing yet another chuckle from her. Lily's own brows came together with the realization that she was completely at ease. Sounds from the bar rushed in her ears— foreign and sudden, as if she'd blocked out the noise. Before she could ponder that, his fingers traced along her collarbone to the tie around her neck holding the coconut bra in place.

"As a native Hawaiian, it's my sworn responsibility to tell you that I approve of your coconuts." The pads of his fingers were rough, as if they'd known countless hours of manual labor and rowdy play. Lily's skin heated under the gentle scrape of his touch along her neck, her knees threatening to give out altogether. Lily gripped the bar; Garrett's hand sank beneath the shade of her hair, following the string to where the ends were tied. It would only take one quick pull—just one—and he'd have the strings free.

Her chest squeezed at the intimate, familiar way he touched her. She should have been indignant, not turned on and mesmerized by the hard and soft pressure of his fingers retreating along the path they'd come. Garrett's hand fell away, but his gaze felt like a caress over her cheek. His voice was low, with a tinge of husky amusement. "So what flavors did you get?"

Her middle quivered as if she were about to perform improv in front of all these strangers. "Flavors?"

Garrett reached under the bar for a large plastic container. "The candy." He produced a handful of packets, throwing them down on the bar. "Root beer. Orange dreamsicle. Berry." He flipped one over. "Black licorice." His smile fell at the same time she made a disgusted face.

She shuddered, a move that seemed to shake off most of the effect of his unexpected—if not welcome—touch. "Throw that away." She laughed.

"Agreed." Garrett tossed it in a trash can behind him. "So?" His eyes narrowed a bit, his head cocking slightly as if he was studying her. She reached between the faux grass of her skirt to the pocket of the khaki shorts she wore underneath and grabbed the packet.

"Oh, this? Orange dreamsicle." Her brain started a little happy dance. It felt good to flirt with him, and, amazingly, her tongue-brain connection was working like a charm at the moment.

Garrett's eyes tracked her movements. "Hmm, do you like that flavor?"

Lily shrugged, drawn in by the heat of his gaze. His pecs bunched close together as he shifted. She had to look; trying not to look at him was like trying to stop the earth's rotation. "Yes."

She'd flirted before, of course. But never with quite this much sexual undertone. Mostly, she had no idea how to respond, though her inner wildcat was trying her damnedest to play this game. It was fun and made her feel feminine and aware, for the first time in too long, that she was young and single.

Garrett slid a hand over to hers, his fingers briefly grazing over her knuckles. "In that case, you know where to come if you want more."

Lily was halfway to taking a drink and nearly spilled the bottle at the grainy sound of his words. Tongue-brain connection lost.

Garrett moved back to help someone while Lily took a deep breath. The clink of bottles and glasses surrounded her; the low tone of Garrett's voice washed over her as he spoke to a customer. He was quick to mix up a couple of drinks, flashing just the right amount of smile and charm as he interacted with a woman next to her. Lily did a double take to her left. A line of women had formed next to her, all glancing hopefully—excitedly—at Garrett. He'd ignored one woman in order to talk to Lily, but this line was too long and estrogen fueled to be defeated.

This was probably her cue that the fun was over. And it had been fun, and freeing and exciting and just the tiptoe back into a male-filled world she'd been hoping for. She turned to leave.

"Don't go."

Lily glanced back to see him holding up one finger in her direction, bidding her to wait as he set the last drink on the counter.

"You're busy," she said. It was true, but she didn't really want to go. Still, being in the way wasn't going to do either of them much good. Garrett's attention was a balm for her ego, no doubt. Especially with the tension that had crept in earlier to eat up her fun.

He sauntered back over, pulled a bar towel from his shoulder and looped it around her upper arm, holding her steady. The sincerity in his eyes was way more than she was prepared for. Garrett gave the towel a gentle tug, making her body lean against the bar and bringing his mouth inches from her ear.

"Not too busy for you."

CHAPTER TWO

GARRETT HAD BEEN in center of a raging house fire yesterday, and yet the adrenaline rush he'd felt fighting that flame didn't compare a lick to the one Lily was giving him.

He'd seen her the minute she'd swayed into his bar a couple of hours ago; he'd had a hell of a time keeping his eyes off her so he'd quit trying. In a sea of stick-thin, cookie-cutter blondes, this tattooed beauty was a midnight dream come to life. She was tall and curvy, and the coconut bra she wore did little to hide the round sides of her breasts. The tie around her back was fashioned into a bow that accentuated smooth muscles and supple skin. A faux-grass skirt hung low on the curves of her hips—full hips that embraced a smooth, soft belly. He loved that she didn't try to cover up her curves. The colorful tattoo sleeve, stick-straight, long black hair and red lipstick she wore only kicked his interest into overdrive.

He hadn't been this attracted to a woman in a long time. Usually the women he flirted with, and ultimately took home, offered the bare minimum of emotional connection. He was all right with that, and, though he was always a gentleman, he tended to seek out women who were single-mindedly interested in the same thing he was: sex without commitment.

He'd been in a bit of a dry spell lately, though. The work it took to flirt and woo his way through the bar scene to find a suitable woman was getting old. Flat. Boring. He kept telling himself it was okay to step back from the dating scene. But as the weeks of lonely nights and an empty bed went by, he wasn't sure he knew what he was holding out for anymore.

Lily had just dumped an ocean all over his dry spell. She wasn't his normal type, but she had *fun* written all over her. Looking at the crystal lights shimmering over Lily's hair and the lushness of her body in that Hawaiian outfit made his libido adamantly agree. But long-term? Hell, no. Marriage led to kids, a house, a dog and all that jazz. All the things that could go up in flames in the blink of an eye. No way. He'd settle for a dry spell rather than let his heart take in too much, only to lose everything.

He'd been down that road too many times now, watching people he cared about suffer tragedy. Bad things happened to good people, wasn't that the saying? Being a fireman, he saw it all the time, even among his own men. Divorce, deaths, affairs, accidents—all the things that jacked up the cost of love. No one was immune when fate decided to play a dark game.

Lily's eyelashes fluttered, and her scarlet-red lips parted slightly. Garrett recognized her sensuality but had a pretty good inkling that she was completely unaware of how siren-like she was—and that she probably intimidated the hell out of the male population in general. She gave off a type of Brigitte Bardot pinup allure with a hard Jillian Michaels edge. Yet, when he'd made her laugh, Lily had looked genuinely surprised—she craved the attention, though outwardly, she tried not to show it.

Women like that—the ones who wanted you to notice them but didn't always want you to know—meant he'd had to work harder to get what he wanted. And he'd never been one to back down from a challenge.

Before he could speak, a shout burst through the room. "Bingo!" A petite woman with bouncy cinnamon curls stood on a stool, shaking her plastic coconut-covered chest with her fists in the air. A collective cheer roared through the room. The woman spotted Lily, pointed at her and damn near bounced right off her stool.

"It's her board. She won!"

Lily put her hands out quizzically. The woman

cupped her hands around her mouth and yelled, "You won the grand prize!"

Well, wasn't that just his luck? Garrett ran a hand over his belly, pleased with this turn of events. He recognized Pete Ambrose, sporting a fire department T-shirt and a smile, as he approached Lily and patted her on the shoulder. Lily spun so her back was to him, and though Garrett couldn't see her expression, he could see that every muscle in her back tensed.

"Congratulations." Pete's deep baritone was loud in the sudden hush of the room. "What's your name?"

Lily didn't reply immediately. Garrett saw Pete's brows drop a little.

"Lily," she said flatly.

Garrett filled a couple of drink orders, still watching Lily from the corner of his eye. From somewhere in the back of the room, a female voice shouted, "Yeah, Lily!"

Pete gave a toothy smile as a camera flashed. "The grand prize includes movie tickets and dinner reservations at Chalet de Blume—and your escort? Did you see the fire department calendar that went out this year? You'll be going with Mr. September." Pete winked and gestured to Garrett.

Lily turned and looked blankly at the bar. If she realized Pete was talking about Garrett, she didn't acknowledge it in any way. Instead, her forehead wrinkled as if she was remembering something or thinking way too hard. Garrett stopped filling glasses as he tried to read Lily's reaction. Most women would be bouncing up and down at the news. Not that he was conceited or anything, but Garrett knew he had a certain effect on women. His pose for the calendar hadn't hurt.

Lily shook her head, cutting Pete off and causing the already quiet crowd to hush even more.

"A date with a fireman?" Her voice was uncertain, her expression dropping into a scowl. She almost looked disgusted. Pete nodded, looking just as confused as Garrett felt.

"No, thank you." Lily pushed away from the bar and squeezed her body between Pete and the crowd. Almost instantly, the curly-haired woman was at her side, grabbing Lily's hand. Their heads leaned low together as they walked to their table. Prickles nagged at the back of Garrett's neck. Her sudden mood change seemed to have left a tangible chill in the air.

Something had set Lily off, and though he really shouldn't waste time worrying about what it was, he did.

Was it possible that she didn't know he was Mr. September? It wasn't a secret—anyone who saw the calendar and came to the bar knew it. But she'd said she wasn't a drinker, so maybe she hadn't seen it, hadn't put the pieces together.

He wasn't ashamed of his sexy no-shirt-pose-against-the-fire-truck picture—hell, it helped sell thousands of calendars across the county. The fire department needed that money, and he was glad to do his part. He was the assistant chief of the department, and, as such, had been roped into being part of the grand prize if the winner was a woman. Take her to dinner and a movie for a good cause. Lily, apparently, hadn't liked that idea. It felt like a flat-out rejection, though a part of him said there was more to it than that. After all, she'd seemed to like him well enough at the bar.

Rejection wasn't something Garrett took lying down. He liked the way she moved, the way she looked, and, after talking to her, he didn't want to give up without at least finding out why she was rejecting the prize. When she slung a purse over her shoulder and hugged her friend, Garrett knew he had to make a decision. He spotted his best friend, Mikey, out in the crowd, cupped his hands around his mouth and yelled his name.

"Fill in for me. You've done it before," Garrett said when Mikey came around. Before his friend could protest, Garrett set a bar towel on Mikey's shoulder. "You owe me for grand theft Budweiser."

Mikey ran a hand through his too-long brown hair. "Dammit."

There were perks to owning the bar, like leaving whenever he wanted to chase a beautiful woman. Because he was pretty sure how this night would end if he could rekindle the spark he and Lily had had earlier—with some hot vertical dancing in his bed. Though he'd settle for a kiss, because those cherry-red lips had been taunting him all night. Lily was the first woman in a long time to make him want to put his dry spell out to pasture, and she'd been interested, too. He'd read that much like an open book.

Garrett pushed through the crowd as Lily disappeared out the side door. The street was deserted, one lone light pole flickering overhead. She'd just reached the sidewalk along the side of the bar when he caught up with her.

"Lily!"

She spun, surprise marking her face. Humidity settled over Garrett's skin with wet hands as a crack of heat lightning flashed in the air. He looked up into a murky night sky and realized for the first time that it was sprinkling.

Lily didn't speak as he approached; her hand clutched the strap of a small purse.

"You left before I could get your number." He started to relax, then immediately cursed himself. Where had that come from? He never asked for numbers because he didn't have to; women always beat him to it. The bucket under the bar filled with slips of paper and business cards with women's names and numbers on them was proof of that.

The corners of her eyes crinkled as the wariness on her face deepened. "You—want my number?"

Garrett chuckled with a quick glance to the ground. "Thought I made that pretty obvious."

Lily ran a finger through her hair before continuing on. Garrett fell into step beside her, hands in his front pockets. She gave him a sideways look, and another crack of lightning gave him a clear view of the shy smile on her lips.

They passed by the empty lot directly behind the Throwing Aces, the for-sale sign mocking him as they walked. He'd been after that lot for months, but the seller wouldn't agree to his terms. He brushed off the thought as a waft of Lily's perfume tickled his nose. They reached the line of trees that separated the empty lot from a competing bar. A small gazebo sat at the edge of the empty lot near the sidewalk and butted up against the trees.

Without overthinking it, Garrett gently grabbed Lily's arm and pulled her onto the grass with him. Music from the hidden bar drifted out into the night, highlighting Lily's light gasp as he tugged her close.

She came willingly, giving him the courage

to just go with it. If she'd tensed at all, he would have backed away, but as Lily pressed against him, Garrett reveled in the fact that she was right where she wanted to be. He wanted to ask what had happened in the bar, but any questions he had flew away.

Garrett tried to hold back the deep groan that welled in his throat as he felt her soft body against him. Her perfume saturated the air and drew him in. His right arm looped around the luscious curve of her back and settled just above the rise of her ass. Maybe her chest was going faster—maybe it was his—but when he held her tighter, their breathing synchronized and their chests rose and fell together.

Yeah, he'd missed this.

Lily's arm curved around his upper arm, her palm flattening against his shoulder blade. Her chin tipped up, her lips parted in a mix of surprise and something deeper—something that looked a hell of a lot like restrained want.

Garrett's throat went dry. He could kiss her. Grab her chin and pull her lips to his. The music trickled into his consciousness, reawaking his plan to steal a bit more of her time. He wanted it—needed it—and he'd hold as many minutes as she'd give him. But he didn't want to scare her off by being too forward. This was silly, but he was going with it. Anything to prolong their moments together.

"Dance with me, Lily." She chuckled softly as he began to move her in a slow circle to the sound of the filtered music. Her hips swayed just slightly, her footsteps a little hesitant. He began a slow caress along her lower back, his fingers gently raking back and forth over her warm, silky skin. "It's not fair, you know."

Goose bumps rose on her skin. "What's not fair?"

Garrett dipped her over his arm, reveling in the sound of her surprised laugh. He brought her back up so fast, her hair whipped across his chest. "You know my weaknesses and I know nothing about yours."

"I call that ammunition."

His turn to laugh. If he wasn't mistaken, her cheeks flamed in a blush. It might have been the lighting from the streetlight, but he doubted it.

"Nice." He gave Lily a spin. "No holding out now." Garrett pulled her tight against him, his lips close to her ear. "Tell me one thing."

A hum came from deep in her throat with a resonance that made his heart flutter. "I, ah… have a cabinet full of marshmallows?"

"Marshmallows?" Garrett spun her again to keep from kissing her hard and full the way he wanted. The ground was springy and soft under his feet. The scent of the damp earth and impending rain cast seductive notes in the air. Her palm met his chest, fingers clutching his shirt. "Stress food."

He nodded in understanding. "Peanut butter and jelly. On toast. With an extra piece of bread in the middle. Another weakness."

Lily made a noncommittal sound, her eyes locked on his mouth, fingers tightening with just enough pressure that her short nails dug harmlessly into his skin through the fabric of his shirt.

"Seems I've developed one more, though..." Garrett smoothed hair from her face, taking time to trace along the beautiful curve of her cheekbone, down alongside her ear to her neck. She shivered as he moved slowly to the rise of her collarbone. Oh, yeah, she was feeling him. She was into this.

"Black hair. Bright red lips. Pretty tattoos."

"Oh," she whispered, tilting her head for him to lean down and take her mouth. Garrett stepped closer to her, his hand reaching for her chin, when the sky suddenly let loose, dumping a torrent of rain straight down.

Lily's eyes went wide. Garrett shrugged off the shock of the rain, cupped Lily's face in his palms and pulled her fully against him. He half expected her to protest or struggle against the rain, but she sank into him, her right hand grabbing his wrist.

Her lips parted just enough to leave no doubt.

Lightning cracked in a brilliant line behind them, making them both jump. Cursing the weather, Garrett grabbed Lily's hand and pulled her to the gazebo. He should have been praising the rain, truth be told, because it was giving him an opportunity to stop this now, take a step back. He had more fire in his blood than he could ever remember having before—and that was saying something, considering the beautiful women he saw at the bar nearly every night.

He raked his fingers through his bangs, spinning to sit on the single bench in the middle of the gazebo. Lily was laughing, and the sound cut off in a heady gasp when he pulled her to sit across his lap.

It didn't matter if her kisses were random and meaningless. It didn't matter that she probably wouldn't wake up in his bed in the morning, despite his willingness to give it a go. He wanted her anyway, and no amount of rain was going to cool that burn. Even if it was just a taste.

Her bottom was seated firmly against his thighs. Water ran in silvery streaks down her jet-black hair, dotting his jeans and soaking through the fabric in cool bursts. Garrett cupped her lower back, reveled in the shiver that coursed through her. She was sweet under that tough exterior and reserved demeanor. Maybe that was what drew him in—the mixture of all the things she was. He stared at her for several beats, only breaking his gaze to blink raindrops away from his lashes. His arms tightened around her—damn, she felt good—every muscle in his chest and neck tightening.

"I'm going to kiss you," he growled. Tantalizing him, thwarting him, Lily leaned closer and put her lips next to his jaw. His senses flared to life.

"I thought you wanted my phone number," she replied, her fingers kneading the nape of his neck. Garrett trembled. The rain beat down harder. Lily's lips pressed into the sensitive skin just beneath his ear. Garrett clenched his eyes, trying to stomp down an insistent burning flare of desire.

"I do."

She pulled back to look at him. Rivulets ran over her high cheekbones, a stray drop curving over her lower lip. Lily licked it off with a slow slide of her tongue. "Then you'll have to work for it."

LILY HAD NO idea where this brazen streak had come from, but she couldn't bring herself to resist it. She hadn't planned this by any stretch of the imagination when she'd first approached Garrett. Okay, maybe she'd had a stray thought or ten about what it would be like to take him to bed, but it had been fantasy. A nice thought—one that wouldn't come to fruition.

But now it was a possibility, and even as Lily considered the "should she or shouldn't she" debate, her body was pulling for should. Definitely should. It had been a long time, and Garrett made it so easy to give in. Plus it might help erase the anxiety that had burst open with learning she'd won that stupid prize. A date with a fireman? Nothing like coming face-to-face with the horror of her past. No, firemen were off-limits. And she wanted to forget....

Garrett was sexy and funny. For the first time in a long time, she felt empowered with an attractive man. He was interested. Despite her initial reluctance, she was interested, too. More than. Especially now that she was out of the firemen-infested bar.

Still, her lack of normal restraint was so foreign, it left her unsure of what to do next. She'd take a few hot kisses. And if that was all that happened, she'd rejoice in it. And if there was the possibility for more... She'd never had a one-night stand, never hooked up with a man she didn't intend to have a relationship with. That wasn't her style.

Just go with it. Lily took a shaky breath and lightly pressed her lips to Garrett's neck. Rough stubble met her touch just below his jaw. His skin was cool from the rain, but hot when she pressed a little harder. His face tilted up just a bit, granting her access, his hands cupping her rib cage and pulling her closer. The cold plastic grass of her skirt became a tangled mess as she straddled his thighs.

Heart pounding, Lily clamped his earlobe between her teeth and gave two soft nibbles. The sudden rise of his chest and stall of his breath made her heart soar. She ran her fingertips down his neck, paused at the collar of his shirt where the fabric was warm from his body and wet from the rain. The hardness of his back muscles made her fingers tingle. Garrett let out a slow breath. It flamed Lily's boldness. She pulled away to look up at him, trailed her hand from his back, over the round perfection of his shoulder, up the smooth length of his neck to cup his jaw.

Garrett's hand went to her hair, his mouth slanting across hers in a swoop that left her dizzy. His firm lips turned soft as he encouraged her mouth with a dance of open kisses and soft, closed caresses. A tug at the back of her scalp flittered into pleasurable little zings as she realized he'd fisted a handful of her hair. Lily gasped at the thrill, becoming aware for the first time that she was clinging to him.

Clinging. And she didn't want to let go. Garrett groaned deeply. She wanted to pull him closer until he wrapped himself around her, claiming her and flooding her with his heat. Desire wasn't letting her talk herself out of this, and Lily was glad about that. She wanted him. He was hot and delicious, and she was taking this chance. She deserved it.

She slid forward until her center was aligned with the hard ridge of his erection. She nearly moaned at the long, thick feel of him. Garrett jerked, gripping her hips as he shifted and pressed himself up against her. His lips trailed over the bare skin of her shoulder.

She needed a lighthouse for the fog in her head. The feel of his hardness right there—where she wanted him the most—was sweet in its newness and achingly raw in its demand. So much time had passed since she'd last been held. Too many times she figured she'd never have those things again.

His palms traced her ribs, dipped into the curve of her waist and over the flare of her hips. The plastic fringe of her skirt rustled with his touch. He spoke low in her ear; his gravelly voice sent heat straight between her thighs.

"You feel so good." He grasped her chin and

turned her head for a deep, aching kiss. Her mind was so busy absorbing his scent, his feel, his touch, that formulating a response was an unnecessary distraction. Garrett cupped the sides of her breasts, his warm palms pressing against soft flesh and the hard plastic of novelty coconuts. She'd never wanted to be rid of that bra as much as she did just then.

"This makes up for you rejecting me." Garrett's voice was teasing and husky at the same time. His hands ran along her sides, making it clear they were playing with a fire neither of them would escape if this kept up.

Lily's middle fluttered with delicious anticipation over the thought of having Garrett inside her. Here on the bench, against the gazebo wall, hell, on the floor—it didn't matter. She was so caught up in her body, she didn't immediately process what he'd said.

"I rejected you?"

He nipped her neck. By the easy way he drew pleasure out of her, Lily had no doubt Garrett would turn her into a pile of mush—a sated pile of mush—in no time. Yet as he embraced her, held her tenderly as though there was no reason to rush, a sense of familiarity and ease settled over her. Being comfortable in his arms was almost as pleasurable as the intimacy.

"I'm Mr. September."

Garrett nuzzled his nose against her jaw. Lily froze. *What?* Fate wouldn't be such a bitch to her, right? Her one time letting loose with a guy like this…. He couldn't be… A knot of unease tightened in her gut, the same as it had each time she'd seen the DFD shirts earlier.

She leaned back. "Are you—are you a firefighter?"

He trailed a finger over her cheek, eyes narrowed and concerned. "Ah, yeah. Assistant chief for DFD."

The gazebo seemed to turn inside out, the space getting smaller just as her chest seemed to shrink, too. Couldn't breathe… She could barely draw a breath, her muscles paralyzed but begging to run. With great effort, Lily blindly slid off him, tears threatening to spill over in a vicious flood. He was just another fireman, one who could have very well been standing around, doing nothing, on the worst night of her life….

This wasn't fair. She wasn't supposed to be reacting this way. She was better now…. Dammit, she was better!

"Son of a bitch!" The words tumbled in her head and fell out of her mouth. She turned and faltered as she moved to the exit. Garrett was behind her in a flash, his hand wrapping gently around her upper arm.

Lily went cold inside. She wanted to pull away

from him, but her stunned nerves were slow to react. "I thought you were just the hot bartender." She put a shaky hand to her forehead. The one time she gave in to impulse, and this was her punishment. Firefighters were off-limits. There was no way she'd knowingly get involved with one.

He carefully turned her to face him, one hand out, palm up. Lily's muscles were stiff; her body resisted his touch. "I own the bar with my uncle Brad, and I'm a firefighter on the department, too. What's going on?"

There wasn't any way to explain what was going on because she didn't fully understand it herself. This bitterness, this…disgust and anger had all come on so quickly, bringing memories with it. Memories of flame, heat, screaming and death. She was unprepared for the emotions, and she found herself equally unprepared for the blend of emotions she could see on Garrett's face—the confusion alone stabbed her with guilt. She was being irrational, but she couldn't help it.

"I can't believe you didn't tell me."

He spread his hands. "Tell you what? That I'm on the fire department?"

She pulled away from him and ran a hand through her bangs. "I never would have… You and I would never have—"

"Whoa—Lily, talk to me."

She could still feel his body heat on her skin

like a brand, but he didn't make another attempt to touch her.

Her lower lip trembled as the dumbstruck sensation was slow to go away.

"Firemen are off-limits."

Each second she stared at him was punctuated by the beat of pain inside her heart and the memory of her sister's face. The firemen were supposed to save Katja that night. But they'd stood by and watched as the building burned to the ground.

On the edge of ugly crying, Lily turned and rushed across the lawn to the street where her car was parked. One quick glance behind was enough to pick at her with guilt under the shock and anger.

Garrett hadn't moved—he was just standing there, watching her leave.

WELL, EITHER THAT was karma for some past transgression or he'd seriously misread the entire situation. Despite his confusion over what had just happened, Garrett was concerned at how genuinely upset Lily was. He moved away from the gazebo as she hurried to cross the street in the rain, positioning himself so he had a clear view of her slipping into her SUV.

As she pulled away from the curb and disappeared down the street, Garrett was pretty sure this had been the strangest encounter he'd had with a woman in a long time. Women loved firefighters, at least in his experience. Lily was the first one he'd met who didn't. Firemen were off-limits? What the hell was that supposed to mean?

He brushed his soaked bangs away from his eyes. Whatever. He'd rushed into thinking their flirtation was going to turn into something more. With all the other responsibilities he had hanging over his head right now, adding a complicated one-night stand was the last thing he needed. Luckily, Lily's true feelings had come out before they'd gone any further.

The ground squished beneath his feet as he crossed to the sidewalk and hurried back to the bar. If anything, he should be glad he'd avoided potential disaster tonight. But the stab of disappointment in his gut said otherwise, and that was almost as confusing as Lily's hot-and-cold attitude.

She was as sexy as sin; he couldn't deny that. Any man would have felt disappointed to lose out on a woman that hot. That was all this hollow sensation was about.

Garrett pushed open the door, immediately relishing the sounds of music and laughter. Nothing like a packed bar to take his mind off, well, everything. His brain was full of so much stuff lately, any little distraction was welcome. He licked his lips, tasting rain and the lingering sweetness of Lily's kiss.

Oh, well, game over. Back to reality. He pushed through the crowd, trying to ward off the multitude of comments and gibes about his soaked clothes and dripping hair. A couple of women took the liberty of running their fingers over his wet shirt, sending clear reminders that female companionship could be found. If he was still interested, which he wasn't.

Rejection was a bitter pill to swallow, wasn't it? Garrett smirked to himself as he slipped behind the bar and moved to the door that led to the back rooms. He had an extra set of clothes in his office, thankfully. He'd just turned the handle when Mikey called his name. Garrett spun to see his best friend sidling up to the bar with a grim expression.

"Where you been? I tried calling you." Concern was thick in Mikey's voice, jangling Garrett's nerves.

"I…walked a lady out. My cell's in the office. Why?"

Mikey's face fell into soft sympathy. "Sorry, man, but your uncle Brad's been rushed to the hospital."

CHAPTER THREE

"NO WAY IN HELL, Doug." Lily turned sharply, prepared for a stare down with her father. Irritation and lack of caffeine had her every last nerve on fire. The message on her answering machine from her ex, Rob, yesterday still made her edgy. Almost a year with no word and he had the nerve to call to see if he could stop by when he came to town at the end of the month. She preferred that he stay in Mississippi with his new girlfriend, because, frankly, Lily had nothing to say.

More unsettling than the unexpected phone call were the nightmares. Every night since the fund-raiser, she'd had the same unsettling dream. Always about Katja and the fire, and Lily, seeing herself lying on the grass as the building burned, reaching for her sister but not being able to get her.

Sitting just to the side within the dream was a fire engine with glaring, revolving lights. Every night, she turned toward the lights and the truck would disappear, prompting her to wake up with a heavy sense of confusion. It was confounding and unsettling, especially since she had stopped having nightmares about the fire a few months ago.

And now her father wanted her to do *this* before she'd gotten her feelings under control.

Lily cocked her head and crossed her arms, mirroring her father's posture. "Can't someone else go?" Like father, like daughter.

Doug Ashden scowled and stuck his chin out. "Everyone else is busy. I know the appointment time is a little unconventional, but it's a bar…and you're young. You like the nightlife, don't ya?"

Lily enjoyed her job as a general contractor for Ashden Construction and Design. Building and designing were in her blood, and as much as she liked the physical labor of creating a structure, she liked generating ideas more. She didn't just meet with clients to consult on their projects, she also drafted out plans and brought them to life. Lily had a pile of drafts to work on, but being second-in-command meant that when the other employees were gone, she picked up the slack.

In this case, it wasn't the meeting that had her stomach in knots—it was the bar.

"Stay and have a drink or dance or something." Doug waved an impatient hand.

Or something. Right. Because the last time she'd engaged in "or something" at that bar, she'd had her tongue down the throat of a man she would rather not see again. Lily shifted her weight from one foot to the other as her body tingled at the memory.

She clenched her jaw hard enough to grind her molars. She needed to forget that night had ever happened. Not only was it out of character for her to get so physical with a man she didn't know, but she'd done it with a goddamned firefighter.

Doug made an impatient sound when she didn't respond quickly enough for his liking. "You look like you could use a drink."

His gruff tone made it clear she was supposed to obey without question, though he knew her well enough to know that she liked to buck him. She was one of the few people, besides her brother, Lincoln, who could talk back to Doug Ashden and make it out alive.

And there'd be talking back, all right. Being the general contractor for Ashden Construction and Design might mean that Lily went where the jobs were, but not this time. She glanced at the new-client form on the edge of her father's desk. *Throwing Aces* was printed across the top. *God.*

"Are you giving me permission to drink on the job?" Her quip was meant to ground her thoughts into work and not on Garrett the Bartender's very talented mouth. The hurt and surprise in his expression when she'd recoiled from him was a doozy, though. She'd almost felt guilty about hurting his feelings. A man like Garrett, well, rejection probably wasn't something he'd come across too often. She'd stomped on his ego a little, but he'd get over it. He'd probably replaced her with some hot blonde the minute he'd stepped foot back inside the bar. Nothing to feel guilty about.

Doug smirked. "It's a bar. I expect it. In moderation, of course."

"Of course." Lily sighed and pushed the new-client form around the desk with one finger. "So Nick can't go because…?"

"He's busy."

"And Raul?"

Doug sniffed and gave her a hard stare. "Out of town. Why are you hedging about this damn meeting? Seriously, Lily. You meet with the client. You talk to him about what he wants. You leave."

Her father's harsh tone could melt weaker hearts into a puddle of submission, but she was used to it—had learned from his no-nonsense personality over the years. They were certainly cut from the same cloth, and if she wasn't careful, he'd see right through her. No way did she need her father wandering in on the hot-fireman replay flickering in the back of her mind. Or the regret she was struggling with.

"You go, Doug." Lily narrowed her eyes. She

and her dad had always had a tenuous relationship, and the habit of calling him by his first name she'd developed when she was a rebellious teen had stuck.

It was an easy way to remember that her dad had never really given her the same affection he had shown her sister, Katja.

Despite being night-and-day different, she and Katja had been as close as sisters could be. Katja was athletic and bubbly to Lily's artsy moodiness, but somehow they'd balanced each other out.

Lily always suspected that Doug identified more with the choices Katja had made—working hard in school, staying away from boys, going to a good college. While Lily had never considered her own choices bad, they paled in comparison. Mediocre grades, changing boyfriends like sweaters, decorating her body with ink and getting a two-year degree instead of a four-year like Katja. Even in their adult years, Doug had leaned toward her sister more, like a plant to the sun, leaving Lily in the shadows.

Doug threw his hands in the air. "No, you're going! And we're done with this conversation. 8:00 p.m., tomorrow night. End of story."

Lily snatched the paper off the desk, tempted to crumple it in her hand. She couldn't keep arguing with her father without bringing up questions she wasn't willing to answer.

Bitterness clawed at her throat. Two years ago, she'd had the chance to move to Nashville to work with her twin brother, Lincoln, but she'd stayed in Kansas with the plan to open a small architectural showroom with Katja. She wished now that she'd gone. Linc had been her one salvation this past year. His quiet contemplative nature had offered her a refuge when the tension with Doug was too much to bear.

Lily blew her bangs out of her eyes. She wouldn't be thinking about missed chances and regret if the firefighters had done their job in the first place. She rubbed her temple with a thumb as that little nugget worked its way in.

"Look, Lily, we need this contract. Brad Mateo is talking major expansion to the bar here. A complete overhaul of the current building, plus landscaping, an outdoor volleyball pit, et cetera. I need—*we* need—you to secure this contract." His eyes softened for a moment, allowing Lily to catch a glimpse of worry. "You know how slow things have been. This contract would carry us through clear to next spring."

She couldn't deny that business had taken a dive in the past few years, thanks to a tough economy. The summer months had brought them enough work to break even and make payroll, but not much to pad the bottom line. She'd already been lowering bids and cutting into profit margins to try to entice signed contracts, but to no avail. The work was simply harder to get than it used to be.

Their situation wasn't unique, although apparently people still liked to drink and party their sorrows away if the Throwing Aces could afford to expand.

"I understand—" she began, but Doug cut her off with a shake of his head.

"I don't think you do. If we don't get this contract, I'll be laying off for the winter."

Lily frowned. Her dad was a builder by nature and trade. He'd rather be on the job, swinging a nail gun and barking orders to the crew, than doing the talking, and sometimes the careful wooing, it took to secure contracts.

That was why Lily was the face of Ashden Construction. She knew how to woo. But sometimes they just couldn't beat another company's bid, and then it didn't matter what she did. Some contracts just couldn't be won, as was the case more than ever lately with so much competition between companies to secure jobs.

"Doug…" Her voice was tight, thanks to the lump in her throat. The men who worked for them all had families, obligations. They'd never had to lay anyone off before, and Lily had no intention of doing so now.

"Bolstom backed out. Postponed the project

for three years in hopes the economy rebounds more." Doug's eyes narrowed, making the effect of his words that much stronger.

Lily let out a slow breath. Grant Bolstom was a land developer who had worked closely with Ashden Construction for almost ten years. He'd brought them in to build town houses in new development areas both here and in Nashville, where they each had secondary offices. They'd had a multimillion-dollar, four-year contract in the works—work that would have carried Ashden Construction for years.

"Jesus, Doug. Why didn't you tell me?"

Doug uncrossed his arms and put his hands on his hips. "It was my deal, my business. Look, Brad Mateo is expecting you. Take good care of him. Give him what he wants."

Lily crossed the office as her dad rattled off a list of things he wanted her to do. She stopped by the peaked windows that overlooked the Greenway golf course. When they'd scouted buildings to convert into an office, the windows of this old brick house had sold it. The foundation needed work and the masonry cried out for some TLC, but it was nothing her father couldn't handle when he finally got some time to tackle it. Carpenters' houses were always falling down, or something like that.

"Okay," Lily interjected at what she hoped was

the right time. In twenty-seven years, she'd gotten good at blocking him out without him realizing it.

The heavy silence made Lily realize her father had stopped talking. She turned to him, shocked to see an almost sweet expression of...what was that? Affection? Whatever it was, it seemed foreign on his stone-cut face and it disappeared like frosty breath in the sun.

"You secure this contract for me, Lil, and then get yourself to Nashville. It's time you took a break."

Her spine tingled. She wanted to run her brother's architectural-salvage showroom. The designer inside her craved it. All those rescued vintage and antique building materials and decorative fixtures just waiting to find new homes called to her.

Since Katja's death, every time the subject of her leaving to work with Lincoln had come up, Doug had pointed out all the reasons she shouldn't go. That plus guilt kept her firmly grounded in Kansas. She couldn't leave Doug alone. With Katja gone now, he'd have no one. No family around him. They might not get along that well, but Lily was all he had.

"You're serious?" Her chest tightened. Doug acted as though he didn't care one way or the other, but the string of excuses he repeatedly blathered on about lent some suspicion that he cared a little. Even if he didn't show it.

"Secure the contract and you'll have my blessing." He knew that was what she wanted— needed. His approval, his love, his support and acceptance. All things he rarely gave. "I need you to do this for us, Lily."

He raked one big hand through his close-cropped silver hair and eyed her steadily. Lily's heartbeat seemed to pause, hovering like a leaf on a strong breeze. Then it started again as the leaf began to float down, down…down. He always needed her when it benefited him. This time, it was more than just them. Their employees' security was on the line.

Katja's image came to mind—expressive chocolate-brown eyes, full lips curved into an enigmatic smile. He'd loved Katja all the time, just because. But he loved Lily when he needed something.

She was a grown woman, for crying out loud. She shouldn't need her father's affection, but she did. The desire for his acceptance had grown even stronger since Katja's death. She needed some sign, some reason to believe that their father-daughter bond was still important.

Her palms grew damp, her fingers chilly, as panic took root. Lily drew in a breath, shook back her hair and grappled with the tremors rocking her. It would pass. It always did. She tried to focus on the possibility of finally going to Nashville—it offered the change she desperately wanted after all—and she felt the panic start to recede. No sense in relaxing too much just yet, though. Dealing with the Throwing Aces was a huge obstacle she had to manage before she could start packing her bags.

"Text me when you're done at the bar. I don't care how late it is, in case you decide to hang out or whatever." Doug gathered up her case containing a company laptop and held it out to her without meeting her eye. She took it, some of the steel she relied on so much back in her veins. Returning to her office, Lily set the laptop down and sat at her desk to try to focus on work.

She'd already done *whatever* and his name was Garrett. Never. Again. Too bad he owned the bar, too, because he'd probably be around at some point during the planning phase. That was okay. She'd play nice and do what was required to seal the deal. Beyond that, Garrett would mean nothing to her. Because Garrett wasn't just a hot man. He was like the best possible vintage in a wineglass rimmed in poison.

GARRETT TRIED TO stop bouncing his left leg as he sat and waited, but it didn't last long. He hated that habit, but he could never get it to stop. As a kid, he was always moving, even in his sleep. He'd frequently ended up on the floor in a mess of blankets from rolling around too much. Now he recognized the leg movement as an outlet for a different kind of energy—the restless kind. The Frasier Realty building was quiet with just the barest of sounds coming from the back room. He was grateful for the quiet. It made a soothing background for the chaos in his mind.

He'd been extra restless since his uncle Brad had gone into the hospital last week with a fever and flu-like symptoms. Since Brad was in remission from bone cancer, any sign of illness had the potential to go south in a hurry.

Seeing him back in a hospital bed gave Garrett a hefty dose of anxiety. Last year they'd almost lost him to the cancer, but Brad had managed to pull through. He'd come out a much weaker man, though he tried to pretend otherwise. After being in remission just a couple of months, Brad had returned to work at the bar a few hours at a time. He'd been adamant that Garrett get a crew together to get started on their plans to expand. It was something they'd been talking about for a long time, but with Brad's questionable health, it had become more of a priority.

When Garrett had visited the hospital that morning, Brad had grabbed his wrist and pulled him close to the bed.

"I'm a time bomb, Garrett. Promise you'll get started on the bar as fast as possible." His uncle's dull eyes were pleading.

Garrett understood. They'd decided to upgrade the bar and expand it to increase the overall value. The bar sat in a prime location and made a profit every year. Selling it wouldn't be a problem, and with the upgrades, the increased price they could get would pay out Garrett's initial investment and sustain Brad's family for a long time. They thought of it as extra life insurance for Brad's girls—enough to put them through college, buy them each a good car. All the things a father worried about, especially if he didn't think he'd be around to watch them grow.

Garrett rubbed a hand over his forehead. He hated watching his uncle's family go through this. Brad had been a pillar for Garrett when his father was killed after a roof collapsed during a structure fire. Determined to be there for Garrett's family, Brad had hung up his own fireman's hat and quit the department.

The firefighting gene ran strong, bonding them in a way other people couldn't understand. Brad had been proud to see Garrett and his brothers, Cash and Sawyer, go into firefighting careers like their grandfather, father and uncle before them. Following in his father's footsteps wasn't a decision Garrett took lightly, especially when the pain of how his father died was always a raw and festering memory. But being a fireman was a part of who he was—a big enough piece that if it were to be taken away, he'd be pretty hollow afterward.

Thirteen when his father had died, Garrett had clung to Brad for strength and advice and support. Now it was time to repay the favor, and he was happy to do so. Seeing Brad in the hospital, once again on the brink of something life-threatening, and the devastated worry on his family's faces only reinforced Garrett's decision to stay single. He didn't want anyone sitting at his bedside in such agony. And although it was selfish, he didn't want to feel that way about someone else. The fewer people he had to worry about, the more he could protect himself.

"Mr. Mateo?" The petite brunette receptionist came back to her desk, a warm smile on her face. "Ms. Frasier will see you now." She gestured with a hand to the hallway.

Garrett covered a grimace by clearing his throat, then stood and smoothed the front of his jeans. Not that it mattered how he looked. He could have walked in wearing an Armani suit, but given their history, Sylvia Frasier's reaction to him would probably be the same: frigid.

He followed the receptionist through the tastefully decorated building to an office in the back. He'd been here several times before and knew the layout by heart. He was equally familiar with Sylvia, and he easily recognized her perfume from the doorway. It was the same perfume she'd always worn and it still made his gut churn. He walked inside with a nod to the receptionist.

"Garrett. How nice to see you." Sylvia's Southern drawl was the kind that mixed pleasantries with insult. In her late sixties, Sylvia Frasier was the epitome of a wealthy business woman. Well dressed, perfect office. Impressive posture and manners despite the hint of poison that always laced her tone when she spoke to him. She gestured for him to sit, the burgundy polish on her long oval fingernails glinting in the overhead lights.

"Thank you for seeing me so late in the day." Garrett sat and tapped the envelope in his hand with a finger.

Her eyes fell to it, a small smile crossing her mouth. She knew why he was there. There was only one reason he would be, and that was to talk about the available plot of land behind the Throwing Aces that he'd been trying to buy from her for months. He needed that plot to complete the bar expansion, including a rear deck and possibly a couple of volleyball courts. They planned to make the property available for parties, vendor fairs and other gatherings, too. Garrett had made Sylvia several offers, but she'd turned them all down. Even though the plot was listed for public sale, she hadn't sold it to anyone else, either, giving him some hope.

He didn't have any more time, and if she wasn't going to sell to him, he needed to figure out a plan B.

"What can I do for you?" Sylvia crossed her hands on top of her desk.

"I haven't heard back from you on my last offer, which leads me to believe you haven't accepted it. But I'd like to know either way."

He took out a copy of the offer from the envelope and slid it across her desk. Their eyes met briefly before she took the paper and glanced at it. Sylvia's perfectly glossed lips twitched just a bit before she gave him that polite yet cold stare he wondered if she reserved for him alone.

"Why are you pursuing this so tenaciously, Garrett?"

He gave a tight smile and glanced down for a second. There was no doubt she'd probably heard about Brad's illness in gossip around town, but he didn't feel that his uncle's personal business was any of hers. Given the intense dislike she'd felt for him since he'd spent a night with her granddaughter two years ago, Garrett didn't feel that confiding about Brad would change anything.

"That's personal. You either decide to sell it or you don't." He folded his hands across his middle.

Getting mixed up with Sylvia's granddaughter, Holly, wasn't the most prudent thing he'd ever done, but to his credit, he hadn't known who Holly was when he'd taken her home. To him, she was a pretty, willing woman who was just as interested in a few hours of mindless fun as he'd been.

Except that Holly Frasier had her sights set on more than that. And when he'd told her there would never be more than that one night, she had gone straight to her grandmother. It wasn't good for any business owner in this town to be on the wrong side of the biggest realty company in the tristate area. When it came to buying commercial property or selling your business, chances were you were going to deal with Frasier Realty. Sylvia was good at what she did, and she was someone you wanted on your side.

"Let's say my decision may well be determined on your intentions for the property." She blinked once, her tight smile tipping up more. "The good thing about being the landowner instead of just the broker is that I get to decide where it goes. Considering I haven't yet shot down your offer, I'd suggest you indulge me a little."

Garrett rested his elbows on his knees and leaned forward. He took a slow breath through his nose. She hadn't shot him down, true. This was as close as he'd gotten to an acceptance since he'd started offering on the plot when it first came up for sale back in March.

He thought of the desperation on Kim's face when she held Brad's hand. Did it really matter if he told Sylvia? Getting that lot would benefit his family, and for that, Garrett accepted that Brad wouldn't mind if his personal business was aired out a little. He licked his lips, mentally forced his leg to stop bouncing when he suddenly realized it was. Before he could speak, Sylvia made a sigh-like sound, her tight smile turning soft.

"Look, I know what's going on with your uncle, and I feel for his family. I've always assumed you wanted the land to expand the bar, but considering I've other offers on the property from a couple of other parties, I don't think I'm out of line in asking what you intend to do with it."

"Who told you?" Not that it mattered. Gossip always rubbed him wrong, because for the most part, the information was always skewed and wrong.

"My hairdresser." *Of course.* Eight thousand people in this town, but all the juicy bits still came through the coffee shop, hardware store or hair salon. Garrett spread his hands, resolved.

"Okay, yes, Brad's been struggling with cancer. He's actually back in the hospital right now. We want to expand the bar, put a deck out back, maybe another seating area. Potentially a small amphitheater that the local bands and theater groups can use. Until we get a contractor out there to show us what's possible, we won't know for sure, but that's the general idea."

"Bring me a drafted plan." Any sign of sympathy was gone, replaced by pure professionalism.

"Excuse me?"

"I'd like to see a draft of your plans for the property. This lot is one of the last open, wood-lined areas in town. As much as I support commercial development, it would be a shame to see such a pretty natural area ruined by bad development. I've owned that land for years and sat on it for this very reason."

He couldn't argue with that. The one-acre plot was parklike, and it wasn't uncommon for people to use it as such. The gazebo Sylvia had erected to make the plot even more enticing to buyers was a magnet for people leaving his bar to spend a few stolen moments.

Just as he and Lily had. His heart kicked up a notch at the thought. Garrett cleared his throat to refocus.

"Understood. We have a contractor coming tonight, actually, so I'll get something to you as soon as I can." He started to rise but paused. "When do you need it?"

Sylvia tapped one nail on the desk. "A week or less would be grand. I'd like to make a decision as soon as possible."

No pressure or anything. After months of jerking him around, she was finally cutting the chase short. Fine. He knew Brad had scheduled a meeting with a commercial contractor for tonight, intending to conduct the meeting himself, but Garrett didn't know any details. He hoped like hell that whoever the contractor was, they offered what he needed. Otherwise, starting tomorrow he wouldn't rest until he found someone who did. He didn't want this opportunity to slip by, just like he couldn't play around with time. Both were too precious to waste.

CHAPTER FOUR

LILY SAT IN her SUV in the Throwing Aces parking lot for a good twenty minutes, tapping the steering wheel with a fingernail. It was a balmy Saturday evening and more people wandered in the front door than out, making her groan at how packed the place was likely to be. Her nerves refused to settle; the hardness at the corners of her mouth refused to soften. This was a job, a job their company desperately needed. If she blew it with a bad attitude and prickly demeanor, people would be laid off because of her.

No pressure, right? Lily finally managed to step out of the vehicle and smooth her skirt. She stared at the building for another minute before heading inside.

The bar was filled end to end. A basketball game played across several screens above the bar, prompting a cacophony of cheers, hollers and groans from the crowd. It took Lily a lifetime to squeeze through to get to the bar. The constant looking over her shoulder didn't speed the process up at all. With any luck, Garrett would be off playing with fire.

"Cute top. Even better ink." A female bartender she recognized from her previous visit gave her a nod while grabbing a glass from a rack above her head. Lily glanced down. She'd chosen the navy blue shirt with little white polka dots and a feminine ruffled hem, gray pencil skirt and neutral pumps carefully. It was about the most professional outfit she owned, and if Garrett happened to show up, she would need all the professional she could get.

"Thanks. Say, I have an appointment with Brad Mateo. Lily Ashden."

The bartender motioned to a door behind the end of the bar. "Hmm, Brad wasn't able to make it in today. But come on back to the office and I'll get someone for you." Lily followed the blonde through the back, past the kitchen and down a dim, narrow hall to a door on the left. She couldn't help but notice how dated the back of the bar was—shabby even—with chipped and peeling faux-wood paneling, missing ceiling tiles and patchy carpet. They'd clearly overhauled the public areas of the establishment, but the rest of it was in terrible need of some TLC.

The woman opened the door and gestured Lily inside. The office looked more like a prison interrogation room than an inviting place to conduct business. The cracked yellow linoleum floor set the groundwork for boring beige wallpaper and a harsh metal desk that looked as though it belonged in a football locker room office. The rickety mismatched chairs were questionable, save for the plush leather office chair behind the desk. Lily gave the bartender a tight smile and sat carefully in the sturdiest-looking chair when the other woman left the room.

Lily's spine felt like a rod, and her shoulder muscles were tight. To distract herself, she pulled out her laptop and set it on the desk. Despite the gloom, a full-bodied scent permeated the room. Musky, with heavy notes of spice and outside air. This was definitely a man's office. She couldn't imagine a woman working here, or the office wouldn't be in this devil-may-care condition.

Time ticked away as sounds from the bar leeched into the small space. Lily was just about to get up to make her way back to the bartender to see if she'd been forgotten when steps in the hallway made her swivel in her chair to the door. A grunt followed the sound of paused footsteps, then a short sound of something being dragged.

"Seriously, Roan, I'm really tired of you passing out on the sidewalk. Next time, I'm just going to leave you there."

Another grunt and something banged against the wall to Lily's left.

"Lie down and sleep it off. I'll take you home in a bit." A door shut, followed by a mumble. "When the hell did I become a freaking baby-sitter?"

The voice became crystal clear as it came closer. She stood, not quite sure what was going on.

LILY'S STOMACH BOTTOMED out as a familiar form stepped into the doorway. Her eyes drank in the sight while her brain rallied against it.

White T-shirt stretched across broad, well-defined pecs. Beaten-to-death jeans hugging long legs for dear life. Work boots. Shaggy blond bangs falling in his eyes, deep golden skin covering the roping muscles of his forearms.

The only thing that would make Garrett more all-American was if his skin tasted like apple pie. But it didn't. It tasted better. Like sex with a side of brown sugar and buttered rum. She'd half risen from her chair but didn't realize it until her thighs started to ache from the odd angle.

"Lily." The brilliant blue of his eyes bore into her. Garrett tugged at the leather gloves on his hands, methodically working each long finger free. "What are you doing here?"

"I have an appointment with…" Her voice trailed away as the tongue-brain connection faltered. "With Brad, but I hear he's unavailable."

Crap, that came out as a squeak. Lily's cheeks heated. This wasn't the reaction she wanted to have. What happened to cool and professional? Out the window, apparently.

He palmed the gloves in one hand. "Wait… you're the carpenter?" He leaned against the door frame as he tucked the gloves in his back pocket. Despite her dumbstruck brain, he didn't seem at all ruffled to see her. Surprised, maybe, but not ruffled.

"General contractor," she corrected. "From Ashden Construction and Design." Lily smoothed her palms over her shirt and tipped her chin up. The move always helped when she needed a composure boost. "Did you…did you just drag something down the hall?"

He cracked an amused smile. "Ah, you heard that? I'm sorry—I didn't know anyone was in here. You're, uh, early. Anyway, yes—*someone,* actually. My buddy Roan had a little too much to drink, and I figured the couch in the employee room was a better mattress than the sidewalk, so…"

"Right." She nodded as if it made perfect sense. *Next time, I'm going to just leave you there.*

She tried to shake off the image his words brought to mind. Someone lying facedown on the sidewalk, passed out and vulnerable. Someone needing help but being left behind. She knew she should say something, but her mouth was suddenly dry.

"I didn't peg you for a contractor." He raked a hand through his unruly bangs, drawing her eyes to every delicious movement. If she hadn't braced her hand on the desk, she might have leaned forward in time with his arm as it moved up and along the curve of his head as he swept his bangs away.

Instead, she turned to the laptop. Looking at Garrett brought back all the sour thoughts she'd had about Katja the last time she was in this bar. He reminded her… That was a problem. He reminded her of firemen and death and feelings she was working hard to get past.

"Well, I guess we're both full of surprises, then." Her chest was already wrenching the breath right out of her. Doug's threat of layoffs gave her pause. This was a game—that was all. One she needed to win. If she looked at it that way—as a challenge she had to face and conquer—it was easier. She liked challenges, had faced and overcome her fair share, that was for damn sure. Lily gathered her composure and faced Garrett again, ignoring the flip of her heart.

"There's an insult in there somewhere." He spread his hands wide. "I feel like I should apologize for something, but I don't know what."

"You don't need to apologize for anything."

Except for not wearing a damn DFD shirt like every other firefighter had been that night so she could have avoided him.

His face took on a boyish quality that made it seem he was teasing her. "Hmm, I'm getting the 'it's not you, it's me' vibe."

"Does it matter? Look, Garrett, I'm here in a professional capacity, not a personal one."

"I'd say the other night was a bit personal." Two lazy strides brought him in front of her. Lily stiffened, though her insides had turned to mush. His eyes fell to her lips. "Talk to me, Lily."

"There's…nothing to talk about. The other night was…interesting, but I don't want more. Frankly, I'm surprised that you're acting as if you do." Garrett's eyebrows shot up. He leaned in just slightly, and the timbre of his voice made her skin prickle.

"Trust me, Lily, if I wanted more, you'd know it already." He leaned back with a smug smile. "I'm just curious about why you bolted. That's all."

She drew away from him, heat flushing from her chin to scalp. He was as arrogant as he was charming.

"I don't get involved with firemen." It was a simple, uncomplicated answer, and he'd have to take it at face value, because she wasn't going any deeper. To his credit, it wasn't as if she'd asked him for his résumé and work references before they'd gotten their make-out session on. It wasn't his fault she kept having flashbacks of her sister's death—it was hers. She owned it, claimed it, and that was good enough.

"Ah," he said, as if it made perfect sense. "You got burned once, I take it?"

Her eyes narrowed. "What?"

He flipped one palm up. "I was just thinking your aversion to firemen could be because you've been burned by one. If so, I hope it wasn't a member of DFD." His impetuousness was almost amusing; Garrett didn't seem to even realize he was being rude. No way was she responding to that, because nothing good was likely to come out of her mouth.

When she didn't say anything, Garrett had the grace to look uncomfortable—for a second. "It's just that I know a few of my guys have their priorities mixed up is all, so…"

"Understood," she said, grateful she'd managed to stay polite when her head was churning with so many snarky replies. Lily recalled how Garrett had made the flirty face with women at the bar before she'd approached him. It was no secret that some of the firemen thought highly of their prowess—Garrett probably included.

He put his hands in his front pockets and spun on one heel, then walked to the doorway. Lily's chest loosened a little. Garrett paused and ran a hand down the ancient trim in the doorway, his back muscles moving effortlessly beneath the thin layer of white cotton.

"Brad is going to be laid up for a while. Is working with me going to be a problem for you?" The challenge in his eyes when he turned to face her was clear; the smug tone of his voice was infuriating. She cleared her throat.

"Of course not."

He tilted his head, observing her quietly for a moment. The intensity of his stare was unsettling and delicious. "Walk with me."

She followed him out front, drawn by the incredible movement of his muscles beneath his clothes and his scent until they were at the packed dance floor. Garrett reached for her hand and grasped it lightly. Before she could pull away, he began maneuvering them through the crowd. They stopped at the empty stage.

"This dance floor needs to double in size. We want to put in another bar so patrons don't have to wait. Another set of restrooms, a second waitress station and a larger seating area."

"What about the property? Do your lines extend enough to allow the expansion?"

Garrett nodded for her to follow him and took her hand again as they walked back through the crowd.

"The property lines are another conversation," he replied as they rounded the bar. "But first, let me show you what else we want done."

He pointed things out, chatted about expansion, showed her what needed to be changed, enlarged and updated. Lily made mental notes, as it was a little hard to write anything down at the moment.

After another twenty minutes, Garrett led her back to the office. He motioned for her to go in first. She did, exceptionally aware of his body heat as she passed by him. Her brain was running numbers, and the preliminary, best-guess scenario would pad Ashden Construction for months to come.

"Of course, this office needs a total overhaul, as well," he said offhandedly as she passed through the door. Lily smirked.

"No kidding."

He chuckled, slipping behind the desk and settling into the leather chair. Lily remained standing, laid her pad of paper down and began scribbling notes. He leaned back, hands folded across his firm middle.

"What's your time frame for beginning this project, Mr. Mateo?"

He rubbed his chin with a thumb before crossing his hands again. "Really? The other night it was Garrett."

Lily's spine stiffened. She closed her laptop

before placing her palm on top of it and leaning in slightly.

"As far as I'm concerned, *Mr. Mateo,* I'd prefer if we didn't let that evening interfere with a professional relationship." Before he could speak, she straightened even more. "Your uncle called Ashden Construction for a reason. Hopefully because he was aware that we're the best commercial construction firm in the area. Let us live up to that instead of letting our mishap cloud your judgment."

His gaze swept over her, leaving behind a warm tingle. "Agreed." He leaned forward and put his elbows on the desk. "I need someone who will give us a fair price, do exceptional work and start as soon as possible. No pressure, right?"

She thought of the twelve men working under her father and the dozen subcontractors who could be called in to help if needed. That, combined with their stellar reputation and her ability to create a solid budget, meant there was a lot less pressure than there might have been.

"No pressure."

"Give me a proposal I can't turn down, Lily." Their eyes locked. "But before you do, come back tomorrow so I can show you the property lines. There's more you need to see. I'm sorry Brad arranged such a late meeting. I'm not sure what his initial plan was for this, but in order for you to get the full scope of what we have in mind, you'll need to be here in the daytime."

Lily finished writing but didn't look up. She had plans for tomorrow already. She wanted to say no, she'd have to come another time, but she didn't want to jeopardize this contract. If Garrett wanted her to come back, she would.

He stood, moving to the doorway as she packed her things.

"What time?" She gathered her bag, pushed in the chair and strode to the doorway. Expecting that he'd move to let her out, Lily's neck tingled again as Garrett simply remained stationary, filling the space.

"Noon." A slow grin made a dimple dig deeply into his left cheek, as if he was mulling over a dirty little secret. "There's more you need to see, but I can't show you in the dark."

Despite herself, Lily smiled before she dipped her head and tried to move past him. Immediate warmth wrapped around her, followed by the heady scent of spicy bergamot and sage. Her right shoulder brushed against him, sending sparks through her entire body. Before she could withdraw, Garrett scooped her elbow in one hand and turned her. Her back pressed against the door frame opposite him so they faced each other, his heat washing over her. Jacking up her blood pressure. Sending her pulse skyrocketing.

When was the last time she'd had such a spirited reaction to a man? Even her ex-fiancé hadn't affected her this way. When Garrett had tempted her with his inviting gaze across the bar last week, something had felt different. The way her heart had jumped in her throat after battling a minefield of nerves had been different. The way her skin had flushed at the sound of his voice... it had all been different.

Nonetheless, she couldn't read anything into her body's reaction. The dreams that had resurfaced since the night of the fund-raiser were enough to set her back. All those firemen had triggered the anxiety she was trying to overcome, and Lily wasn't going to risk going down that road again.

Despite her resolve, her gaze flicked to his lips. They were model perfect, soft yet undeniably male. The kind of lips that could kiss you tenderly good-night or grind you to aneurysm-worthy pleasure.

She squeezed her eyes shut and sidled to the left. The space was narrow, causing her chest to bump his, making her gasp and stiffen. He dipped his head, his hair tickling her temple as his gravelly voice filled her ears.

"Are you a vegetarian, Lily?" His expression was a tease and a dare rolled into one sexy smolder as he shifted to let her out of the office.

"Yes."

Garrett paused before replying with a light chuckle. "Seriously? I was expecting you to say no. Either way, plan on staying a bit tomorrow."

Lily pulled in a slow breath. There would be no staying. She was inspecting property lines, not—

"I'm the client, remember?" he said. She must be wearing her reluctance like a perfume. "Indulge me a little. Please?"

"The client." Her voice trailed off before her brain broke free of its sexy-Garrett stranglehold. "Of course. However—"

There was loud thump from the room next door, followed by a long muffled groan. Both of them looked at the wall, as if they could see what was happening on the other side. From the sound, it was obvious Roan had fallen off the couch.

They turned back to look at each other, and Lily didn't miss Garrett's eye roll and sigh. He ran a hand over his face and was suddenly transformed into a man who looked as if he could sleep for a week. It was as though he'd taken off a mask, reducing him from cocky, confident Garrett to someone with a lot of weight on his shoulders.

"I'm going to check on Roan." He thrust a hand out. Lily took it for a firm shake, interest in his transformation niggling at her. It shouldn't matter, but it piqued her even so because in that moment he wasn't a hotshot fireman. He was just a man who radiated hidden sadness and deep responsibility.

And that rubbed her both ways: wrong and right. Wrong because she didn't have time to care what was going on under Garrett's surface, and right because she'd be a complete bitch not to at least wonder.

Their hands parted more slowly than she would have liked, prompting Lily to make a half turn toward the hall and her exit.

"I'll clear my schedule and meet you here at noon."

"Okay." He followed her down the hall until he stopped at the employee lounge. "Oh, and, Lily?"

She didn't look back. If she did, he'd see how badly she was trembling. "Yes?"

"I'm not opposed to you wearing that coconut bra again."

His voice was lighter, and the sound made her pause and look back. His weariness was gone and the usual confident charm had returned. His cocky grin seemed a bit out of place, as if it was a mask he hadn't quite gotten to fit right. True colors? It was hard to tell which were really his. Not that she'd be finding out.

Lily turned back to the exit without a reply. The last thing she needed was to try to figure out a complicated man. She just wanted to secure this job, pack her bags and get the heck out of Danbury.

"THREE WEEKS?" LILY slid to the edge of her bed, taking the comforter with her until it bunched against her butt. She held the phone away from her ear, stared at it a moment to be sure she wasn't still asleep.

Doug's gruff voice floating through the receiver made it clear she was awake.

"It's what you wanted, right?"

The blanket—and Adam the cat, who Lily hadn't noticed—landed on the floor when she abruptly stood, excitement prickling her skin. Hell, yes, this was what she wanted. She just wasn't expecting to have it so soon.

"Lincoln's having an open house in the showroom and he could really use you there. That way you can check it out, see the sights—see if moving to Nashville is what you really want. Linc's getting too busy with the construction end. Thankfully, he's doing better than we are, but he could use some help."

The Ashden Construction and Design office in Nashville wasn't just an office, it was a showroom. Junk artists, master furniture builders, concrete and textile artists all had work on display. Lincoln managed both the construction business and the showroom, but he'd been trying to dump responsibility for the showroom for the past couple of years.

Lily wasn't much of a crafter herself, but helping others support a career doing just that was close enough. The poetry of artisan construction elements had always fascinated her—bathroom sinks made from decorative concrete, mosaic tabletops, hand-carved finials and molding created by loving hands were as beautiful as stunning architecture. Managing the showroom would be a dream come true, especially since Lincoln was talking about starting an architectural salvage yard. Instead of watching reruns of *American Pickers,* she could be living it.

Her father had been reluctant to approve Lily's request to transfer there—always citing that he needed her in Danbury more than she was needed in Nashville. Lily knew that her father played on her guilt over leaving him alone, so she stayed. Until recently, she hadn't felt completely ready to move on, but the loneliness of her days and nights made her realize now was the perfect time.

The sound of swallowing came through the receiver. Scalding coffee, she suspected, black and strong enough to disembowel a T. rex.

"Linc's excited that you're coming, Lil. He wants you to give him a call when you can."

Lily paced her small bedroom, barely feeling

the scratchy carpet that usually irritated her bare feet. Leaving her father alone with no family in Kansas seemed cruel. But Doug seemed to be managing, as far as she could tell. Maybe he was ready for her to go.

He'd never said either way, because they never talked about how their relationship had changed since Katja had died, or about the tension between them. Knowing Doug, he never would. She'd tried so many times to get him to talk, to no avail. It was just easier to give up trying and keep her emotions bottled up.

"We need to talk this through a little more, Doug. I mean, if I do decide to move there, who will replace me in the office?"

She'd decided a long time ago that moving to Nashville was a no-brainer, and before she and Katja had decided to open a salvage yard in Danbury, she'd been ready to go. It was Nashville, for crying out loud. The nightlife. The shopping. The men. Guilt was the only thing holding her back now, and Lily was starting to see that was an obstacle she could skirt around.

"How'd it go last night? You didn't text me like I asked."

She sighed heavily at Doug's deflection, but it didn't dampen her excitement. The chance to meet new people, make new friends. Maybe find someone…who wasn't Garrett. The thought prompted her to grab the alarm clock from her nightstand to check the time. Eleven o'clock. She'd tossed and turned last night, finally waking up after another nightmare only to spend hours staring at the wall.

"Doug, I have to go. Talk to you soon, okay?"

He hung up without a proper response, as usual, leaving Lily to rush through a shower with no time to dry her hair. A flowing, lacy top from her favorite store, Magnolia Pearl, and slim, well-worn jeans did the trick. She slicked on a touch of red lipstick on the way out the door.

Lily was still on an endorphin high when she pulled into the Throwing Aces. It was great to have something to focus on, something that helped drown out the reality that the first anniversary of her sister's death was fast approaching. She'd been thinking about that a lot lately, wondering how she'd handle it—whether Doug would acknowledge it or ignore it. For once, Lily hoped he'd face the tragedy they'd been through, maybe talk about it—*something*.

Lily pushed her thoughts away as she tried the front door, frowning when she found the lobby completely dark. The building was eerily quiet and a little calming in its emptiness. She wandered through the main room of shadowy tables with upturned chairs, drawn to a soft glow coming from behind the bar.

Her excitement started to fade and apprehension about being alone in the deserted bar with Garrett crept in. She frowned. There was no reason to feel nervous. *Sheesh.* It was a business meeting, not a date.

"Hello?" Lily paused at the bar, running her fingers along the silky wood as she moved toward the door that led to the back. The door was slightly ajar, letting a sliver of light through. Then it suddenly swung open, startling her and revealing a smiling Garrett, wiping his hands on a towel. Lily jerked back, nearly dropping her canvas workbag. The impact of Garrett's smile was nearly as intoxicating as the savory scent wafting out from the kitchen.

"Hello yourself." He whipped the towel over his shoulder.

Her lips did that tingly thing so she clamped them to make it stop. It didn't help. "Mind if we turn on some lights?"

He nodded and moved behind the bar. Two clicks later and the place was flooded with light. "There you go."

Lily placed her bag on the bar and leaned against it. The smell filling her senses was incredible, reminding her that she hadn't eaten yet.

"What are you cooking?" She looked up, her words trailing off as Garrett went through the swinging door and disappeared into the kitchen.

When he returned, he had a steaming coffee mug in each hand.

"Freshly ground, black, and of the thought that weak coffee is for weakhearted losers, which clearly you are not. Did I get it right?"

A slow grin tugged at her mouth as she accepted a mug. He was delicious and adorable. And a mind reader. And completely correct. *Off-limits*.

"Yes. Thank you."

Garrett leaned a hip on the bar and gripped his mug in both hands. She looked away, then was compelled to turn back again. The appreciative smile on his lips warmed her to her toes.

"To answer your question, you'll just have to wait and see."

The tanned perfection of his face made her brain dance in a slow fog, prompting her to forget what she'd asked. Luckily it came rushing back before she made a fool of herself. She leaned back against the bar and took a small sip from her mug.

"I forgot something. Excuse me a sec?"

Garrett set his mug down and went back through the kitchen door. Lily took out a notepad, pen and tape measure from her bag, trying to keep her hands busy.

Being nervous was ridiculous. Maybe it wasn't so much a case of nerves as it was a sense of shyness from being with a man she'd kissed and then run away from, and the knee-jerk distaste that welled up in her when she remembered that Garrett was a fireman.

Irritated with her train of thought, Lily reached for her mug, and her elbow pushed her nearly empty bag off the bar and onto the floor on the other side.

"Dammit," she muttered, moving to the end of the bar and going inside to where the bag lay. Lily reached for it, her eyes drawn to Garrett's name written on the side of an ice-cream tub. It was filled with pieces of paper, some folded, some not. It only took a second to recognize that the slips contained phone numbers and women's names. A few lay open on the very top—one from Stacy, another from Ivy and one that just said "Call me."

Lily scoffed as she straightened and smoothed the front of her shirt with one hand. *Typical.* He'd asked for her phone number, too, hadn't he?

Seemed her instincts had been dead-on. Garrett was right up there on the playboy firefighter list. If her discomfort because of her sister weren't enough, getting tangled up with another player after being dumped by her fiancé would have been the nail in the coffin. Walking away from Garrett the other night was the smartest thing she could have done—aside from never kissing him in the first place.

She slung the bag strap over her shoulder as a sound to her right drew her attention. Garrett stood there, sliding his mug over the bar surface, an intensely curious look on his face.

"Lily?"

"I dropped my bag," she explained, wondering if he'd seen her looking at the bucket o' numbers. If he had, he didn't let on.

"Should we get started?" He motioned for her to come back around the bar with a sweep of his arm, reminding Lily that she was still standing there. *Yes. Please.* She followed, deposited the bag and grabbed her notebook, holding it to her chest. As if that would do anything to calm the nerves that seemed worse than ever.

It didn't.

IT WAS A beautiful late morning, and despite only a few hours' sleep last night, Garrett was refreshed and pumped with energy. Maybe it was the plan in his head or having Lily by his side. He didn't know—didn't care.

He sneaked another look at how the lacy top clung to her feminine shape, outlining her full breasts and narrow ribs and flaring prettily over the top of her hips. Her arms were bare; the tattoo on her right arm was an eye-catching work of art as the sun highlighted the many colors. He led her out back to the empty parcel, glaring once at the realty sign.

"So the property lines end here."

He pointed them out, already knowing they had enough property to do the expansion. That wasn't what he was worried about. Taking it one step further could mean a huge burst in property value for the bar, and for that he needed this damn lot.

"This empty lot is what I really wanted to show you. May I?" He reached for the pad and pen. "It's probably easier if I just jot it down since it's so clear in my mind."

Garrett turned the paper, drew an outline of the lot and started adding things in.

"So a friend of mine, Mikey, has a brother, Bodie, who's disabled." He focused on the drawing, taking a second to scoff at his own inability to draw a decent-looking rectangle.

"Art class was always a pain in the ass." He winked. "Anyway, Bodie is an amazing metal artist. We can give him a pile of scrap metal and a few days later, he'll have made all this amazing stuff. Sculptures. Wind chimes, that kind of thing. Mikey started looking into groups or classes Bodie could get involved with to, you know, help him socialize a little while he creates. Turns out, there's quite a large community of art-

ists in and around Danbury, but they don't neces-
sarily have an outlet to meet or sell their stuff."

He held out the paper, very aware that Lily was
hanging on his every word. He slid the notebook
to her. A confused expression crossed her face,
making him laugh.

"That is supposed to be a pavilion. And that's
a small open amphitheater or stage. We'd like
something where bands can play, theater groups
can put on a show. Whatever. We'll add a deck
off the back of the building, including an outdoor
server station and bar."

Lily's eyebrows arched. She almost looked impressed. "While you sell alcohol and supper to
the crowds they attract."

"You got it." He took the paper back and made
a few more awful additions to the design. "Cur-
rently, there isn't a place like what we're propos-
ing in the area. This all started as a way to give
Bodie a place to maybe sell his stuff. But it kind
of turned into something more. Really, it could be
a great space for any community group, and the
Throwing Aces, of course, would benefit from
that, too."

Lily turned to face him, her head tilting as
though she was trying to figure something out.
"It's an incredible idea, Garrett. In fact, I'm
something of a junk-fair connoisseur, so I have
to wholeheartedly cheer on your plan."

Her cheeks flushed pink, the color adding warmth to the appreciative expression on her face.

"Well, then, you're going to come in quite handy."

He closed the notebook and handed it to her. They talked about sizing for the outside structures and the deck and all the nuances of the projects he was planning. The more they planned and discussed, the more he found himself drawn to her.

Lily wasn't just sexy as hell, she had a sharp mind and a visionary way of making him see what the Throwing Aces could be like once the expansion was done. She zipped through possible code and zoning problems and their solutions as if she'd written the city manual, and he didn't for one second consider that she didn't know what she was talking about.

Excitement shone on her face, and Garrett found himself getting more excited about the possibilities, too. As they walked around the acre plot, chatting about all the things the land could be, the project took on a lightness it didn't have before. Almost as if the ties to Brad's illness weren't there.

They strolled along the property. "I can really visualize what you're trying to do here," she said suddenly, giving the gazebo a cursory glance. "It's just…a great idea."

"Thank you." They walked back toward the bar. Lily stayed just far enough away that they wouldn't bump shoulders, but close enough he could reach out and touch her.

"My brother, Lincoln, owns a showroom in Nashville that sells architectural salvages and artisan decor. I'd love to see some of Bodie's work sometime. Maybe some of it would be a fit for Lincoln's store." Her blue eyes twinkled in the sunlight; her pale, heart-shaped face was framed by waves of damp, inky-black hair that fell past her shoulders. Garrett had a hard time looking away from her.

"Yeah. That would be fantastic. Bodie's sold a few pieces in the bar, but an opportunity like that would be great for him. I appreciate that, Lily."

She smiled warmly. The red lipstick she'd had on had worn away, leaving behind a ruby stain. He faltered, and that irritated him as much as the crazy breathless thing he'd had going on just a moment ago.

God, he really needed to start getting more sleep.

Before he acted on impulse, Garrett led her back inside. They reviewed some of the things they'd spoken about last night and he helped her take measurements and sketch a rough draft of the inside renovations. Lily laughed softly a couple of times at his juvenile attempts at sketching, prompting Garrett to laugh, too.

"Good thing I use computer drafting software," Lily teased, taking the pad of paper from him. "I think I have a general idea of what you're after here."

They finally headed back toward the bar. Their coffees were cold, but the room was warm and fragrant with the smells coming from the kitchen.

"How fast can you get me a decent drawing of our outside plans? I just need a sketch better than that chicken scratch I made," Garrett explained.

Sylvia's one-week timeline could suck a dirty sock. No matter how many hoops he jumped through for her, Garrett had the nagging feeling she'd still decline his offer. If that was the case this time, he was going to plan B, which included smaller expansion plans that wouldn't cross their current property lines. That would mean none of the community space he was hoping for, but ultimately he had to be concerned about the Throwing Ace's renovations and property value.

He pulled out a chair for her at a small table near the kitchen entrance. She hesitated before sitting.

"How fast do you want it?"

"Day after tomorrow."

It wasn't much notice, but he needed it. Besides, Lily wasn't naive. Giving him what he wanted would only reflect well on her company and help seal the thousands of dollars' worth of work he'd sign them to do. Her light professional smile told Garrett he'd nailed it.

"Well, I'll plug it into our computer design system and—"

"I can stop by Tuesday evening about six-thirty to get it. Can you meet me then?" He went behind the bar for fresh coffee. It took Lily a moment to respond. When she did, she looked slightly amused.

"You're demanding, aren't you?"

"Arrogant, too. Stubborn. Impatient. I could go on, but I don't want to tarnish your opinion of me." He picked up a small remote and clicked a radio on. The sound of old country music came through, filling the space with twang and scratch. Before he could set a fresh cup of coffee down for her, Lily was sliding the chair back.

"I think we're done here." She started to stand, but he set the cup down with a pointed *thunk*.

"Not quite," Garrett said. "You were going to indulge me, remember?" Her eyes showed a flicker of surprise before she sat back down.

He went into the kitchen. When he came back out a few minutes later, she was looking more relaxed as she tapped on her cell phone. The phone slid from her hand and fell onto the table when she eyed the tray he was carrying.

"Wow."

Garrett set the tray down and sat across from her. "Is that a disappointed wow or a get-that-in-my-mouth-ASAP wow?"

"Definitely in my mouth ASAP." Her gaze was wide and appreciative as she took in the steaming platter of marinated roasted vegetables and a smaller one of steak. Garlic, rosemary, lemon and spices he coveted from his home in Hawaii had blended together to soak the meat and vegetables for hours before he'd slow roasted it all in the oven.

There was a perk to insomnia: coming in at four in the morning had delicious results.

"Since the bar's getting an overhaul, we figured the menu should, as well. Marinated prime-rib sandwiches for starters. But since you're a critter hugger, veggies for you."

He shuddered and made a face that drew another blush from her. He sat, stabbed a ribbon of meat and gave her a little salute with his fork before taking a bite.

He tracked Lily's fork as she slowly brought a baby carrot to her mouth, his brain going on sensual overload at the blissful expression on her face. Those scarlet-tinted lips closing around the fork, her crystal-blue eyes closing in a fan of midnight lashes made his brain forget about bar menus and a bigger dance floor.

Jesus.

Garrett shook off the slight stupor. He and Lily had already had their chance, and it hadn't ended well. There was too much going on to even think about trying it again. She didn't get involved with firemen, and he didn't go back for more with the same woman. Done deal.

"It's delicious," she said spiritedly. "The marinade is spicy and sweet, but something else. A little smoky…or…what is that incredible flavor?"

He smiled around a mouthful and swallowed. "A Hawaiian secret."

"Right. You mentioned that's where you came from. Lucky bastard." Her candor made him laugh out loud. Lily's eyes lit up as she made her way through the meal. "What's a Hawaiian boy doing in Nowhere, Kansas?"

Garrett rose to grab two root beers from the bar tap.

"Well," he said as he set the glasses on their table. "My uncle Brad's wife's family is from Danbury. It looked like a good enough place to open a sports bar, so he bought this building six years ago and started a slow remodel, bit by bit. When business started to get better, he needed help and suckered me into it…sweetened the deal by waving an opening on the fire department in my face. That was five years ago."

"That was pretty nice of you to leave Hawaii for, ah, Kansas." The humor in her eyes warmed him.

"I owed him. Brad's like a father to me." Well, he hadn't meant to share quite that much. Garrett wiped his mouth with a napkin. *What the hell, why stop now?* "A little over a year ago, Brad was diagnosed with cancer. I'm just glad I'm here to help him out."

Lily was halfway to taking another bite, but she lowered her fork and took a hasty sip of soda instead. "Do you still have family in Hawaii?" The words were strained. Garrett pushed his plate to the side and crossed his forearms on the table.

"My mother, some cousins and another aunt and uncle. My eldest brother, Cash, is…was…a fire medic in Honolulu. He runs the family hotel there now and works in fire investigation. My middle brother, Sawyer, is in fire search and rescue in Colorado."

"All firefighters?"

"Family tradition, I guess. My father and Brad both worked on the Honolulu department. And so did my grandfather before them. For us boys, it was never a question of if we would follow in their footsteps—it was a matter of how fast we could get started."

Her face flickered with emotions, the most prominent being sadness. Everything else came and went before he could begin to read them. She moved food around on her plate before putting her fork down. "I see."

Lily's flat tone wasn't the reaction he was used to when discussing his role as a firefighter, especially from women. While he didn't thrive on being fawned over, he was used to it, and Lily's indifference was like a neon elephant walking through the room. Her distaste of firefighters in general wasn't something he had experience with. It heightened his curiosity more than bruised his ego. She met his eyes as her fingers splayed over her napkin.

"So you're a golden boy from paradise. You care for your ailing uncle, you cook—wonderfully, I might add—and you come running when someone yells, 'Fire.'"

Garrett leaned slightly over his crossed arms. "I donate blood and mow the lawn for my elderly neighbor, too."

She raised her eyes to the ceiling, but not before he caught the amused twinkle in them. "Of course you do."

He picked up his glass, saluted her with it. "You're wondering why I'm still single, aren't you, Ms. Ashden?"

Lily gave him a narrow glance. "Maybe."

Garrett studied her over the rim of his glass as he took a drink. Her eyebrows arched prettily over those big almond-shaped eyes. The paleness of her skin cast an almost pearlescent glow next to her black hair. Green and orange popped from the ink on her arm, leading him to wonder if she had more tattoos elsewhere.

"And maybe I wanted to tell you how impressed I am with you," he said.

It was true—he was impressed. And also curious why *she* was still single. Lily was a whole recipe of things that made her delightful and interesting and sexy—all attributes men beat each other bloody to get at.

She tapped a finger against her glass. "Really." Her voice was unconvinced.

They were getting way out of the professional zone, but it was an easy line to cross. Besides, teasing her helped him forget all the noise in his head. "Look at this face, Lily. Does it look like the face of a man who'd lie to you?"

She leaned forward, making the space between them smaller. The back of his neck prickled at this sudden bold turn on her part. "It looks like the face of a man used to sweet-talking his way with women."

He gave a self-incriminating groan and dipped his head in mock shame.

"Would you believe I'm reformed?" It was the

truth. Six very long, very frustrating months. And, strangely, he didn't miss it all that much.

"Reformed?" Lily choked a little, tried to hide it and a small smile behind her hand. "I seriously doubt it."

Garrett liked surprising her, even if it was at his own expense. Despite the fun of it, he knew it was time to refocus. He was impressed by Lily Ashden's business mind and was eager to see the plans she'd come up with. Jeopardizing a working relationship with flirting wasn't going to help his cause any.

Garrett leaned away from the table. "Anyway, I'm very glad you like my ideas for the bar, and I appreciate your insight. If you need any other info to get the draft together, you can reach me here." He dug out his wallet and produced a business card with his cell phone number on it. "Otherwise, I'll plan on seeing you Tuesday evening."

Before she could reply, his cell phone rang at the same time his fire pager went off. Lily jerked in her chair; Garrett grabbed his cell so quickly that he almost dropped it.

He flipped it open. "Yeah?"

Mikey's voice burst through the phone. "Got your pager on? I know you're off today, but we could use you...."

Garrett stood as Mikey related the information. A four-car pileup on the interstate, with one vehicle up in flames. He looked at Lily as his brain processed the information. The Throwing Aces was four miles from the fire department, too far for the guys to hold up a truck to wait for him. Lily was watching him intently, her expression hard to read.

"I'll grab my gear and meet you on scene." He ended the call.

Adrenaline shot through his blood like a potent combination of Red Bull and whiskey: burning and with a rush of energy. He looked down at the mess on the table, already sending off a text message to one of the bartenders on shift tonight to see if he could come in a bit early and clean up. Good thing it was Sunday and the bar didn't open until five.

Garrett held up a finger to Lily, sorry that he had to rush about like this, but he was antsy as hell to get to the department to grab his turnout gear. He rushed into the kitchen and made sure the oven and all burners were off and threw the leftover food in the refrigerator. When he hurried back out, Lily was gone.

CHAPTER FIVE

FIVE MINUTES AND fifty-five seconds.

Metal popped and squealed as Garrett steadied the equipment in his hands. Good old Jaws of Life—they'd cut the car's top in under six minutes. Had to be a new record.

The mangled piece of metal and plastic that had once been a Ford Taurus shuddered as Garrett cut the last support to free the top of the vehicle. "Popping the top" was the fastest way to get the victims out of the wreckage, and even though he'd done it more times than he could count, Garrett always loved slicing a vehicle apart. He was in work mode, yeah, but the little boy in him loved playing with big, cool toys like the Jaws of Life.

Four firemen removed the top of the vehicle and pulled away what was left of the passenger door. High speed meets guardrail wasn't a good combination, and, from the looks of it, it had done a number on the human bodies inside, too.

Garrett handed off the jaws and registered silence for just a second as the loud, rattling grind of the equipment was turned off. That silence was quickly filled with moaning and crying—someone trying to scream but managing a gurgling yodel instead.

The three other vehicles involved in the pileup were being tended to by teams of other firemen, and the noises mixed into a chaotic blend. Sweat rolled down his back and matted his hair to his head. At eighty degrees outside, he was burning up inside his heavy turnout gear, but Garrett didn't care.

He leaned into the vehicle and the smell of alcohol hit him like a wall. Two patients. Driver slumped over the center console, the passenger trying like a wild boar in a straitjacket to get out of the prison his seat belt had become. Blood and lots of it, covering them both. Empty beer cans were scattered all over the place. He reached across the screaming patient to the one who lay still—gave him a pinch on the meaty part of his shoulder. No response.

Traffic accidents were the worst part of this job. Fires could be tamed or not—either way, they could fight and try to win. If they couldn't beat the fire, they could contain it; they could keep it from ravaging more than the timber and fiber it had already consumed. He knew how to jump in and wrangle the flaming beast—knew how to put every ounce of knowledge to work to try to fix it.

Accidents like this left him feeling helpless, useless sometimes, and he hated that. The faster and more effectively the firemen worked, the quicker the medics could get in and help the victims. It was all about time—the narrow window standing between the next breath and the last.

Once the car was cut apart and gas or other dangerous chemicals contained, Garrett could step back and let the medics in—watch as they put their impressive knowledge to work to try to wrangle whatever threatened to take life away.

He couldn't fix people. Sometimes, many times, the medics couldn't, either.

Like when his father had fallen through a fire-engulfed roof. It had taken too long for the firemen to find him—too many seconds had gone by as the fire grew stronger and whatever chance Teddy Mateo had had of survival ticked away. Every second counted. Every damn one.

"Let the medics in," Garrett yelled over his shoulder, taking a pair of shears from his pocket. He held them up to the patient to show his intention. "Hold still, okay?"

He cut the seat belt to the sounds of boots behind him. Someone touched his shoulder, asked him to move back. It was the same old routine, one he'd been through a hundred times—secure the scene, cut the victim out, help the medics with moving patients and whatever else they needed.

The steps didn't always follow the same pattern, but they were all there. And the end result would be the same, no matter if the patients lived or died—the high. Garrett was filled with an adrenaline rush and a potent sense of purpose that nothing else could re-create. Forget drugs—they had nothing on the pristine boost he got from pulling his turnout gear on and rushing into things other people backed away from.

He was on autopilot, his heart racing, his brain as sharp as it'd ever be. Chasing the high—it drove every fireman on this squad. This feeling, this sense of knowing what to do and when, the human connection in doing everything you could to help save a life and property was about as good as it got.

Going after that feeling, reaching for that high, kept them all working as hard as they could. It was what his father had been after the day he'd been swallowed from a rooftop into a belly of fire. Garrett figured that luck would keep him alive while he chased the high, but the absence of good fortune and enough seconds would see him out with honor the way his father had gone.

He wrinkled his nose at a stream of blood oozing from the unresponsive driver. He backed off, thankful it was the medic's turn. A good adrenaline rush didn't just keep him going, it helped block out, for a little while at least, that the lumps of flesh and bone were actually human, and that the tragic things in front of him were actually real.

Later, when the high wore off, Garrett would remember the grisly details and be flooded with the sickly reminder that bad things happened to tear people and families apart. It always served as a reminder of why he was alone and why it was easier that way.

"See that?" Mikey Cain wiped a soiled leather glove over his face and jerked his head toward the hazy August sky.

Garrett lifted the grimy eye shield on his helmet and glanced up. It had been overcast all day, with a slightly green hue coming and going. Everyone around these parts knew that could be bad or just a false alarm.

Given the heat and the balmy breeze that had only gotten stronger throughout the day, and now the massive swirl of gray and purplish clouds above their heads, Garrett was going with bad. Alabama had been hit with two tornadoes yesterday, Texas with a random handful earlier in the week. A system was always cooking this time of year.

"Been brewing all damn day," Mikey muttered.

Garrett's hand went reflexively to his pager. If a tornado had been spotted, the 911 personnel pagers were the first to go off. That it hadn't, combined with the town's quiet weather siren, made him feel a little better.

"Got that right. Did you hear the forecast?"

Mikey shrugged, his eyes trailing back to the wrecked car. "Nope. 'Nader coming, if I had to guess."

The medics extracted the patient using a long orange board, and then placed him onto a cot positioned beside the wreckage. The patient wasn't obeying the paramedic's instructions and pushed frantically at the rigid splints they were trying to put on his arm. His right arm flopped at an unnatural angle. Garrett and Mikey cringed at the same time.

"Damn." Garrett turned away and began gathering equipment.

"Yeah." Mikey pulled in the hydraulic lines that connected to the Jaws of Life before slanting his head back up to the sky. "Reminds me of when that tornado hit right after we worked that wreck this same time last year. Remember? Engine One got tipped clear onto its side."

Garrett paused a moment to think. "Nah, I was out of town then." He'd heard about it, though. There were enough pictures of the overturned engine hanging up on the fire station bulletin board, and stories still floating around about it to make it feel like he'd witnessed it himself.

Mikey walked to the fire truck, his arms loaded.

"Right—you were off prancing in your bikini in Hawaii then."

Garrett smirked. At thirty-one, he was one of the youngest on the squad and was used to taking his share of razzing from the other firemen. Since he'd worked his way through the roster of much older and more experienced men to the role of assistant chief, the razzing had only gotten worse. But over the years, the comments had turned from a way to test him into a good-natured display of male respect. He took it with a smile. Mikey was only a couple of years older, but he acted like an old-timer, despite being the brunt of many jokes himself.

"Don't be jealous of my bikini body, man." Garrett patted Mikey's belly over his heavy jacket. Mikey smirked and knocked Garrett's hand away.

The scene was starting to wind down. The other firemen gathered equipment and tidied away bits of metal from the road. Garrett remembered the mess he'd left behind at the bar, his thoughts straying to the disappointment that his morning with Lily had been cut short. At least they'd gone over everything they'd needed to for her to get started on his bid, and that had been the point.

Garrett looked up at the sky just in time to see a streak of lightning glisten behind the azure clouds. The wind gave an impressive gust, considering it had been a relatively mild day. He was glad the vehicle fire had already been put out, because this wind was just strong enough to fan flames and make their job harder.

Mikey began pulling on the end of a rope coil. "That's when you were in Hawaii for Cash after his accident, right?"

Garrett held his arms out for Mikey to wind rope around them into a neat oval and gave a tight nod in response.

The reminder of his brother's accident gave him a pang. Cash Mateo had been the big, strong and silent type before a beam had fallen on his head during a fire rescue attempt and he'd suffered a traumatic brain injury. Now he was just big, strong and ornery as hell.

The seizure disorder and short-term memory loss he earned from that accident had turned Cash into a hollow man—one who'd slipped into a scary depression after his wife decided she couldn't handle what had happened and divorced him. He was better now, seemed to have settled into the fact that his firefighting career was over and accepted that his new job as a fire investigator was a suitable replacement.

"You had a bad year, Mateo, between Brad getting sick and Cash. It's time something good happened to you."

Garrett couldn't argue with that. His family had taken its share of hits, that was for sure. He was ready for...something else to happen, too. Something fun and good to remind him that there was more to life than disaster and death. Like a four-wheeling trip with lots of mud and beer involved. Garrett paused at that thought, but instead of mentioning it, he found himself saying something entirely different.

"Remember the woman from the bar the other night? The 'I don't get involved with firemen' one?"

Mikey widened his eyes. "Yeah. Did she change her mind?"

Right. "Ha, no. She's my new contractor. Ashden Construction? Lily Ashden."

Garrett eyeballed Mikey, who'd stopped looping rope, his face thoughtful. Mikey tipped back his helmet and wiped a dirty glove over his face. A couple of dark curls of his too-long bangs sneaked out from beneath his helmet.

"Got that *Twilight Zone* feeling?" Garrett asked, watching Mikey's lips pull tighter. "Does she sound familiar to you, too?"

"Yes." Mikey cocked his head, shrugged and went back to rope looping. "How do I know that name?"

"I don't know," Garrett replied. The adrenaline was starting to fade, leaving him tired, hot and wishing he could get out of his gear and let the breeze cool him off. He was ready to be done. "Ashden Construction is pretty well-known. I'm sure her name's been thrown around here and there. Then again, I don't really care as long as she can get the job done."

Remembering their conversations as they'd walked the empty plot behind the bar, Garrett felt a bit guilty that he'd only given her two days to complete the draft, but Sylvia hadn't given him much time to work with, either.

That was it. He couldn't take it anymore. Garrett unstrapped his helmet and pulled it off. Sweat coursed over his face as he puffed out a tired breath and glanced around. The scene was pretty much cleared. All the patients had been taken away, the vehicles moved to the side of the road and debris cleared so traffic could get through. With any luck, he'd have enough time to stop by the hospital and see Brad before his shift at the fire station started at six.

"Anyway, Lily's brother owns a shop in Nashville. She asked to meet Bodie to see if some of his work might be a fit for the store."

Mikey's expression perked up. "Yeah? Sure. Anytime. You know, you should take her to the Pit and show her all of Bodie's work there." Someone shouted from behind the engine. Frowning,

Garrett pulled on his helmet, moving to the front to see what was going on.

"I was thinking that, too." Not that he expected Lily would go anywhere with him unless it was related to the job. Did he even want her to? Hard to say. He was attracted to her, sure, but was it a good idea to mix personal aspects into business?

Another voice rang out, followed by the screech of brakes and tires. Garrett peered around the front of the fire engine just as a small red car whizzed past and slammed into one of the wrecked cars that had been pulled to the side of the road. The crunch of metal on metal cut through the air.

"Goddamn rubberneckers!" The curse preceded the stomp of boots as several firemen ran over to the fresh collision, Garrett included. It wasn't the first time this had happened, people driving by too distracted from looking at the scene to realize they were about to crash themselves.

Garrett's heart pumped with renewed vigor. Apparently he wasn't done yet.

"THANKS FOR MEETING ME." Macy smiled around the straw of her frappé. Mama's Java was packed, everyone making a mad dash for midafternoon coffee. Lily popped the top of her to-go cup to let the steam out. It might be hot and humid outside, but coffee was akin to fresh air. Had to have it to live.

"Of course," Lily replied. "Besides, you sounded weird on the phone." Macy was a kindergarten teacher and usually spent her summers traveling, but since breaking up with her boyfriend a month ago, she had decided to cancel their joint travel plans and hang around Danbury instead.

"Well, I got a strange phone call last night." Macy eyed her steadily. "From Rob."

Lily curled her upper lip. "Rob? What did he want?"

Lily had already had two voice mails from her ex-fiancé, and she had no intention of calling him back. As far as she was concerned, there was nothing to say. The bastard had walked out on her at the lowest, most devastating time of her life. Instead of supporting her when Katja died, Rob had left.

Macy tucked a curl behind her ear. "He's coming to Danbury and he wants to see you. Wondered if I could relay the message since you won't call him back." Her face scrunched. "What's this all about?"

Lily spread her hands. "I don't know, and to be honest, I don't care. I'm sorry he called you."

Macy's eyes lit up. "Maybe he's dying from some horrible bastard-killing disease and he's coming to throw himself at your feet to beg forgiveness."

They both laughed at the crude justification in that. Lily had wished a pox on Rob more than once—never seriously, of course—but it was hard to not feel vindictive when her heart had been breaking.

Even as she thought about it, a familiar pang hit her. Rob had never said why he'd left, and though it shouldn't matter after all this time, it sort of did. There were times, more than she wanted to admit, that she wondered what had prompted him to go, and it left her unsettled. Closure was a good thing, and though she'd mostly achieved that, Lily had a little hole that Rob could fill with an explanation. Even if it was one she didn't want to face.

"I'll send him a text to stop calling. I'll change my number if I have to. Seriously, that is how badly I don't want to speak to that man." Lily didn't miss the tight corners of Macy's usually smiling mouth, or the tired little creases next to her eyes.

"Yeah," Macy agreed with a sigh. She looked down and picked at something on the table. "If only it was that easy, right?"

Concern hit Lily hard. In all the years she'd known Macy, Lily had never seen her look so… flat. She touched Macy's hand.

"What's up, Mace? Don't say nothing…."

Macy shook her head as if it wasn't a big deal. "Devon keeps calling me. I know what it's like, the calls—not wanting them. Wishing they'd just leave you alone so you can move on. You know?" Macy and Devon hadn't been together that long.

"So you haven't been sad that the two of you broke up?" By the disgust on Macy's face, Lily figured she was right.

"God, no. I'm frustrated because he won't leave me alone. Calls at all hours, drives by my house. Sometimes he just sits there and stares at the front door, like he's waiting for me to come out."

Lily's throat went tight. She leaned in closer over the table, wanting to simultaneously hug Macy and shake her silly. "Macy Marie, why didn't you tell me? What...what can we do?"

The smile Macy produced might have fooled someone else, but not Lily.

"It's fine. I haven't heard from him or seen him in over a week. I think he's finally moved on." Macy took both of Lily's hands and cocked her head.

"I didn't say anything because you've got enough going on. Katja's... The anniversary of that day, and all the projects you're working on. Speaking of which, how is our hot Thor/bartender/fireman doing?"

Lily slumped in her seat and took a long drink of coffee. "Nice deflection, Macy."

Truth was, she'd wanted to talk to Macy about how muddled her emotions had been since meeting Garrett, but the opportunity had never presented itself. She checked the clock on her cell phone, saw that she still had plenty of time to finish up Garrett's drafts before he stopped by that night. She folded her hands and pursed her lips. No time like the present.

"I've been having nightmares again, ever since I met Garrett. It was like the moment he told me he was a firefighter a switch in my head turned on and let all the demons back out."

Lily grabbed two sugar packets, ripped them open and dumped them into her coffee. She didn't usually like sweet things, but it gave her hands something to do.

"I haven't slept much since the night of the fund-raiser," she continued. "Every time I close my eyes, I see Katja's face, and I get this *feeling,* like she wants me to… I don't know." Lily grabbed another sugar packet, but Macy plucked it from her fingers and put it back.

"Wants you to what?"

Lily's chest grew heavy. This was silly. "Nothing. I just…I have this feeling that she wants me to find out *why.*" She puffed air between her lips. That was probably the craziest sentence that had ever come out of her mouth. Ah, the fun of emotional trauma.

Despite how foolish Lily felt, Macy didn't look surprised. Her brow was furrowed, her green eyes inquisitive.

"Are you saying you're seeing Katja's ghost?"

Shivers burst along Lily's arms and scalp. It wasn't that she didn't believe in the supernatural, but the thought of her sister's spirit roaming the earth was too much to bear. If Katja had to be gone, it was better for her to be gone completely.

"No, no. That's not it. It's just that, when I think about her, I get this sensation that she wants me to find out *why.* Why the fire happened. Why she died. I never had that feeling before the fund-raiser. I think it was being around all those firemen."

Lily and her father had never gotten a firm answer on what had caused the fire, and the case had been closed as accidental. Lily knew she should be grateful to have made it out alive when eight others hadn't—and she was—but the memories made it hard not to be bitter. All those firemen, and not a single one had been able to get Katja out....

"Maybe you should talk to Garrett about it." Macy raised an eyebrow and nodded as if that made perfect sense.

Lily shook her head. As much as she liked to see things through, she had long ago accepted that she'd never get closure in Katja's death, not completely.

"He's a client. Why would I discuss my personal business with him?"

She grabbed another sugar packet and ripped it open before Macy could stop her. The little granules glittered in the sunlight streaming through the window as she poured them slowly into her coffee. Macy plucked the sugar container off the table and made it disappear under her side of the table.

"Because he's a firefighter. Maybe he'd be able to help you understand a little more about that night. He wasn't there, so maybe he'll have an unbiased, professional view on the whole thing. Or—"

Macy's cell phone rang. Her shoulders tightened and she clenched her jaw as she dug it out of her purse. She checked the number, visibly relaxing.

"Or you could just sleep with him and enjoy yourself." Macy's wink was wicked as she answered the call, leaving Lily with her mouth open.

Sleep with Garrett. There were so many reasons that would not happen. She thought of all the phone numbers in Garrett's personal pick-a-girl bucket. She'd fallen for his charm once and luckily stopped herself before she'd become another number.

Macy hung up, her smile genuinely happy.

"Ha! That was my hairdresser. She can fit me in right now. Call me later?"

This girl and her hair. Macy took naturally curly to a red-carpet level and didn't care how much it cost. "You got it."

"Think about what I said?" Macy slid out of the booth, Lily right behind.

"About sleeping with Garrett?" She rolled her eyes, giving Macy a little wave as she headed to the door while Lily went to order new coffee.

"That, too!" Macy called out before the door shut behind her.

That, too. No. Way.

LILY WHISTLED WHAT should have been Maroon 5's "Payphone," but it came out more like the screech of a dying cat as she walked into the Ashden building. Her talents had never extended to music, but it didn't stop her from trying. Especially since she knew how much her father hated whistling. She thought he might still be at lunch, but Doug stuck his head out of his office as she passed by.

"What the hell is that noise?"

Lily whistled louder in response. Girl time with Macy had been just what she needed, though she now had more clutter in her head than before. Namely, worry over Macy's confession about Devon being a creeper and the hope that he really was gone for good. Next in line was Macy's lovely suggestion about spilling her guts to Garrett.

She pushed that advice away as a sick feeling churned in her gut. Talking to him about Katja would probably lead to her having a meltdown, and she wasn't about to put that kind of emotional baggage on a man she barely knew. Besides, Ashdens didn't have meltdowns; they just found more work to do until they got over it.

"Deal with it, Doug," she called out with sticky sweetness as she walked into her office. And stopped dead. Her purse and laptop bag slipped off her shoulder, dumping her computer onto the carpeted floor.

At least a dozen yellow roses sat on her desk in a glass mosaic vase.

"If roses will keep you from whistling, I'll get you some every damn day." Lily barely heard Doug's quip as she made her way to the desk and gingerly touched the delicate petals. There were fifteen, artfully arranged around a backsplash of baby's breath and greenery. A little card sat on a stick in the center. Heart pounding, she plucked it from the holder. Her father's breath washed over her neck as he leaned over her shoulder.

"Who'd ya impress, there, girlie?"

"Doug, please. It's probably a mistake."

Doug smacked his lips. "Yep, that's why the card says 'Lily' on it."

Her cheeks flushed when she realized her name was scrawled across the white envelope. She'd never been sent flowers before. In the four years they'd been together, Rob had never sent the token, insisting that she wasn't the "flowers type."

Until now, she'd never considered flowers her thing, either, but apparently all it took to change her mind was for someone to make the attempt. The roses were gorgeous, and her office smelled amazing. And with the beautiful mosaic vase, the arrangement was most certainly her style.

Someone had guessed well. Her fingers trembled as she eased the card out of the envelope, already suspecting what name she'd find. Her tummy quivered when she saw she was right.

Enjoy. Garrett

Lily dropped the card onto the desk. She couldn't stop the smile that crossed her lips or the flash of joy that sparked in her heart. As she tucked her hair behind her ear, she realized she was shaking. A mixture of jubilation and fear tumbled into her. She was way too happy at Garrett's thoughtfulness. She liked this too much—she couldn't like this, could she?

She read the note again, as if an explanation would magically pop up, something like "thanks for meeting with me" or "thanks for dealing with my cockiness." The little he had written left his motives open to interpretation.

"This *Garrett* isn't a client, I hope," her father said from behind her.

"Jesus, Doug. Don't make me chop you up into little pieces and scatter you across five states."

"Lily." The firmness of his voice dampened her joy, but it also made her want to laugh. Was he trying to be protective or watch out for her interests…something *fatherly?*

When her engagement to Rob had ended, her father had given her a pat on the back and extra work to "take your mind off things." Nothing more was ever said about it, nor had he encouraged her attempts to bring it up. So she'd locked her pain and anger and withering self-worth away, in the same little compartment of her heart where her grief over Katja's death lived.

She wasn't about to put herself out there with her father now. "Garrett happens to be the co-owner of the Throwing Aces. I've been meeting with him since Brad Mateo is apparently out for a while. These are just a nice gesture, that's all."

Lily retrieved her laptop and set it down be-

fore turning to the windows behind her desk.
Golden rays of sun struggled to break through
the overhead clouds. Little shadows of yellow
dotted the grass and leaves outside, not unlike
the pale golden hue of the flowers on her desk.
My own perfect sunshine. Lily hugged herself,
wishing to hold on to the contentment. That
peaceful feeling was unfamiliar, yet so very,
very comforting.

Doug cleared his throat behind her. Moment
over. Lily turned, frowning at the blueprint that
looked up at her from her desk. She cocked her
head at her dad and picked the paper up. "What's
this?"

"Lincoln sent that over for you this morning."

Lily's gaze returned to the drawing. She immediately recognized the old shoe factory. A turn-
of-the-century brick structure, the shoe factory
had housed a handful of businesses in Danbury
over the years since closing its doors to shoe making in the 1930s. It sat just at the edge of town
on a lot that was both quiet yet easily accessible
from the main road. The blueprint showed the
stately three-story building redesigned as a showroom. Across the top was Lincoln's fancy script
handwriting. "Lily's Showroom. Big Plans for
My Brilliant Sister."

"Shoe factory's for sale." Doug's nose twitched.
"Lincoln thought you might like to see how eas-

ily the building could be converted into a showroom like we have in Nashville." He sniffed and turned to the door as if he was going to walk out, but Lily called his name. Unable to take her eyes from the miniblueprint, she waved Doug back to her side.

"Wait a minute." She and Katja had planned to open a showroom in Danbury. The town was growing, thanks to the state college being so close. Tourism had increased, and people were slowly investing more in their homes. The success of a showroom was promising, though Doug had never seemed very supportive of their plan.

After Katja's death, his indifference to Lily's passion for local artists was a big reason she'd given up on the idea of the showroom and resolved to just move to Nashville. Lincoln was always welcoming and supportive. Even now, Lincoln was giving her something to believe in, a reason to stay in Danbury and be close to their father. She pushed down a sad sigh. Too bad work had to be the reason she stayed here with him.

Lily ran a finger over the carefully drafted blue lines on the drawing. It was standard-size paper, just right for sending via fax machine, but she could still envision the scale. Lincoln had drafted out the bottom level as a store for architectural salvages to be sold, the middle floor as an artist showroom and the top floor for offices.

It was large enough that another business could be hosted there, too. It was perfect.

Doug's breathing was loud in her ear as he leaned over her shoulder to peer at the print. She turned to him. The blasé look on his face should have stopped her, but she didn't learn easily, apparently.

"What do you think?"

He shrugged. "It's just a building. I suppose it would work fine."

"Do you think I should pursue it? Stay in Danbury?" She caught her father's eyes. As usual, they were devoid of any discernible emotion. She searched his face, looking for some soft spot, some sign that he might be coming around.

He sniffed. "It's just a drawing."

Tears bit the back of Lily's eyes. She blinked them away. She knew better than to ask…didn't know what she was hoping he might actually come out and admit. That he wanted her to stay in Danbury? That he believed she could manage an extension of their business here, the way Lincoln believed she could do in Nashville?

Lily's chest tightened. Saying that he loved her would have been a nice start. Foolish, stupid, idiot thing to even hope for. But she couldn't stop herself from trying, just once more.

"Do *you* want me to stay in Danbury?" The sweet feeling the roses had given her faded.

Doug waved an irritated hand at her. "Lily, you're going to do what you're going to do." He spun around. "Hey, I need you to pull the file for the Masterson bid and make some changes ASAP. I just sent you an email about it."

He walked out, his voice driving nails through her foolish hope that someday her dad would tell her that he wanted her to stay. Not because he needed her help with the business, but because he loved her.

Talking with Garrett about his plans for the empty lot had given her a little blip of excitement. Between his development to host fairs and sales and her showroom to draw contractors and designers, they could easily work together to cross promote their venues while helping support the community. That was a partnership that made sense, one where she'd be important.

Lily set the blueprint on her desk and turned back to the window. It had been a nice thought— a quick passing thought. Because there was no way she was getting any more involved with Garrett Mateo or hanging around Danbury for her father to walk all over her any longer.

She kept herself busy the rest of the day, torn constantly between the flowers and the blueprint. How she managed to actually get any work done with all the daydreaming was a miracle, but by the time Doug had left for the day, Lily had finished the draft for Garrett and tidied up several lose ends for other clients.

Cranking the radio, Lily clicked through templates on her computer drafting program until she found one that was a pretty close match to the lower level of the shoe factory. She plugged in her own design ideas, her focus and more daydreaming draining her of any sense of time.

Her hair had started to fall from the green-and-white silk scarf she had it tied up in, wisps curling around her eyes and tickling her neck. The heat was sticky, despite the fan she had running, making her top cling a little more than was comfortable. She shut down the computer and spun in her chair, wishing Garrett would hurry and pick up the draft so she could head home and dunk herself in a cool shower.

That might soothe her skin, but she knew it wouldn't do anything for the burn of her emotions. Lily tilted her head and studied Lincoln's draft and compared it with the one she was working on. Each time her eyes fell to Lincoln's version, she thought of Doug's crappy attitude and some of her creative juice would dry up.

He'd never been a talker, especially about anything emotional or personal. When they were young, Katja and Lily would ask him about their mothers, but even then he hadn't been forthcoming.

Katja's mother had been Doug's first wife, Greta, and from the little Lily had been able to get out of him over the years, she'd been his greatest love. She'd been from a political family, which had had enough influence on Doug that he'd agreed to give Katja her mother's surname instead of his own. Greta Ober died when Katja was two.

Doug remarried shortly after and had Lincoln and Lily, only to have their mother walk out and never look back. Lily and Lincoln had been four, too young to really remember their mother, but old enough that Lily could recall the grief Doug had gone through.

Every time Lily and Katja asked about their mothers, Doug would pretend not to hear them or change the subject. In the rare moment he felt cornered enough to comply, his answers were truncated and unencouraging. It didn't take long to realize painful things weren't something they talked about in the Ashden household.

He'd been a caring enough father as they all grew, but only to the extent of a pat on the head or a one-armed hug. He was in shutdown mode more than anything, so the girls had naturally drifted to Lincoln for support and affection and love. And he'd readily given it.

Lily leaned back in the chair and held the shoe factory draft near her face. Since Katja's death,

Lily had distanced herself from Lincoln, too. It was a sobering reality, but it was true. She'd turned inward, despite therapy, despite knowing she needed to talk about what happened the night of the fire. It was easier to hold it close to her heart and leave it buried inside than to share it with someone else. It was easier to accept that Doug only wanted her when he needed her to do something than to confront him about it. It was easier to just be an emotional hermit.

Even if it meant she was turning into Doug.

She closed her eyes. She didn't want to be Doug. She wanted... She wanted things to be normal. Whatever that may be; whatever that meant. Because the tension brewing between her and Doug—and the way she'd distanced herself from Lincoln—wasn't normal, and she couldn't accept it anymore. Soon they'd be facing the first anniversary of Katja's death, and, dammit, they all needed to find a way of dealing with that. Together.

A light knock rapped on the open door. Her stomach flipped as Garrett peeked his head in.

"Hey," he called warmly.

She bolted upright in the chair and gave him an inadvertent once-over—it couldn't be helped. He was in his firemen's uniform. Black pressed pants, a light blue button-up shirt with firefighting patches on the sleeves. He looked good—

amazing—but the sight of the firefighter crest on his sleeve gave her a sour taste in her mouth. Garrett glanced down and smiled sheepishly.

"I didn't have time to change." He smoothed one wide palm down his middle and strode to her desk. She slid Garrett's draft out of the folder she'd set it in.

"Wow, that looks great!" He picked up the print, blessedly oblivious to how her body was at war with itself over its reaction to him.

His hair was a mess, lying in seductive disarray over his forehead with curls licking around his ears. The top three buttons of his shirt were undone, revealing just a peek of golden skin. Lily tidied up the top of her desk, desperately needing something else to focus on. An hour-long conversation with Macy last night had turned into her fishing for more scoop on Garrett. Lily had begrudgingly admitted he was too handsome for his own good.

God. That is a freaking understatement.

"I just finished, actually. We can make any changes if you like. I can open the program back up."

Keep it professional, Ashden. She almost laughed out loud at her inner reprimand. He turned his back to her desk, studying the print as he paced. After a moment, he turned and met her eyes.

"This is amazing, Lily. It's exactly what I had in mind." He came around by her chair and hunkered down next to her. "What are these marks here?"

"Landscaping outlines. It gives you a general idea of where trees and flowers could be planted to increase the appeal of the space." She pointed to the sheet. "These lines give you options of walkways—paths—that could be put in to lead people from the new deck off the bar outside. For instance, if you wanted to allow vendors to put up booths, it would make sense to do that here and here, and put paths between them."

They went back and forth over options. Lily found she had to concentrate on his questions a couple of times. He smelled too good, and that, combined with his closeness, muddled her focus.

He finally straightened, his eyes straying to the vase of roses behind her desk. "Huh. I wonder what exceptionally good-looking, thoughtful gentleman sent those?" His eyebrows arched playfully as he sauntered to the shelf where the vase sat.

Lily rolled her eyes, not that he'd see. Those flowers had been taunting her all day—not just with their divine scent but the overall gesture. She could still feel a pleasurable tingle all the way to her toes when she remembered seeing them on her desk that afternoon.

"Thank you for the flowers, Garrett. You didn't have to do that."

"I felt bad for rushing you into this project." He eyed the vase, fingered a flower. "And I may have had an ulterior motive, too."

Garrett wore his self-confidence like a well-tailored suit. He read her well. She'd spent almost an hour staring at the flowers when they'd sat on her desk, touching the petals, thinking about him. Finally, she'd moved them to the shelf near the bookcase behind her desk out of frustration, but the lovely scent wouldn't let her forget.

She tipped her chin up and crossed her arms. "There it is. You need something."

The amused sound he made could have brought her to her knees had she been standing—a deep, sexy sound. "It's not as horrible as you're making it sound, I promise."

So he did need something from her. Of course. Flowers couldn't just be flowers. They had to be a way of getting something out of her. She'd had enough of being used, thank you.

She was about to make a snappy retort, when Garrett pushed his fingers through his hair, turned away from her and stared at the bookcase. Garrett narrowed his eyes at her for a moment before focusing back on what had caught his interest. He'd found Katja's picture and was studying it with a slight cock of his head.

Lily's stomach flipped a little. She tried not to think about the irony of having a fireman in full uniform staring at the picture of a woman who'd died in flames. He turned back, hands in his pockets again, his face displaying that his mind was chewing something over. But whatever that was, he seemed to shake it off.

"Okay, so I have a very impromptu meeting tonight with someone I'd like you to meet." Garrett slid the print off her desk and rolled it carefully. "Do you know Sylvia Frasier? Of Frasier Realty?"

Every developer and contractor for three states knew Frasier Realty. "Of course. You can hardly buy property in this town without dealing with her." Suddenly Lily understood. "Aah. She owns the lot behind the bar. I saw the sign."

Garrett tapped the end of the rolled paper against his palm.

"Unfortunately, Sylvia and I don't have a warm, fuzzy history. I keep offering on the land, and she keeps turning me down and raising the price. But I'm running out of time." The passion with which Garrett spoke planted questions in Lily's mind. "I made a promise to Brad to get this development done before—"

Silence dripped between them while Garrett's eyes were bright with inner fire. He didn't need to say any more for Lily to understand.

She traced the edge of her desk with a finger, feeling a sudden sadness for what the Mateo family was facing. She hadn't met Brad, but it was obvious from Garrett's emotions that he was close to his uncle.

"Here's the thing," Garrett said. "Developing the land isn't fundamental to the Throwing Ace's future, not like the overall renovations are. But it's something that would add value while enriching the community and giving people like Bodie an outlet. I want to give the land purchase one last shot. I'd like you to present this design to Sylvia."

Some of the tension seeped out of Lily— tension that had built up because she was trying so hard to stay closed off from Garrett. Yet the more time she spent with him, the more it became apparent there was a lot going on beneath his golden-boy exterior—a lot to be admired.

"You have a ton of people counting on you."

He smiled and looked down. "It's not just that. I don't fail."

There was no cocky edge to the words, just a solid self-confidence. And when he did get told no? It was probably such a foreign concept, Garrett had no idea how to handle it except to take it personally.

"Okay. But I don't understand why you need me. Why can't you present the idea to Sylvia?"

Lily reached for her purse from beneath the

desk and slipped it over her shoulder, but remained seated. Garrett gestured for her to come over to him, held out a big welcoming hand. The gesture was simple but gentlemanly, and it tugged at her resistance. She relented, crossing to him, where that beautiful hand found her lower back as he ushered her out of the room.

He cleared his throat, his voice hard. "Sylvia is under the impression I don't respect women."

"Care to explain why?" She slid him a sideways look, saw that he was frowning. Garrett held the front door for her, then waited as she locked it.

He remained tight-lipped until she was settled in the front seat of his truck and he'd started it up. Garrett turned to her, ran a thumb over his chin.

"I had a very short relationship with her granddaughter. By 'relationship' I mean a casual night, no strings attached…at least, not for me. Holly had other ideas. I guess I hadn't been clear enough that long-term hookups aren't my thing. I broke her heart, she threw me under the bus with Sylvia and here we are."

Lily thought of Rob, how he'd packed up and left when she was least expecting it. It was crushing to find out the man you were intimately involved with had life plans that didn't include you.

The tension started to sink back in, her mind wandering to the bucket of phone numbers under the bar. She untied the scarf from her head, pulling harder than she intended, making her scalp ache.

"Were you cruel to her about it?"

"What?"

She fished a comb from her purse and began running it through her hair. Why was she so irritated right now? She shouldn't care a lick about Garrett's personal life, but it bothered her anyway. "When you broke it off. Were you cruel to her?"

He shook his head, brow wrinkled as though she'd wounded him with the question.

"God, Lily, no. Never." He turned, put the truck in gear and pulled out into the street. "It's just... I've never made a promise I can't keep. I never promised her or any other woman anything beyond a few nights together. A couple weeks after I called it off, I...unknowingly got involved with one of Sylvia's Realtors. Nail, meet coffin."

A small laugh bubbled in Lily's throat. That he was confessing his tomcat ways was a little unsettling. Classic womanizer. He'd come on to her after all, but why? Because she was female? He said he was reformed, but that was hard to believe. It didn't matter. He was the client, end of story.

She gave him a sideways glance. Maybe there was a part of her that hoped Garrett saw something special in her. It had been a long time since anyone had seen anything beyond what she could do for them. Even if she couldn't—wouldn't—get involved with him intimately, it was still nice to think that he found her…what, attractive? Interesting? Despite her reservations, she was attracted to him. There was no denying it. But it seemed he just found her useful, like everyone else in her life.

"So what exactly did you see in me?" She stared straight ahead, grappling with the anger brewing. "Did you know who I was the first night we met?" He needed her, not for *her,* but for the reputable Ashden name and the company she represented.

"What? No. I had no idea who you were."

She swallowed hard. To think she'd given in—welcomed his kisses and caresses—before she had realized he was a fireman. It had been easy to convince herself that Garrett was genuine, but now she realized she needed to nip this in the bud. He wanted her to help him out? Fine. But she wasn't going to make it easy on him. That much she could control.

"I'm assuming that you need me to meet with Sylvia tonight because number one, I'm a woman in a high position with a successful development company, and number two, simply because of the good reputation of my last name. She'll be so impressed that you've hired a woman that she'll overlook her original impression that you're a pig and sell the lot to you."

Garrett stopped for a red light, giving her a quick glance before simply staring. "No. Yes... but, Lily...a pig? Really?"

She tossed back her head, watched the cars crisscrossing through the intersection in front of them and began to retie the scarf in her hair.

"Yes, I do think Sylvia will be impressed by you, not only for the reasons you mentioned, but because you're intelligent and..."

Lily's chest tightened with anger. She didn't have time for any more of this nonsense. God, Nashville couldn't come fast enough.

"There's only one reason I'm still sitting in this truck," she said. "And that's because I made a promise to my father that I would do what it took to show you we're the best company for the job. I owe it to our employees to keep my word. I'll woo Sylvia Frasier, you'll sign the contract that I'll have delivered to you in a few days and then we're done dealing with each other. Understood?"

CHAPTER SIX

THAT HADN'T GONE WELL. Garrett knew enough to keep his mouth shut the rest of the way to the club where Sylvia was having her routine Tuesday-night cocktail. Spilling his story about Holly—hell, with women in general—probably hadn't been the smartest idea, but he wasn't one to hold things back. There was no reason not to be honest.

What exactly did you see in me?

Lily's question nagged at him. He wanted to address it, wanted to wow her with some amazing answer, but the truth was, he didn't know. That first night in the bar, yeah, he'd been attracted to her looks and then the sound of her voice, her laugh and her humor. He'd also been reasonably sure that she was just as attracted to him. But their subsequent meetings had highlighted her intelligence, wit and dry humor. There was more, but he couldn't put his finger on it exactly.

It shouldn't matter anyway, and her sudden anger made no sense to him. She'd already said he was off-limits because of his job. It shouldn't matter to her what he did in his private life—unless there was more going on under the surface than she was letting on.

He watched from the corner of his eye as she applied a slick of red gloss to her lips and ran fingers through her black hair. She sat stiff as a board against the seat, looking anywhere but at him. She was pissed, all right, but it didn't dampen the desire he had to trail his fingers over her cheek as he kissed that lipstick clear off.

Garrett shifted in his seat, cursing the flush of heat the wicked thoughts brought on, and pulled into the parking lot of the Chandelier. He swore a cool breeze wafted off her, and if she sat any straighter, she'd probably give herself a migraine from all the muscle tension. He didn't make a habit of pissing women off—at least not without knowing he'd be able to soothe them later. He doubted there'd be much chance to soothe Lily anytime soon.

"I shouldn't have sprung this meeting on you." His voice was soft with sincerity. She let out a pent-up breath but didn't look at him. Sunlight was fading, letting in a bloodred glow.

"Nope." With only that cool reply, she opened the door and slipped out.

Garrett walked around the truck to meet her, took her arm lightly. Her frigidity was really messing with his ability to figure out what to do or say next. He pulled her to a stop, grateful the early-evening air had lost some of its humidity.

"Thank you for coming with me." Lily simply glared at him. "If she sells, I'll get a tattoo of your name on my arm. Deal?"

Where that tease had come from, he had no idea. There was no way he was getting jabbed with needles to ink the name of a woman with about as much affection for him as a wild boar on his body. But one corner of her mouth tipped up, and in that second, the quip was worth it.

Lily shook her head as she walked past him to the door, her shoes tapping on the pavement in sassy, confident clicks. The lacy mint-green skirt she wore had an asymmetrical hem that fluttered in time to the sway of her walk. A white blouse made a perfect contrast with her black hair. She wore it stick straight today, and a green-and-white silk scarf acted as a shimmery headband.

Garrett could have stood there admiring her until the sun set completely, but three big strides caught him up to her. He put his hand on her lower back, a move he was starting to enjoy. He enjoyed it even more that she didn't shrug him off. Inside, they were greeted by warm golden light from a large chandelier in the entryway. The elegant carpet boasted a red-and-black damask pattern; the walls were beautifully finished in gray leather and walnut. Lily's expression went from irritated to impressed as she glanced around.

A hostess welcomed them with a brilliant smile. "May I help you?"

"Sylvia Frasier is expecting us." Sylvia hadn't been all that pleased when he'd asked to meet her tonight. He wouldn't be one bit surprised if she'd left instructions to turn him away. By the look on the hostess's face, he figured that was exactly the case.

"I'm sorry, sir, Mrs. Frasier didn't leave a guest list." *Damn woman.* She was going to make him work for a minute of her time the same way she kept making him work for the land. Cat and mouse.

Lily looked at him sharply. Garrett put on his best smile, the one that always won people over. It was a gift, and he wasn't above using it to his advantage.

"I'm really sorry for the inconvenience, Molly," he said smoothly, reading her name tag. "Perhaps she simply forgot. Could you tell her Garrett Mateo is here, please? I'd owe you one."

The hostess's eyelashes fluttered, her cheeks going pink. Lily made a loud disgusted sound and looked away.

The young woman nodded. "Yes, of course. Just a moment, Mr. Mateo." Her voice dripped honey. Now, *that* he was used to.

Turning to Lily, Garrett tapped her arm with his hand, barely able to contain a grin.

"We need to have a serious talk about your manners, Ms. Ashden. Making snorting sounds in public is unprofessional." Provoking her wasn't smart, but it was fun. Ah, there it was—that I'm-going-to-kill-you-slowly fire in her eyes.

"Yes, well, neither is flirting with jailbait."

The hostess returned before he could reply and showed them to Sylvia's table. As soon as Garrett caught sight of her over the dinner crowd, he clenched his jaw. His plan might backfire. Sylvia might be completely taken aback at Lily's blunt attitude. Worse, she might just assume Lily was his lover and he was using her to his advantage.

Garrett ground his molars unintentionally, realizing he'd clenched too hard when a small pain shot through his jaw. Well, he was using Lily to his advantage—sort of. He felt a little ashamed of that, but in the end, he'd make it up to Lily. Somehow.

"Sylvia Frasier." Lily's sweet voice cut through his rumination. She'd stopped at the private corner table, her hand extended to the woman Garrett figured ate puppy livers for breakfast. Sylvia's cool blue eyes took on an eager gleam when her gaze slid from Lily to Garrett. "I'm Lily Ashden, from Ashden Construction and Design. I hope

Mr. Mateo had enough manners to let you know we were coming?"

Sylvia's wicked smile deepened, her eyes clinging to Garrett while she took Lily's hand. After a firm shake, Sylvia turned back to Lily, regarding her intensely for a moment before her expression softened. "Yes, yes, he did." Her brow scrunched as if she was trying to recall something. Then her mouth made a little O. "Lily *Ashden*. Of course. I'm so very sorry for your loss, my dear. Such a tragedy."

Lily gave a nod of polite acknowledgment. "Thank you."

Garrett looked from one woman to the other, completely lost. What tragedy? Sylvia waved down a waitress.

"I was just about to have prime rib. Care to join me?" Sylvia's tone made it clear they were joining her, no question.

Garrett's stomach turned happily at the mention of steak and his lips parted—he hadn't eaten since early that morning.

Lily gave him a dramatic wave of her hand. "Oh, thank you, Sylvia, but I ate before we came. And Garrett, well, I'm sure you didn't know, but he's recently gone vegan."

She smiled and tilted her head at him. He glowered. What the hell was she doing?

Lily crinkled her nose. "Sylvia, we won't keep

you. In fact, I'll be honest. It's a major inconvenience that Garrett forced me to come along tonight, so why don't we make this brief?"

Garrett slid a chair out for Lily, extremely tempted to yank it out from under her as she sat. She gave him a wary side eye as if she knew what he'd been thinking as she lowered herself into the seat. Garrett smoothed the front of his shirt and sat next to her, the sickening notes of Sylvia's floral perfume giving him an instant headache.

Sylvia steepled her fingers. "I detect a mutual dislike for Mr. Mateo, Lily. Yes?"

"Mmm, yes."

Lily reached for the rolled-up design. Garrett scowled but handed it over, crossed his arms and leaned back in his chair as she spread it out on the table.

Almost twenty minutes later, she'd relayed Garrett's plans for the lot, and he couldn't help the surprise coursing through him at how interested Sylvia appeared to be. She hung on Lily's every word, thought and idea. *Ha.* He knew bringing her along was a good idea, even if he had the feeling he was going to pay for it somehow.

"The thought here is to create a place where artists can gather. Have you ever been to the junk and art fairs in Truman or Picard? Both offer venues large enough to host four-times-a-year shows that attract tourism and bring outside dollars into the community. Picard alone attracts one million a year in tourist dollars. In time, there's no reason why Danbury can't tap into that, as well."

Sylvia asked a few more questions and studied the design with a sharpness to her expression that clearly displayed her interest. After a bit, she sat back in her chair and pointed a finger at Lily.

"I have to say, Lily, I'd rather sell the plot to you."

Garrett held back a disgusted groan. Of course she'd go that route. He was about to object, but Lily held a palm up to his face. Anger flashed. That was the second time she'd taken that liberty with him. He grabbed her hand and lowered it with a squeeze that left no doubt she was crossing the line. Lily's eyebrows arched. She gave him a pointed look, something in her eyes asking him to trust her. Maybe that was wishful thinking on his part, but he was going with it. He let go and she smiled, reaching for her purse. Turning back to Sylvia, Lily withdrew a checkbook and opened it.

"Done." She raised her pen. "Deposit price?" The pen shook in her hand as she slowly began to write Sylvia's name on the line.

A stunned silence hung over the table. Finally, Sylvia gave a light laugh and patted Lily's hand. "Well, it's not really a legal sale, my dear."

"It shows my good intentions until the contract

can be drawn up." Lily paused in writing. "Look, I don't have the time or inclination to develop the property for myself, but I really believe in the plan Garrett has for it. He's doing something great for the community. I'm leaving for Nashville in a few weeks, and I'd like to close this deal before I go. I'm more than happy to make the sale and transfer the property to Garrett if you'd rather not deal directly with him."

Lily slid Garrett a look. "The purchase price will be added to your first bill. Cool?" *Damn, she's good.* He would have mulled that over a little more if he hadn't been so disappointed by her Nashville comment. In the span of a few minutes, he'd learned more juicy tidbits about Lily than he had after spending an entire morning with her—and he wanted to know even more.

Sylvia finished her drink, waved a finger in the air to call the waiter back. "That won't be necessary." She ordered another gin before leaning over the table and tapping a finger on the design. "I like what I'm seeing here. Please, just tell me one thing, Lily."

Garrett's chest tightened. Was she saying that she was willing to sell? He gripped his beer glass.

"What's that?"

"You're not *involved* with him, are you?" Sylvia said it just loudly enough that Garrett heard, then laughed as if it was the biggest joke ever.

His left eye twitched, his leg bouncing as though it were on fire. He scooted forward in his chair, consciously stopping his leg and considering the possibility that Sylvia had been drinking too much. She was always cool toward him, but not usually so brash. Maybe she just liked having someone to show off to. Whatever it was, he was ready for this meeting to be done.

Lily indulged in a few hesitant chuckles of her own, her nose wrinkling slightly. "Oh, Sylvia. Now you're just insulting me."

Both women turned to look at him. Garrett grumbled, took a long, deep drink from his beer and concentrated hard on not shattering the glass in his grip.

"You've been remarkably quiet, Mr. Mateo," Sylvia said sweetly.

He smiled around the rim of his glass, took another drink and set it down. "I have good self-preservation instincts."

Sylvia looked from Lily back to him. "I'll be in touch to discuss the purchase agreement. I have to admit, Garrett, I'm impressed."

Garrett fisted his hands together, hope rushing through him like blood. They'd already been playing that game for months, but the lighter edge in Sylvia's tone made him think she was serious this time. "Great." He didn't dare say anything more.

"Very good, then. If you don't mind, I'd like to order my steak." She saluted him with her glass. Garrett forced his lips together and rose, holding a hand out for Lily as she did the same, but she made a very clear step away from him.

"Have a nice evening, Sylvia." Lily handed a business card to Sylvia. "Please call if you need anything from me."

Lily pushed her way in front of him and strode through the restaurant with a haughty air that made his mouth go dry. He wanted to pull her into his arms and tell her how amazing she was, how impressed he was with how she'd presented herself in front of Sylvia, even if he'd been the target. But none of that would come out the way he intended, he was sure.

He growled in her ear as he opened the door for them. "A vegan? Really?" She'd pulled that as a jab to the groin, just because.

She smirked. "Out of that entire meeting, *that* is what you're focused on?"

The sass in her voice nearly made him come undone. No, he was focused on a lot of things. He wanted to know what tragedy Sylvia had referred to and why the hell Lily was leaving for Nashville and where that commanding business presence of hers had come from.

But mostly, right now, he was irritated, thrilled…aroused. This was as close to getting that land as he'd ever been. Garrett kept his hands to himself, even though he was sorely tempted to touch her. He was about to open the passenger door for her when the thin hold on his resolve snapped. Garrett spun her around, backing her gently against the door. She gasped, her eyes widening before they fell to his lips. Her chest rose and fell hard; the movement made her shirt brush his chest. He'd been attracted to her before, but now...now he wanted to kiss her in the worst way. His hands lightly grasped her upper arms.

"You owe me a steak, woman."

She wore a look of self-satisfaction. "And you owe *me* the pleasure of watching you cry like a baby while you get a tattoo, because I'm fairly certain we just made a deal in there."

A second of near-palpable heat pulsed between them before they both laughed. She was right, and he was on cloud nine. Being this close to getting things rolling for Brad was uplifting. And he had Lily to thank.

Without thinking, Garrett brushed a stray piece of hair away from her cheek. The backs of his fingers tingled at the softness of her skin, his heart racing as she lightly leaned into his touch.

He leaned closer to her ear. "You were brilliant."

Lily's eyelids fell to half-mast, her breath holding for a beat. The pulse at her neck was tapping quickly against her fair skin, filling Garrett with ridiculous satisfaction that she was as into this moment as he was.

"I don't even care that it was at my expense."

His hand wrapped around the back of her neck. Her fingers dug into his shirt, clutched the fabric, but she didn't push him away. Garrett searched her face, took in the scattered bit of freckles over the bridge of her nose and the perfect rise of her cheekbones. Dark eye shadow and liner made the brilliant blue of her eyes stand out. And that red lipstick… It had become the bane of a good night's sleep. He couldn't see red lately without having a passing thought of her, which had been especially challenging at the firehouse, where every truck was crimson. Red was ruined for the rest of his life.

"What are you doing?" Her palms flattened against his chest. His skin heated under her touch. She'd been the last woman to touch him, that night in the gazebo, and his body remembered the sensation of her hands now. His fingers crept into her soft, smooth hair.

"Thinking about kissing you."

"Just thinking about it?" The admission in that statement cost her. He could tell by the way her shoulders stiffened and her neck went tight. So there was heat under the ice.

Garrett cupped the back of her head in his

palm. "Should I be thinking about it?" He tipped his head just right, moved in until her sweet breath touched his lips. "Or acting on it?"

Lily leaned into him, pressing until she simply fit—the length of her molding to the length of him everywhere that made his body buzz. If that wasn't encouragement, he was really losing his ability to read women's signals. Garrett pulled her head up for his kiss. It was soft, this first touch of lips, and didn't come close to easing the demand coursing through him.

Lily moaned in a breathy sigh, her mouth parting to urge him on. Her shirt ruffled as he traced his palm down her ribs to the flare of her hip. Lily arched slightly, her spine taking the curve of the truck door as he leaned into her.

The take-control woman she'd been in the restaurant was nowhere to be found, and he was just as pleased that he had the ability to turn her to jelly as he was to have the control. He kissed her longer, flicking her lips apart with his tongue, blending her mouth with his. Her hand slid into his hair. The strong, tender glide of her slim fingers along his scalp was delicious and sent a shiver over his body.

Garrett knew he should pull away. She'd been so standoffish about anything unrelated to their working relationship, yet she leaned into his kiss as if she'd craved it. As if sensing his thoughts,

Lily abruptly pulled back. She covered her mouth with one hand, her eyes wide. Garrett realized just then how hard he was breathing, how hard she was.

They stared at each other a moment before Lily's fingers fell away from her lips. Garrett waited for it—expecting a sharp word to come from her. Something. But she didn't say anything.

Voices wafted their way from across the parking lot. The sound seemed to propel both of them into motion. She moved aside; he opened the truck door for her. She gave him a quick glance before sliding in, and was silent and looking out her window when he slid in behind the wheel.

The sudden awkwardness was fitting punishment, Garrett supposed. He'd gotten caught up in the excitement of the moment. So had she, apparently. They could set this aside, focus on the job and get it done. He opened his mouth to say so…maybe to apologize, though he wasn't especially sorry, but Lily held up her hand and gave a curt shake of her head.

"Don't say anything."

"What?"

She took a deep, patient breath. "Don't. Speak." Her eyes were pleading when she finally looked at him. To his relief, there was no regret, no anger, in her expression. "I'd like to be in my own head right now, please." She clicked her seat belt and went back to looking out the window.

Garrett ran a palm over his mouth, struggling to stay quiet when there were things he wanted to say. Now that the heat had cleared, he remembered she'd said she was leaving for Nashville soon. The ping of unease the thought gave him was the same one he'd experienced when she'd first mentioned it.

He stopped at a red light, took in the glow of streetlights sparkling off Lily's hair. Whatever this effect she was having on him, Garrett wasn't sure how to interpret it. He easily imagined her right there, in the seat of his truck, as he took her out to dinner. Making conversation as they headed out of town for a road trip or simply went back to his place. There was a growing familiarity between them, at least on his end, the kind that said something deeper and more meaningful could easily follow. Underneath it all was that nagging sensation that he knew her from somewhere.

It didn't sit well, this attraction to her. It was different…more complicated than anything he had experience with. Figuring it out—any of it— was the last thing he had time for. Seeing how she still wouldn't look at him, Garrett figured Lily probably felt the same.

She got out of his truck with a wave when he

pulled in next to her SUV at the Ashden building. Garrett waited until she'd started up the vehicle before pulling away. He licked his lips. Lily's taste was still sweet on them. Kiss number two? He was going to forget all about it.

Starting tomorrow.

CHAPTER SEVEN

MAYBE SHE WAS seeing Katja's ghost. Lily crossed her arms on her desk and rested her forehead on top of them with a yawn. What she was experiencing at night seemed to extend beyond a normal dream.

It always started out the same way: she and Katja surrounded by an orange glow as they ran down a hallway. And then Katja stopped, mouthed the words *go ahead,* turned around and ran back to her apartment. Lily reached for her—screamed her name and, in a blink, was lying on cold, wet grass.

She pushed herself up, saw the apartment engulfed in flames, and the sensation was always the same as it had been in real life. Terror, panic, the well of nausea and grief. But beyond the sickly realism of her dream memories, Lily was flooded with the feeling that she was missing something. That she needed to know *why....*

She shouldn't have kissed Garrett last night. Being with him always made the dreams worse, and the kiss they'd shared seemed to have launched her subconscious into overdrive. This morning was one of the worst she'd had.

She made it to noon before she was ready to burst. Luckily Doug was out all morning, so she could struggle with crunching numbers and prices for the Mateo project in peace and quiet.

And what a struggle it was. Her mind jerked between the thought that she should feel guilty over kissing Garrett but didn't, and the guilt that arose because she didn't feel guilty.

Each attempt to work the numbers now on the computer screen or plug information into the spreadsheet resulted in staring at the haphazard drawing Garrett had made of the empty lot. She'd placed it near her mouse pad and there it remained for no specific reason.

She should have thrown that thing away after she'd made the professional draft yesterday, but she couldn't. The squiggly lines and circles and doodles were little more than chicken scratches. But each of those pen marks represented something profoundly important to Garrett, and they came to life on the paper as a design of the man he was beneath his fireman's uniform.

He was determined, cared about other people, conscientious of the community's needs and full of remarkable business intuition. He'd believed in her yesterday, believed that she could negotiate with Sylvia on his behalf. Maybe it had been a purely selfish move on his part—who was she kidding, it had been a purely selfish move on hers, too—but he'd still given her his trust, and she'd gotten the job done.

What had happened next had kept her sitting on the edge of her couch last night, elbows on her knees, staring off into space. The wickedness of Garrett's kiss, the way he'd pressed her up against the truck in the middle of an open parking lot had been delicious.

She and Rob had never indulged in any public displays of affection. Always normal sex, in a bed, fast and convenient. And the warm, connected, wanted feeling she'd had in Garrett's arms last night was something she hadn't experienced with Rob for months leading up to his leaving. Those were the kinds of feelings a girl could get used to, that was for sure.

Just not with Garrett. He wasn't the kind of man who stayed; he'd said it himself. Not that it mattered. She wasn't looking for anyone to stay, and certainly not a man who reminded her of the pain of her past.

He was a fireman. Lily closed her eyes and sank into her office chair. It always came back to that. Even if she only took a few days with him, enjoyed him, his profession would always be there, hanging over her. Prodding her, pulling anger and resentment out of her subconscious.

Wouldn't it?

A light rasp on her door frame made Lily jump. A deliveryman stood in the doorway with an amused expression, holding a vase of red roses. A ton of them.

"Ms. Ashden?"

Oh, my God. She stood, her brow furrowing at the beauty—and number—of red roses arranged in a blue glass vase.

She waved the deliveryman in. He smiled and put the vase on her desk. "Have a great day," he said before leaving.

Lily stared at the roses, eyeballing the white envelope peeking out of the blooms. Perfume filled the air, tugging at her heart and making her pulse pound. Thirty roses, no, thirty-one, all bloodred, all amazingly perfect.

She finally plucked out the envelope and opened it with an expectant smile…only to find it blank. No writing. Nothing. "What the…?"

She flipped the card over. On the back, a line was scribbled:

Didn't know if I could speak yet or not. G.

She sank back into her chair with a disbelieving laugh. Roses once? She could accept that, even if an ulterior motive had been attached to them. But roses twice? Once again, Garrett had left his intentions up for interpretation.

Lily tapped a finger on her desk. What could he possibly be buttering her up for now? She glanced at the Mateo file, which lay open on her desk, and pulled her cell from her purse. No more surprises. If he wanted her to do something, he was going to have to ask. Lily dialed his number and studied the nuanced variations of crimson on each rose as it rang.

"Yeah?"

She wrinkled her nose. He sounded like she'd interrupted him. "Garrett?"

A rustling sound came through the line, and then the deep, clear tone of his voice.

"Lily. Sorry, I… How are you?"

She leaned back in her chair and looked at the ceiling. Now that she had him on the phone, words were harder to form than they had been in her head a few seconds ago. "Bad time?"

More rustling. "Not at all."

She thought about how to start, then shrugged off her usual tendency to overthink. Might as well be blunt. "I'd say thank you, but I have to ask something so I know if I should feel grateful or irritated."

"You got the flowers." He sounded pleased with himself. Too pleased. She paused, waiting to see if he'd volunteer his motive, but he paused in return and the line filled with silence.

"I appreciate the gesture, Garrett, but I'd rather you just talk to me about what you need instead of trying to butter me up first." Another small silence ensued, followed by a noncommittal sound coming from his end.

"I sent them as a thank-you for dealing with Sylvia last night." A loud bang burst through the background, followed by his very hushed curse. "Sorry. Look, no ulterior motive this time. I promise. I really appreciate you helping me out last night. That's all."

Lily sat up in the chair and ran her fingers over the tops of the roses. He'd chosen well, but for some reason that didn't surprise her.

"Oh. Well, then, thank you. I'll let you go. You sound…busy."

"Actually," he said in a rush, "I know it's Wednesday afternoon, but it's my only day off for the next century and I was just about to head out of town for a ride, and I… Well, any chance you can take a couple hours off?"

The corner of her mouth hitched up despite her immediate reluctance. "I really can't." She wanted to mean the words, but they lacked credibility, even to her own ears. "I'm working on your proposal, actually."

"Well, then, as the client, I say forget about my

stuff for the rest of the day. There's something I think you'd like to see, and believe it or not, it's related to my project. Consider it field research."

Lily swiveled in her chair to look out the window, her eyes catching Katja's picture sitting on the bookshelf. That smile...those eyes. Lily actually winced, as if bracing herself for her sister's image to morph from beautiful joy into an accusing stink eye. Of course, it didn't.

"I...suppose..."

"Great. Are you at the office?"

"Mmm-hmm," she replied absently, barely aware when he said he'd be there in a few and hung up.

Lily stood and turned away from the bookshelf. She should be able to see Garrett, both in and out of work, and it should be okay. He wasn't just a firefighter, he was also a man. A regular man. One she liked spending time with. There shouldn't be any guilt in this, but it was hard to know if she was just being too hard on herself, or if the feeling was justified. Macy seemed to think Lily was overthinking things, as usual, but her friend had never been through a loss like Lily had.

The front door slammed. She knew it was Doug even before he called out a gruff greeting and went into his office.

Maybe she needed the opinion of someone who

could relate. How would someone else react in her position? What if Lincoln found himself attracted to a female firefighter? Would he have the same mixed feelings as Lily did? Granted, Lily figured Lincoln didn't have nightmares like she did—he hadn't almost died in the flames as she had—but he might have perspective that would help. She retrieved her phone and dialed her brother, knowing by the third ring that he wasn't going to pick up. It went to voice mail just as she hung up.

Antsy for some sort of an opinion, Lily walked to Doug's office. She'd probably have better luck torturing a navy SEAL for classified information than getting any kind of advice from her dad, but it was worth a shot.

"Hey, question for you."

Doug didn't look up from sorting mail. "No, you can't have a puppy."

His eyes crinkled with a smile. Lily leaned against the door frame, curious and a bit shocked over his light mood.

"I haven't wanted a puppy since the Mutt Incident in fifth grade." That comment actually drew a laugh from Doug, making his broad shoulders move just slightly.

"Right. When Katja brought that mess of a stray dog home and it ate the heads off your Beanie Babies and peed on your art project." To this day, Lily wasn't convinced the thing Katja had brought home really had been a dog. Devil's spawn, sure, because there had been nothing cuddly or cute about that mangy animal. Katja had been convinced all that the puppy needed was someone to love it; Doug and Lily had resolved someone else could tackle that improbable task as they'd dropped it off at the pound. Katja had sulked, and Lily had realized she was a cat person.

Doug looked up and caught her eye, and for a moment, something passed between them. The connection of a shared memory. This was the closest they'd come to talking about Katja since her death. But in a blink it was over. Doug sat back, a scowl replacing the almost smile.

"What was your question?"

Lily crossed her arms over her middle. "Let's say we'd really loved that puppy Katja brought home, and we took it to the vet, and he gave it, I don't know, the wrong medicine and killed it." Doug looked at her as if she was nuts. "And a while later, you meet an attractive woman who also happens to be a vet, but not the vet that killed your puppy. She reminds you of your dead dog, but you still—"

"Lily, I wouldn't have felt sad a minute if a vet had killed that puppy."

"Stay focused, Doug." She strode to his desk,

absently picked up an envelope and flipped it over. "You're attracted to her, even though she reminds you of that damn dog. What do you do?"

Doug leaned back in his chair, a pencil tapping his lower lip. After a second, he waved the pencil before dropping it on his desk.

"I hated that dog, so I can't help with your scenario."

Lily didn't know if she should laugh or strangle him. She should have known better than to approach him with this, even hypothetically. "Oh, my God, Doug."

"I say you be honest with the vet. Talk about the dog. Don't shut her out, and see where it goes."

Lily spun around at the familiar voice, glancing up to see Garrett's brilliant smile. Her pulse sounded in her ears as she momentarily forgot how to breathe. His long, broad body was in well-worn jeans and a heather-gray T-shirt. A white ball cap was pulled low over his forehead with curling tips of his blond hair peeking out. He stood a couple of feet behind her in the foyer, his hands in his pockets.

"H-hey," she finally managed as she straightened and smoothed the back of her hair. Oh, God, he'd heard what she'd been saying. If he had any inclination that she'd been talking about him, his expression didn't betray it.

Doug came to stand beside her at the door, his presence shaking her from her stupor.

"Doug, I'd like you to meet Garrett Mateo. From the Throwing Aces." She emphasized the bar's name, hoping it would put off the grand inquisition. Garrett immediately removed his hat and held a hand out.

"Garrett, my father, Doug Ashden." Her father's eyebrows flicked up as he shook Garrett's hand maybe just a touch too long.

"Good to meet you." If Doug's steely stare affected Garrett at all, he didn't show it. "You the Garrett who sent Lily the flowers?"

Lily's mouth dropped open, but Garrett just looked proud of himself.

"Yes, sir." That was it. No explanation. She was slightly impressed that Garrett didn't feel the need to clarify his reasons.

"Mmm." Doug cleared his throat and looked at Lily. "How's his proposal coming along?"

She and Doug had discussed the Mateo project just once since her first meeting with Garrett. Since then, he'd given her free rein to take care of it herself. "It's going fine."

Garrett slipped his ball cap back on. "It's going exceptionally well. Should we get going, Lily?"

Oh, he was smooth. Sliding his way out from having to stand there and make any more awkward small talk with Doug. Lily moved away from her father's office door and his questioning look. She grabbed her purse from her office before joining Garrett.

"I'll be out the rest of the day, Doug. See you in the morning." She didn't give Doug an opportunity to start pressing as she headed for the door.

Garrett held the front door for her, his eyes settling on her lower half long enough to make her skin heat up. When they stepped out into the sunshine, she glanced down at her knee-length hemp skirt and sandals to see what he was staring at.

"What?"

He shrugged. "That'll work."

"For what?" she asked.

"Straddling me." He pointed to his big black truck parked at the curb. A four-wheeler sat in the back. "Straddling the Yamaha, *behind me,* while I drive, I suppose. Or just me, whichever you prefer."

Lily bit her bottom lip. She never had cause to ride an ATV before and wasn't sure she liked the idea of it now. Especially since what Garrett teased about was completely true. She *would* be straddling him…her thighs wrapped around his hips, her hands hanging on to his tight middle.

This would be great, just great, for her resolve to keep it professional.

"I don't ride four-wheelers," she managed to sputter.

Garrett just grinned. "You do now."

CHAPTER EIGHT

"YOU CALL YOUR father Doug?"

Garrett tapped a finger against the steering wheel to the soft country music coming through the radio. Sunlight shone brightly, the sky was crystal clear and the palette of late-summer colors was brilliant in the flawless day. His uncle Brad was going to be released from the hospital soon, and Garrett had eighteen hours of freedom left before he started a three-day string of on-call time at the firehouse. He'd decided to celebrate by ripping his ATV through mud and over the rocky hills outside town, but when Lily had called, his mind had taken a different direction.

And it was perfect. He'd just been daydreaming the other day about something like this—him and Lily just taking a ride. Seeing where it led.

He felt a lick of fear he didn't want to acknowledge. He was playing with his own rules here, because he genuinely liked her company. He wanted more of it. If he wasn't careful, Garrett could see himself falling into something as close to a relationship as he'd ever had. He did a lot of things that might scare the hell out of other people, but for him, letting Lily in was more terrifying than having a flaming building fall down around him. He could resist it a little more. He could.

She rewarded him with dimples curved prettily beside her mouth, her eyes lighting up in a way that made her seem content and naughty at the same time. "You just met him. Does he seem like the warm, fuzzy daddy type to you?"

"That would be a no."

His own father had been a big man, like Doug Ashden, but he'd had a ready smile that offset any intimidation his size might have otherwise caused. Everything about Doug seemed intimidating, from his buzz-cut silver hair to his biker mustache, huge neck and rock-solid body. How a man like that produced a woman as feminine as Lily was a mystery. Luckily, the only physical thing Doug seemed to have passed on to her was his blue eyes. If Garrett had to speculate, he'd say she got her stubborn, sassy streak from him, too.

"Admit it—you call him Doug because it drives him nuts."

She laughed. "True."

It was a soft place to be, with her looking relaxed and beautiful, and he wanted to hold on to this as long as possible. This serenity was an amazing contrast to the confident, smart-mouthed businesswoman, and the one who could be quiet and introspective. Ah, the many sides of Lily Ashden. And he was wickedly attracted to them all.

"What about your siblings? Are they as G.I. Joe as your father?" Garrett caught a glance of her from the corner of his eye as he made a right turn. She looked out the side window, her smile gone.

Out of the blue, he recalled what Sylvia had said—*such a tragedy*—and dread filled him. Maybe he'd just made a fatal mistake, asking her about her family.

"Thankfully, no. I only have a brother, Lincoln, and he's as kind, levelheaded and easygoing as anyone could wish for. We're twins." Her face lit up.

"Really?"

"Yes, but Linc is more easygoing. He's more like our mother, from what I hear. And I've got Doug's stubborn side." She picked at her skirt. "My mom… She and my dad split when we were four, so I don't really remember her."

He pulled his lower lip between his teeth. Could that be what Sylvia had been talking about? Possibly, but he wasn't convinced. Divorce was unfortunate and sad, but hardly a tragedy. Given that he'd already dampened her mood, Garrett didn't want to press by simply asking.

"I lost my dad when I was thirteen. I don't think it matters what age they leave your life. It still has an impact, you know?" He turned onto a gravel road, kicking up mud from the recent rain. She gave an agreeing nod.

She pulled the elastic off the end of her braid and began working it free. Garrett did a double take as her fingers drew through the strands. *Damn.*

"What happened?" she asked. "To your dad?"

He thought about how to answer, because there was so much he could say in response. It had been a long time since he'd spoken about his father to anyone besides his brothers and Brad. Lily had turned her upper body to almost face him completely. She didn't apologize for asking, and he had the sense that his answer was in some way important to her.

"His department was working a factory fire. My dad and his team were up on the roof, making ventilation holes. The fire got so hot, everyone was called off, but my dad didn't come down in time. We'll never know why—if he got hung up or thought someone was still inside. He fell through the roof and there was no way anyone could get inside to get him. It was just too hot."

Lily's face paled.

"They couldn't get him out?" Her voice was weak and distant, as if she wasn't really speaking to him at all. That nagging familiarity he had off and on when he was around Lily came back full force. It was driving him crazy, this feeling that he should know something but didn't.

"I saw a melted helmet in a case behind the bar, the first time I was there."

He couldn't read her expression, but heaviness seemed to fill the space around them. "That was my dad's. It was recovered in the rubble. We're protected from heat, but nothing could withstand heat like that."

Her hand slid to his knee, and the unexpected touch made him quiver. Lily's fingers squeezed gently, and then she turned back to the scenery as the road narrowed and led up a hill, then down to a thick grove of trees.

Silence fell between them. Lily's hand was still on his knee, and he didn't say anything else. And as much as he wanted to clasp his fingers over hers, he didn't do that, either, because something had just happened here—something he had no idea how to interpret, but he felt it all the same.

Signs announcing private property ahead dotted the side of the road as they approached the grove, then became swallowed by the trees, until a clearing opened to the right, like a small park. An older camper, a picnic table and a huge wooden swing were scattered throughout the freshly mowed space. Garrett pulled in next to the camper.

"Where are we?" Lily unbuckled her seat belt.

"We call this the Pit because the lake down there is man-made from an old gravel pit. A friend of mine owns it. There's something here I thought you might like to see." Garrett opened his door and moved to get out, but Lily crossed her arms and contemplated him, making him pause.

Her voice was raw yet soft. "I'm not sure how to take you."

"What do you mean?"

Lily cleared her throat, her lips parting as if she was trying to find the right words. "The flowers—no one has ever sent me flowers. And you sent them just because. It's not my birthday. It's not—"

"No one has ever sent you flowers?" He frowned. That was hard to believe. "I'm afraid to ask, but what kind of men have you been dating?" He chuckled, but the humor quickly died when her face clouded.

"The leaving kind." The sadness changed as she smiled softly and shook her head as if to erase what she'd just said. "Just…thanks for the flowers."

She opened her door and scooted out before he could think of an appropriate reply. Anger made a sharp appearance as he processed her confession. Some loser had sliced her to pieces. *The leaving kind.* He thought he was starting to understand. A fireman, most likely, if he had to guess. No wonder she was gun-shy and not too keen on trying again.

Half an hour later, he had the four-wheeler backed down from the bed of the truck and Lily securely seated behind him. Her thighs, God help him, squeezed the backs of his legs in a death grip. Her right arm looped around his middle as if she were hanging from a cliff. And he hadn't even started the machine yet.

"I'm going to go real slow, Lil. Want me to chain you to my body?" Her forehead pressed against his back and she shook with a laugh.

"Shut up, Garrett. I've never been on one of these things before." She held on harder and he took that as a sign she was clinging on tightly enough. He started the ATV, and her nails dug into his belly.

He winced and swiveled to look at her. "Okay, there's only one time I like to be clawed, and this isn't it."

She actually threw her head back and laughed, smacking him with her thankfully un-clawed-from-his-gut hand. "You're terrible."

He smoothed his fingers over her cheek. Their eyes met. Her lips parted just a bit, making him lean in. A replay of their kiss against his truck last night made his heart skip a beat. He pulled back and turned to the handlebars. Kissing her wasn't going to keep him from getting involved any further. He'd brought her here to see the Pit, that was all.

"Ready? Now hang on, *gently.*"

Garrett couldn't remember the last time he'd driven his ATV at such a geriatric pace, but the way Lily's body relaxed against him made it worth it. They went slowly down a trail that led away from the camper and through a young copse of trees. The roar of the machine made conversation difficult, so he just enjoyed the scenery and the feel of Lily's hand pressed flat against his ribs.

Usually beating the hell out of the four-wheeler through the mud or taking it full tilt over rocks and hills was his way of blowing off steam. The soft mounds of Lily's breasts pressed against his back and the comfortable feeling of her being close made this a pretty good second choice.

He turned his head to look over at her. "Close your eyes."

"Why?"

He made a *tsk-tsk* sound. "Just do it." Garrett checked over his shoulder twice to make sure she was obeying, both times drawing a giggle from her. He veered off to the left and parked the ATV, swiveling to place a hand over her eyes as he slid down.

"Come on down. I've got you." He steadied Lily as she slid down, leading her to the mouth of a new trail. He glanced up, his heart swelling as the sun beat through the tree canopy in just the perfect amount of light.

"Welcome to Wonderland."

He removed his hand, watching her face as she blinked to clear her vision. Her mouth morphed from a surprised smile to a serious, disbelieving line and then back to a curve of wonderment. The little dimples in her cheeks deepened as loose strands of hair waved around her face in the breeze.

Garrett didn't need to look down the trail. He'd seen it all many times, but watching Lily see it for the first time was like unwrapping the most anticipated gift he'd ever wished for. He stepped closer. Touched his lips to the warmth of her cheek. When Lily turned to look at him, the impact of her eyes robbed him of his breath. So this was what it felt like to be rendered breathless by a woman.

He didn't want to ever breathe again.

She took several big steps forward, made a half turn to take in both sides of the trail, then turned completely. Her hand made a sweeping arc in the air.

"This." She turned around again, looking up. Looking down. Looking at him as he sucked in a deep breath. "This is incredible!"

And then she was gone, walking through the

maze of metal art that hung from the trees and lined the edges of the trail.

Birds created from metal pieces and found objects sat perched on rods driven into the ground. Gazing balls cradled in hands of mosaic glass and metal pedestals glistened in the sunlight as they lined the path. Above their heads, wind chimes of all descriptions clanked and tinkled and sang on the breeze. Lily inspected each item, her fingers trailing, touching, cupping, her face expressing every nuance of joy and appreciation.

They came to the opening of the trail, where a long wind chime crafted from antique skeleton keys and silver utensils waved in greeting. Lily fingered the keys, and the brilliant smile she gave him took Garrett's breath away.

"Who did all this?"

Her joy was filling him up, warming his blood, giving him a syrupy sensation he'd never experienced before. He peered into a gazing ball held in a metalwork dragon's mouth just to try to get his head together.

"Remember that artist I mentioned, Bodie? He's my friend Mikey's brother. Came back from Iraq three years ago with a blast injury to his head." Lily grimaced. "It was a miracle that he survived at all. But something happened to him after the doctors patched him back up. He...well, he pretty much has the mentality of a twelve-year-old and he never sleeps. But this…this is all from him."

Garrett pointed up, drawing her gaze to an intricate red, white and blue eagle that sat in the tree branches above. "He started making things out of tin cans. He'd be up all night, making and tinkering. So Mikey and their sister, April, started getting him scrap metal—let him use the welder under supervision. Pretty soon, he was off and running on his own."

She shook her head. "I definitely think we could put a few pieces in the Nashville store. Lincoln will love it."

"You mentioned you were going to Nashville."

"Yeah, soon. I could take a couple pieces with me, if that's okay with Bodie and his family—"

"Are you coming back?"

She turned to him, her fingers trailing over a gazing ball before dropping away. "Temporarily, I think. I'm going now to help Lincoln with an open house in the store, and after that, I'll likely move there." She turned back to looking at the art. "Time for a change, you know?"

Garrett could understand that. The need for a change and a purpose had brought him from Hawaii to Kansas, and while he missed the Hawaiian weather, he wasn't unhappy with his choice. But relating to her desire to change her life didn't ease the tension in his gut. Lily moved on down the path back the way they'd come.

"There's not much left for me in Danbury. Not since…" Her voice trailed away. Garrett followed behind her, the sway of her hips drawing him along like a puppy on a leash.

"Since?" It was his turn to dig. She pulled her hair over one shoulder and waved him off.

"You don't want my sob story."

Wrong. He wanted it. He needed it, needed to know what made Lily Ashden tick. Garrett grabbed her hand and gently spun her around.

"I do." He caught her gaze. "Besides, I told you mine. Fair is fair." Her hand clasped around his wrist, her fingers imprinting heat into his skin. She wasn't going to get out of it; he'd press if he had to.

"Okay. Truth is, Garrett, I owe you an apology anyway." He pulled back a little. That wasn't what he'd been expecting. "I misjudged you, and I'm sure my behavior reflected that. I'm sorry for judging you solely on the fact that you're a firefighter."

He ran his palms down her upper arms. "Now comes the part about *why* you dislike firemen."

He was sure it was a man who had hurt her, and the darker side of him wanted to know if it was someone from his department. So he could what? Kick the guy's ass? He didn't know—but the thought of her being hurt by one of his own left a very sour taste in his mouth. Lily moved to walk down the path again and he fell into step beside her.

"My sister was killed in a fire last year. I… barely made it out myself and I've been really angry with the fire department because of what they did—or, rather, what they didn't do—and that's all I really want to say about it. I've held a pretty big grudge against firemen since then. I shouldn't have assumed anything about you."

The back of Garrett's neck started to prickle. He pressed a palm there to stop the sensation at the same time that his brain went into overdrive. That wasn't the confession he'd been expecting. Her sister? He thought of all the fires he'd attended in Danbury in the past year or so, but he couldn't recall any deaths other than one elderly man. As if reading his mind, Lily went on.

"It wasn't even your department, but meeting you has brought back some of the nightmares I used to have about that night."

Garrett took her hand and held it with what he hoped was a comforting squeeze. To his joy, she returned the gesture as they walked.

So much could go wrong at the scene of a fire, and for bystanders watching it all unfold, the process the firemen went through could be confusing. Sometimes they were chastised for risking their lives too much; sometimes they were blamed for not doing enough. And sometimes, no matter what they did, a fire could go completely, horribly wrong. Garrett's instincts told him the latter was the case for Lily's sister, and while he wanted to know more, Lily had said she didn't want to talk about it. She didn't have to go into detail for him to recognize how much pain she was carrying around.

Her admission brought something to mind that he hadn't thought about in many years.

"When I was a student at the fire academy, one of my instructors set a glass of water on his desk. He asked us how much we thought the glass weighed. As we all guessed, he picked up the glass and held it in front of him at arm's length." They paused on the trail. "He said that in the end, it didn't matter how much the glass actually weighed because the longer you held it, the heavier it would get. At first, you could hold it no problem. After a few hours, your arm would start to shake. After a day, your muscles would be screaming at you until, soon, that simple glass of water would pull you to your knees if you didn't let it go."

Garrett glanced at the ground as the words sank in. He hadn't thought of that analogy in years, but now it seemed fitting.

Lily rubbed her thumb over the back of his

hand, her fingers twining more tightly with his as they resumed walking. "What if you're holding more than one glass?" She said it kind of jokingly, but he wasn't fooled.

"I suppose just set them down one by one. Can't juggle them forever."

"Smart thinking."

The end of the trail was nearing, reminding Garrett that one of the most relaxing afternoons he'd had in recent memory was coming to a close.

"Firefighting has its really tough moments, and that little bit of wisdom is to remind us when to let go of some of the hell we carry around. I can hardly think of a fireman on my squad who isn't carrying around a glass. Mikey, Roan, Chief… Pretty much all of them." They were quiet for a bit. The crunch of dead leaves and twigs was loud in the silence of the woods.

As they neared the end, he tilted his head. Time to change the subject, lighten the mood. "So…any chance that tragic-puppy analogy earlier had anything to do with me?"

Lily's cheeks flamed red, but she stopped and took both his hands, her gaze steady and soft. He thought he saw the shimmer of tears hidden somewhere in her blue eyes.

"I know you don't do relationships, and I'm not looking for one considering I'm moving soon, but if either of us were in a better place, you'd be a pretty awesome guy to get involved with, Garrett."

Garrett didn't wait to think it through; he didn't try to talk himself out of it. He pulled Lily against him. Her hands found his hair at the same time his lips crushed hers. Her mouth was hot, her lips supple and giving as she relaxed against him, her fingers knocking off his ball cap to wind into his hair to hold him close.

There was nothing scary about this, about having her in his arms, where she fit like a puzzle piece. It filled him, filled the empty space he'd carried around for as long as he could remember. And although he'd have to live with that emptiness again someday, he could let Lily fit for now. It was temporary for both of them, right?

Her clothes molded to her body as Garrett ran his palms over the delicate length of her ribs to the indent of her waist and flare of her hips. This time he didn't have to pull her closer; Lily leaned her hips into him as she opened her mouth, welcoming the slide of his tongue along hers. Garrett pressed a hand to her lower back, holding her, filling himself up with her.

"I walked to the office from my apartment. Take me home," she said as she broke away. Her eyelids fluttered as he searched her face. "That's an invitation, in case you're wondering."

Exactly what he'd been wanting since their time in the gazebo. But now...

"Lily. I can't give you more than a couple of nights." He tucked her hair behind her ear, wishing for the first time ever that he could give a woman—Lily—more.

What would it be like, coming home to her every night? Maybe thinking about a family... doing all the things lovers did? Vacations, dates, picking out an apartment, petty fights and nights of laughter.

On the flip side of all that happiness was the cloud of uncertainty. That heavy hand of fate that might come slamming down at any moment and take all that joy away. The cost was just too great.

"I saw your bucket of phone numbers at the bar. I'm well aware that you're not a one-woman guy." She put a finger to his lips before he could explain that he'd never called a single number out of that bucket, not once. It had been kept around as a running joke.

"I'm tired of being angry at the world, Garrett." She took a deep breath. "A couple of nights with you sounds perfect."

The late-day heat was slowly dying down, leaving behind a hazy burn in the air. It mimicked the sizzle in his blood. He kissed her again and closed his eyes against the well of deeper emotion trying to grow inside. Instead, he fell back to his old standby: covering it up.

"So much for being reformed," he quipped, grabbing his hat before clasping her hand tightly as they headed back to the ATV and started down a sweet path he was reluctant to see the end of.

THE DAY HAD been so perfect that Lily was afraid to shut her eyes for too long in case she woke up and it all went away. Garrett was everything she'd secretly hoped for and nothing she expected. Each second that he made her laugh or set her pulse racing with a simple touch was one more time she started to see him as someone she could easily fall for. In the span of a few hours, he'd made her feel more cherished than she could recall in her recent past. His thoughtfulness and the way he put her at ease were like slow-burning aphrodisiacs. In the back of her mind, Lily understood that wanting him was normal, healthy. And she did, so much.

They made it back to Danbury in record time, Lily sitting as close to Garrett as she dared while still making it possible for him to drive. The need to be near him was so strong that they barely made it through her front door before they were tangled up in each other's arms. He kicked the door shut and she spun him around, walking him backward through the small apartment as they kissed and tugged at each other's clothing. They stumbled their way to the bedroom, tripping over a startled Adam the cat, who ran out of the room. It was surreal and silly and her heart soared.

Lily reached for the buttons on her shirt, undoing them one by one. Garrett's eyes trailed her hands, until she reached where the shirt tucked into the waist of her skirt. In one swift move, he flipped her down onto the bed and straddled her, one arm on either side of her shoulders. He bent his head and parted the loose sides of her shirt over her breasts with his teeth. A low groan rumbled from his throat as his fingers found her bra strap and followed its length.

"Damn, Lily." The red-and-white gingham bra had been an afterthought when she'd gotten dressed that morning, but she'd wanted something feminine to match her good mood. As Garrett's fingers trailed over the eyelet lace peeking from the top of the cups, she was exceptionally happy with her choice. She bent her left leg, the hem of her skirt sliding up her thigh and bunching around her hip.

"Panties match." The resulting groan was deeper, more needful. Garrett moved lower until his breath washed over her belly. He tugged the shirt with his teeth, freeing it from the waist of her skirt before nibbling his way back up. He had a wicked gleam in his eyes. Lily's breath came out in a rush when his mouth closed over her nipple through the bra. Garrett teased her breast with hot, moist pulls of his mouth as his fingers found the front clasp and popped it open.

Lily slid her fingers into his hair as Garrett's lips met her bare nipple. The quick sensation of cool air collapsing against the heat of his mouth created a frenzy in her brain. He found her mouth as he cupped her breasts, kneading them softly, swirling his palms over her taut nipples.

There was no separation between conscious thought and the fog of pure sensation as Garrett's hands and mouth took over her body. He caressed her with long, hot strokes of his rough fingertips, tracking over her ribs to her waist, then back up. His lips traced her jaw, her neck, her breastbone, as his fingers found the side zipper of her skirt and lowered it.

Garrett's mouth tugged at her left nipple at the same time as he whisked her skirt down her hips and sent it flying. Her slight panic over the newness of being bared to him melted under the glory of his mouth. The need to feel his skin was nearly as overwhelming as the need to have him in her—hard and insistent and unrelenting. As he found her other breast, Lily reached for the back of his shirt and pulled it off.

She raised her head from the bed just enough to see his naked torso. Supple, hard, sleek and covered in a soft dusting of golden hair…a ridge of hard muscles leading to the V that disappeared inside his jeans.

"Touch me." Garrett gave her nipple a firm tug, sending a million little shocks over her body.

Her hand stopped, suspended in front of his chest, so close but not close enough. Making that first contact…letting her fingers wander over his incredible body would be giving in. Surrendering.

Receiving pleasure was one thing, but giving it back—that was an intimacy, a personal connection that terrified her. She was about to give herself over to a firefighter, but she didn't want to be saved this time. She craved an out-of-control spiral—a leap with no safety net.

He placed a kiss between her breasts, shifted just a little and began kissing a trail down her middle. Her palm cupped warm, firm muscle and supple skin. It was good, so good, to feel his skin under her hand…to caress up his neck until stubble scratched her fingertips. Lily slid her hand down to the flat plane of his shoulder blade. Long, smooth-edged curves of muscle met her touch as she ran her hand as far over his back as she could reach.

Garrett pushed up on his hands to look down at her. His eyes were a deep blue, clouded with desire that pushed delicious warmth down her body to the tips of her toes.

"I promise you'll know with every touch, every kiss, how much I don't take this moment with you for granted."

His palms cupped her hips and pressed inward. The movement sent sparks through the deep heat that pulsed between her legs. And then he was kissing her again, hard and soft, deep and light, while he brought her hips up so her pelvis met his. Garrett leaned into her, drawing the length of his erection down the middle of her, making her gasp.

"When you leave for Nashville, you'll remember this. My hands on your body, my lips on your skin, the way I move inside you." Garrett hooked his fingers into the sides of her panties and began to pull them down.

"You'll remember how much you loved it and you'll crave more of me."

She bent her knees to allow the panties to slide down more easily, her fingers gliding through his hair with a desperate need to pull him back up—to feel his body on top of hers again. He was right. She would remember this. She was naked with a man too beautiful and considerate to be real. He was a wish materialized, and she was going to take him in, hold him close, before all of this wafted away like dandelion fluff on the wind.

Garrett's touch became a storm of sensation as he smoothed his hand up and down the length of her, his lips loving her mouth, her neck, her breasts. She fumbled with the button of his jeans, too flooded with adrenaline to be coordinated about it.

By the time the button popped free, Garrett had parted her thighs with a gentle touch of his hand. His palm rested over her mound, making her arch and demand with a thrust of her hips. His fingers slid inside her, and she forgot about everything except the way he moved over her, her eyes locking with his, and the gleam of passion looking back at her, making her body respond that much more.

Tension began to build and split in two directions—one leading her to the edge she wanted to jump off so badly and the other to a place that couldn't let go. She closed her eyes, aware that Garrett was watching her. He shifted his hand, driving two fingers inside her while his thumb resumed its play over her nub. A gentle kiss on the side of her neck; a sexy voice rumbled in her ear.

"Fly for me, Lily."

She dug her nails into his shoulder. "Not without you."

He groaned against her lips, his fingers increasing their wicked assault. Despite herself, Lily felt the sweet edge getting closer. She longed for it—chased after it in her mind—begged for it.

Garrett wanted her to let go—wanted to absorb every nuance of expression on her face as he helped her get there. He cupped her breast, brought his mouth to it while increasing the pressure and speed of his touch. Her body arched and then went still.

And then she let go with a cry that snared him, pulled him in and threatened to drown him in its beauty. His heart swelled. He brought them together, chest to chest, held her while the pound of her heart thumped against him. But Lily was having none of it. She squirmed against him, her lips finding his neck, her fingers digging into his back.

"Please, Garrett…" He was sliding his jeans down before the plea left her lips—fished a condom from his wallet before throwing the jeans to the floor. Her eyes swept him up and down, settled on his groin.

"Oh, my." Her hand reached for him, closed around his length and made a full sweep from base to tip. He nearly lost it and pulled away before she could do it again. Too many weeks, months, days had gone by since his last time, and there was no way he wanted this to end too quickly.

He settled the condom in place and gathered Lily against him again, tilting her hips as he lowered himself. Her eyes were wide with anticipation, the clench of her jaw at his slow entry, encouraging and so damn arousing. Her body was snug and hot, taking him in with a race of pleasure he felt clear to the bottom of his spine. Lily muttered a soft, passionate expletive against his ear as he filled her, then held still so he could absorb the sweetness of this first connection.

Need quickly took over his intention to take it slow, driving him to move—harder, faster, each tilt of Lily's hips and moan from her lips encouraging him. His fingers found her tender nub, pressed it firmly while he thrust. She squirmed, uttered a protest before sinking into the aftershocks he knew his touch caused.

It didn't take long. Garrett smiled as he rested his forehead against hers. Lily's body tightened around him as she released again, urging him to follow until they both melted into a tangle.

Garrett rolled onto his side and pulled Lily against him. Her hair tickled his chest as her fingers lazily caressed his ribs. He blanked out for a while, time having no meaning except for the fullness inside him—the satisfaction that settled into his consciousness. It wasn't just the fulfillment of sex, it was something…else.

"Garrett." Lily's soft voice drew him out. He snuggled her closer and kissed the top of her head, wishing he could hang on to this feeling of—whatever it was.

"Yeah?"

"Just...*wow*." Her voice was light and filled with amusement. Garrett chuckled, reveling in the relaxed set of her body and how well she fit against him.

"Agreed." He could sink into sleep like this, no problem. Staying the night would be a first for him, but so was whatever was going on between him and Lily. He'd never been so interested and invested in a woman before. Not in the way that made him want to know all her secrets and her plans, how her day had been, when he could see her again.

They lay there, silent, his fingers moving up and down her arm, until Lily's breathing settled into a slow, even rhythm. In another minute or two, she'd be sound asleep and he'd be right behind her. But as much as he loved the idea of staying just like this, he had to work early in the morning. Besides, there was no sense getting too comfy. It wouldn't be good for either of them.

He trailed a finger down her tattoo and traced the delicate metal loop bracelet on her wrist. Garrett brought her wrist up to his view more to keep himself awake than anything. Three thin leather cords intertwined with copper and silver wire.

"That's an interesting bracelet."

She half opened sleepy eyes. "It was Katja's— my sister's. She found it at a junk sale in Texas."

Garrett wasn't sure if she was completely

awake and smiled at how adorable she looked curled into him. *Katja.* The name rolled around in his head, unusual but with a pang of familiarity.

"Pretty name."

"She was a pretty girl."

Was.

Lily's eyes opened as color swept her cheeks. She blinked a couple of times, her mouth pulled into a line.

The familiarity of the name nagged at him, but Garrett couldn't recall where he'd heard it before. *Katja Ashden?* He'd remember that, he was pretty sure.

Lily ran a hand over his chest, the warmth of her palm a sensual comfort against his bare skin. He looked sideways to the window and the inky blackness outside. It was only nine, but he had to get ready for tomorrow and keep himself from getting any more comfortable than he already was in Lily's bed.

He kissed her temple and sat up. "I'd better get going."

He moved from the bed to the adjoining bathroom. When he came back out, Lily had turned on the bedside lamp and had slipped into a long T-shirt, her messy hair pulled over one shoulder. He was a little afraid of seeing regret on her face, but her eyes were soft. The flush on her pale skin was a beautiful by-product of what they'd shared.

He dressed as she watched him—was tempted more than once to forget the clothes and dive back under the covers. He didn't want it to end, and the way she watched him, Lily didn't seem to want that, either.

Despite his contentment, something nagged at him—something forgotten that wanted to be remembered. Garrett shook it off as Lily walked him to the door. They hadn't said much, and, honestly, he didn't know what to say. Words didn't really seem to be necessary anyway. She reached up and kissed him, a soft press of her lips that quickly turned into something else. Garrett finally leaned away and swept a thumb over her lips. Any more of that and he wouldn't be going home.

"Good night," he said as he opened the door.

"Good night." She smiled softly as he walked out, then closed the door with a *click* that resonated in his head.

The drive back to his place seemed to take forever as his mind ran through the sweetness of this day. He stopped at a red light a block from the Ashden building. A flash of an image played in his mind. A black-and-white photograph—like an image printed in the newspaper. He rubbed his eyes but the image popped in again, clearer this time. That sensation of déjà vu came back with a bang.

A newspaper. An obituary.

Not Ashden. Olson…Oder. Yoder. *Ober.*

His stomach bottomed out. *Katja Ober.* A flashback of the same picture in Lily's office— daughter of Douglas and the late Greta Ober. Leaving behind a sister, brother and father.

Oh.

Shit.

A horn blared behind him. Garrett's eyes flew to the rearview mirror, barely processing the cars behind him as his head swam. He shook his head, snapped back to the stoplight. It was green. He dragged his attention back to the street and passed the light, wiping a hand over his face to try to clear his mind.

Katja Ober hadn't died in Danbury, but he'd been there anyway. She'd lived in an apartment complex in Barron, the next town over.

When the complex caught fire, the Barron Fire Department had tried fighting it alone. But it quickly got out of hand and two other departments had been called in for mutual aid, Danbury among them.

By the time they'd gotten there, the building was beyond saving. Back draft had made the flames too dangerous for the firemen to fight from the inside, and people had still been trapped; the heat had risen to well beyond what the firemen's turnout gear could handle.

It had been one of those no-win situations. The fire had spread in the middle of the night, leaving people confused and scrambling to find a way out. With all the flammable things inside a complex that size, the fire had a million sources to feed from, and it had grown well beyond what one department could handle.

Nobody won that day. The fire had beaten them and changed Lily's life forever.

God, he had to tell her. She'd probably recoil and he'd lose even these last days with her. Blame him on principle. The thought panicked him. He couldn't risk that—she was leaving Danbury soon and he didn't want her to walk away despising him. Hell, he didn't want her to walk away at all, but since he had to let her go, it should at least be with sweet memories.

Not with ashes raining down on what they'd shared.

Garrett pulled in next to his apartment and sat gripping the wheel. He'd be on at the department for the next three days, plenty of time to think of the best way to tell her. Three days without seeing her.

It sucked, but he could deal with it because it would give him time to figure out how to lie if he had to.

CHAPTER NINE

MACY WASN'T GOING to let up an inch. Lily rolled her eyes and tried to change the subject, but there was no deterring her friend's single-minded determination to wring out every piece of dirt on Garrett Mateo that she could.

The junk fair in Yoker was as packed as Lily had ever seen it, and she'd been coming for the past six years, give or take. It was a combination of antiques, handmade wares, architectural salvage and flea-market goods that promised lots of bartering from vendors with, to put it politely, interesting personalities. She'd already bargained down the price of a vintage handbag from a seller with no front teeth and a beaver skull glued to his felt hat, and was pretty exhilarated that the one-eyed dog standing guard under the table hadn't bitten her leg off in the process.

She turned the patent black Lucille de Paris handbag back and forth in front of her, marveling at the excellent condition of the leather while Macy pouted like a three-year-old.

"Lily. Ashden. I want to know *all about* the

sex." Macy tipped her head back and groaned her impatience, floppy curls spiraling every which way. "Come ooon. Spill."

The sex. How did she begin to describe it when she couldn't even fully rationalize it to herself? Saying it was the best experience she'd ever had seemed cliché, even if it was the truth. Spending time with Garrett did something for her, gave her something she needed. Nourished her, almost. The art in the trees, holding his hand, talking about heavy glasses and realizing he was right about that, the intimacy. Trying to explain it to Macy would be pretty difficult, since Lily didn't completely understand all the subtleties herself.

"Your hair is very cute today," Lily said with a grin.

Macy hit her in the arm hard enough to make her nearly drop her bag. "All right," Lily relented. "The sex was awesome. Now will you stop?"

Macy looped her arm through Lily's and led her down the dirt aisle between vendor booths. "That is not a description. My last oil change was awesome. Your maw-maw's purple hair was awesome. Okay, not really, but you get my point."

Lily's heart flipped when they passed a booth with turn-of-the-century hardware. Light switch covers, door hinges and knobs. A pair of pink plaster rosettes sat on a foam display board next to another set hand carved from oak. She ran her fingers over the wood, amazed by the fine detail of each line and curve.

"Really, since you're leaving me for Nashville and all, the least you could do is—"

"Macy." Lily sighed.

Her eyes were drawn to the table and a little wooden box filled with antique skeleton keys. She thought of the wind chime hanging from the sapling near the Pit. Lily rifled through the keys, marveling at their different widths—some wide, some narrow—and lengths. Each had a different pattern on the thumb hold. Considering the amazing chime Bodie had already made with skeleton keys, there was no telling what he might do with more. Garrett had texted her earlier to see if she wanted to stop by the Throwing Aces tonight since he was off shift at the firehouse. She could drop the keys off with Garrett to give to Bodie.

"How much?" She picked the box up and waved it at the woman behind the table.

The woman spat on the ground, her bottom lip stuffed full of chewing tobacco. She was knitting something, didn't bother to look up. "Not for sale."

Lily smiled at Macy, dug a ten-dollar bill from her pocket and held it out. There had to be thirty keys in that narrow box. She knew she was pressing her luck, but she had to start somewhere. The woman made no acknowledgment.

"Are you blind?" Lily asked sweetly, knowing how this game was played. The thrill, and fun, of the barter was half the excitement of coming to junk fairs like this. There were a couple of good ones she liked to travel to in the tristate area, and she couldn't wait to see what she'd find in Nashville.

"Maybe," the woman replied, looping yarn over her knitting needle. "Or maybe I just don't see anything worth my time." Lily shook her head and added another ten. No response. She added one more. The old woman waved a hand in front of her own face.

"My vision…it's starting to come back to me." Macy giggled as Lily added another ten-dollar bill. The woman snatched the bills from Lily's hand with a grunt.

"Well done. I'm cured. Enjoy."

Lily tucked the heavy box into her canvas market bag. She didn't know Bodie, but his story was inspiring and she couldn't wait to ask Garrett for a chance to meet with him and talk about his art.

She could already visualize his wind chimes decorating people's front doors, his gazing balls adding that missing touch to backyards. She could give him the chance to offer people his beautiful things via the shop in Nashville.

Or by opening one in the shoe factory. The idea hadn't left since Lincoln had planted it in her mind with his drawing. She'd poked around a little by calling Sylvia Frasier's office to find out what the asking price was. There was an open house happening this weekend, and, encouraged by the reasonable price, Lily decided her next stop today would be a browse around the building.

Lily relished the wealth of possibilities. She had options. For the first time in a very long time, she had a choice, and with a bit of determination, she could make a place for herself no matter what she chose.

"What are you going to do with all those keys?" Macy tucked a curl back and glanced over her shoulder.

"Give them to someone special."

Macy was looking behind her, her lips pressed together. Lily looked, too, not seeing anyone familiar. "What are you looking at?"

Macy's grip on Lily's arm tightened. "I think I just saw Devon." Lily moved to look behind them again, but Macy stopped her. "Let's just go, okay?"

Adrenaline ticked through her blood, making Lily suddenly jittery and hyperaware. She'd never cared for Devon, and this crap he was pulling was simultaneously pissing her off and creeping her out. She could only imagine what Macy was going through.

"Time for a restraining order?"

Macy made a *pfft* sound and shook her head. "Do those things ever do any good?"

Lily pulled Macy closer until their shoulders bumped. "I mean it. I'm worried about you."

They wove their way through the crowd and to the parking lot. Macy's phone rang, making both women look at each other. Macy just shook her head and kept walking.

"I'm not even sure it was him that I saw," she said. "Maybe I'm just paranoid. Either way, he was accepted to Missouri State to finish his degree. He'll be leaving anytime now."

It didn't sit well with Lily, but Macy looked determined to dismiss it. "Fine, but you're coming to the shoe factory for the tour with me."

Macy made a face. "Why would you want to tour that old pile of bricks?"

Lily laughed, her excitement over possibilities flamed with the chance to talk about it. She clicked the remote unlock to her SUV as they approached and gave Macy a wink.

"Well, my dear, you may be sorry that you asked."

GARRETT BLINKED AGAINST what felt like sand in his eyes and poured a fourth cup of strong coffee. He'd pulled his last shift at the firehouse, and it had gone out with a bang in the wee hours of morning.

A resident at the nursing home had thought it would be great fun to pull the fire alarm, not once, not twice, but three separate times before he finally let the nurse give him a sleeping pill. Geriatric joke or not, Garrett and his team had gone each time to check it out—couldn't be too careful—and Garrett had ended up sitting and chatting with Mr. Bentley until his nighty-night pill kicked in around six in the morning.

Garrett had made a half-ass attempt to reprimand the old man for pulling the alarm, but he'd let it drop. He'd been the one to get an earful instead, learning about the car dealership Mr. Bentley had run for over half his life, how only twelve of his twenty-nine grandkids ever came to visit him and how his wife of sixty-one years, Minnie, had died last year from heart failure.

The unmasked sadness in Mr. Bentley's voice when he spoke about his wife had riveted Garrett to his chair with gentle hands. There was something special about sharing the ups and downs of the human experience with a man who'd lived a long life, seen tons and loved well. The quiet sadness in the old man's voice when he spoke about Minnie was layered with the sweet affection that came from remembering someone special.

"She put up with me, raised eleven children

and put up with me." The old man's heavily lidded eyes brightened with a chuckle as he poked fun at himself. "She had a damn fine heart. Even a heart that good needs a rest, don't ya think?"

Garrett had agreed with that and Mr. Bentley had worried his gnarled fingers together. "She'd better rest up good, 'cause I'll be there soon to get that ticker of hers going again."

Garrett had pondered those words as he left the nursing home. His parents had been happy together. In fact, he couldn't recall a time when they weren't. Even when they'd argued, it didn't take long to blow over. Teddy Mateo had first wooed his wife when she'd come to his beach on spring break. He'd continued to woo her with the beauty of the land, soothing whatever disagreement they'd had or boredom she might feel by taking her to the islands. She'd finished her teaching degree at the University of Honolulu and made Hawaii her home, teaching fourth grade while raising three kids and helping run the family hotel. They'd been a close unit, Mom and Dad, him and Cash and Sawyer.

And then Teddy had fallen through the roof of a factory engulfed in flames. The devastation that ripped through his family after that had occurred with a powerful force Garrett would never forget. And it was something he'd never put a family of his own through. Damn fine hearts and sixty-one-year marriages were for some people, but not for him. If he didn't get too involved with a woman, he kept her safe from loving him, safe from worrying about him, safe from being left alone if he died. And he kept himself safe from suffering if fate reversed its hand and took his family away from him.

Making love to Lily went against that idea, but there wasn't one second he'd spent with her that he could feel guilty about. The memory of her sweet body, the supple, curvaceous feel of her under his hands, was slow to fade. In fact, he hadn't forgotten a moment of it; he could still taste her mouth and hear the cadence of her moans and sighs as he buried himself inside her. The wonderment on her face when she saw the metal art and the joy of having her pressed against him as he took her on her first ATV ride—these were supposed to be casual things. Things that would have never mattered with another of his onetime flings. He'd never cared before, but each experience he shared with Lily was important to him.

She'd captivated him. It would be easy to let their intimacy tumble into something more. He wanted more of her. Underneath her skittish exterior was a woman who could last sixty-one years with a man, and then some. She was just tough enough to put a man in his place and soft enough to keep him coming back for more. Whoever had let her go was a fool, and whoever caught her heart for keeps would be one lucky son of a bitch.

Now that he'd remembered who her sister had been, Garrett was even more certain that letting his mind wander to a lifetime with Lily was the worst possible torture he could give himself. Not that it mattered; she'd made it clear that she wasn't interested in a relationship with him. But when she found out... *God.* He'd asked her to stop by tonight because he was going to tell her. He had to.

"The hell, man, you look terrible!" Mikey wandered up to the bar and sat on a stool next to Garrett.

It was four o'clock. The bar had opened a half hour ago, but patrons were slow to filter in. Not a problem as far as Garrett was concerned. He had a full staff of bartenders tonight, so he could nurse his coffee until a problem arose or he succumbed to exhaustion—whichever came first.

He wanted to retort, but his tired brain wouldn't cooperate, so Garrett flipped his friend off instead. Mikey slapped him on the back and waved for a Coke. Garrett shook his head as Mikey's long brown hair flopped into his eyes. "I'm going to get some chick to braid your hair and make you look all pretty."

Mikey raked the hair back with one hand and smirked. "I'm already gorgeous. But I'm not opposed to you finding me a chick. Preferably before my fire shift starts tonight."

"Fix your own dry spell, jackass."

Garrett waved down the bartender to refill his coffee. Mikey wasn't a frequent flyer in the one-nighter club. Every woman Garrett had known him to go out with had been a permanent fixture in Mikey's life for a while. After his brother, Bodie, had come home from war, Mikey had stepped in as a part-time caregiver, sharing the responsibility with his sister. Between that, working for the fire department and working construction on the side, Mikey had been single a lot longer than he'd been attached.

"Speaking of a dry spell—" Mikey knocked Garrett's shoulder with his own "—what ever happened with tattoo chick?"

Garrett tapped a finger against the handle of his mug as he gathered his thoughts. "Remember the fire in Barron last year? That apartment building that lit up?"

"I burned my ass when the embers got in that rip in my turnouts, remember? I still have a scar."

"Jesus, Mike." Garrett chuckled despite the seriousness in his heart. "People died in that fire."

Mikey gave a somber, respectful nod. Garrett turned sideways on his stool, fixed his eyes on Mikey's.

"Hot tattoo girl has a name—Lily Ashden."

Mikey's eyes went round and amused, obviously not seeing the connection. "Her sister, Katja Ober, was one of those people…and she has a serious issue with firemen."

"Damn. You didn't tell her you're a fireman?"

"She knew."

"But…"

"She doesn't know I was working the fire that killed her sister."

Fifty men had been on scene, doing everything possible to contain the fire and get the trapped victims out. When everything possible turned into nothing working, they'd been called off and had stood watching helplessly as the fire had consumed everything and everyone left behind.

"Well…does it really matter if you're not going to see her again?"

"I slept with her." Garrett gave his coffee mug a shove so it slid to the edge of the bar. "And that's just it. I want her…for more than sex. I mean, I could, easily… *God*."

"Well, this is a cold day in hell," Mikey teased. There was a pause as Mikey looked at his hands. "There was nothing we could do. Hell, man, she's got to understand that."

"I don't think there's anything I could say to make it better for her." They were silent a minute, Mike staring across the bar, Garrett tracking the Coke can in his friend's hand as he turned it round and round.

"She's going to hate you, just on principle." The apologetic grimace on Mikey's face wasn't reassuring. Garrett sighed and waved at the bartender for a glass of water.

"I know." Lily wasn't the kind to hint at anything going on in her pretty head until she was ready, but he didn't think she'd bother holding back her feelings on this particular subject.

"Well, then, September, you're just plain screwed." Mikey turned on his stool to look out over the tables. The place was filling up now.

Yes, he was screwed. Or had been. Completely, wonderfully screwed. A smart man would end this now, cut his losses and move on. The raise of Mikey's eyebrows said he was thinking something similar.

"You'd better plan how you're going to break it off, and do it ASAP. Let her move on, find someone who doesn't have such a painful connection to her past."

Garrett snorted and took a drink. "Thank you, Mr. Therapist."

"Well, she's probably a nice girl, right? Deserves to be happy with a guy who doesn't remind her of her dead sister every time she looks at him."

"Seriously, Mikey? Ouch. And, yeah…damn you, I suppose you're right."

Mikey spread his hands and gave a nod of his head toward the front door. "Someone like that guy." Garrett looked to the door, darn near slid off his stool. Lily was just inside the doorway, a man beside her, her face tipped up as the man leaned down and kissed her.

LILY WAS ABOUT to come unglued. She'd run the gamut of emotions in about eight seconds, from shock, to anger, to disgust and now annoyance. Running into Rob on the sidewalk outside the Throwing Aces was the last thing she'd expected. She hadn't even recognized him when he'd scooted ahead of her to hold open the door, thinking it was just someone being a gentleman. She'd looked up to thank him and caught a glimpse of eyes she knew so well. She must have wavered a little, because his hand was on her back, supporting her and ushering her inside the building.

"Lily." Rob leaned low. She could feel his breath on the side of her face.

In that moment, she realized he was about to do what he'd always done—kiss her cheek. The thought of his lips on any part of her body made her physically ill. She leaned back, avoiding his mouth.

Rob frowned, making the length of his nose with its sharp point appear almost beak-like. His brown eyes swept over her slowly as a grin spread across his wide mouth.

"What are you doing here?" She'd texted him last week to tell him to stop calling and not to bother stopping by. He hadn't replied, so she'd assumed he'd gotten the message.

Rob gestured to an empty table near them. He moved to it, but Lily didn't follow.

"I'm wondering the same about you. Lily, in a bar? I never thought I'd see that." He gestured again for her to sit, and when she didn't, he made a sound that used to seem endearing and now was ridiculously annoying. "Lil-*y*," he whined. "Please, sit. Just for a minute."

She whisked hair from her face and stayed put. He'd been gone eleven months, and Lily realized for the first time that she'd stopped feeling hurt by his abandonment. He didn't invade her dreams or her spare moments. She didn't find herself staring into space, thinking about where Rob might be…what he was doing. Lily almost laughed. She just didn't care anymore.

Not since Garrett had wiggled his way into her life.

At the thought of him, Lily turned and scanned the room, catching sight of Garrett standing by the bar. His body was ramrod straight, his eyes homed in on her. Her middle quivered as anticipation and a blend of other things she couldn't name rippled through her.

"I don't think I will." She tossed Rob a dismissive look before taking a step toward the bar.

Fingers curled over her shoulder, making her jerk. Rob's chest came into contact with her right side, then Garrett was moving through the crowd so quickly, he was nearly knocking people over to get to her. A man behind him put a hand on Garrett's shoulder, whispered something in his ear that made him stop. Lily whipped her head around, pulling free of Rob's grasp.

"Lily, I actually…I was coming to see you. I just stopped off for a drink first. I know you said you didn't want to see me, but this can't wait." He put his hands up in placation, took a step back. "Will you just give me a minute?"

She looked back to Garrett, could see his chest rising and falling. He'd seen Rob grab her arm and was in full-on protector mode. She melted a little inside. They barely knew each other, yet he was ready to stand up for her. When was the last time anyone had supported her other than Macy?

"You have about five seconds, because there's someone I need to see." Rob followed her gaze.

The veins in his neck popped when he spied Garrett. He shoved his hands in his pockets.

"Okay, fine. Lily, you never returned the ring." His nostrils flared a little. "I need...I need the ring."

The heat drained from her face. *The ring?* She glanced at her left hand, knowing full well it wouldn't be on her finger. They'd cut the engagement ring off her finger as a precaution in the emergency room. It had been returned to her in a plastic baggie. With Katja's funeral and the depression Lily had sunk into afterward, she'd never put the ring back on. Lily searched Rob's face, trying like hell to remember what had happened to it.

"I did return it."

He shook his head, dark hair wisping around his ears. "No. No, you didn't."

Lily raked a hand through her hair. She'd woken up in the hospital room, alone. No Rob. Completely, devastatingly alone. And then Macy and Lincoln had rushed in and held her while the doctor explained Katja had died.

When Rob had finally shown up, he'd never once held her or reassured her while she rocked on the bed, too emotionally and physically traumatized to even shed a tear. He'd come infrequently while she'd been in the hospital, explaining he had to keep a normal work schedule to help him cope. And the day she'd been released—

"I had to call Macy to leave work and drive me home the day I was discharged from the hospital because you were nowhere to be found. A week later I came home from therapy to an empty apartment and a *note*. A note, Rob!"

He had the grace to look chagrined, but it didn't cool her anger. Lily pinched the bridge of her nose. "You never let on that you wanted to leave me. I mean, four years together and not once did you say a word about being unhappy. You waited until I was broken."

"I know, Lily. I know. I'm a coward. I'm a bastard. You have every right to be mad at me. But I still…I still need the ring back."

She tilted her head and took a small step away from him. She'd thought about this very moment, the moment she could face him and ask him why. She thought of the analogy Garrett had shared, and right now it seemed like a damn good opportunity to let go of a heavy glass. "I need to know why you left."

Rob threw his hands in the air, his mouth opening and closing without a sound. He ran one narrow hand down his front, looked at the ground. "Because I didn't want to deal with the aftermath, Lily. I'm not good at disorder and chaos. Your father was enough for me to handle all those years, and then the fire happened and Katja…and I couldn't do it. I couldn't see you through that. You're right—I'd been unhappy for a while, but it took that to make me really realize that I wanted out. Goddammit, I'm getting married. It was my grandmother's ring, Lil, and I need it back."

Some of the tension leeched out of her muscles. It was like cool water dousing an ember that had been slowly getting hotter and more destructive. Hearing Rob admit why he'd left her was the closure she'd never had. And it only confirmed her impression that she'd already wasted too much time on him.

She let out a pent-up breath, felt almost like laughing. "Thank you for leaving," she gushed, turning her eyes to Garrett. "Really, thank you."

Across the room, Garrett's impressive body was still rigid, his stance wide, his arms crossed over his broad chest. Rob was tall and whip thin. She'd originally been attracted to his midnight hair and the gorgeous dragon tattoo running down the side of his neck and taking up his entire back. Looking at him now, she was well aware that his form, his character, in no way compared to Garrett's. She turned, but Rob's hand caught her arm again. He tugged her back this time, causing her to shriek. Something toppled, there was a rush of footsteps and then everything became a blur.

He'd stood by long enough. Mikey had convinced him to wait and let the scene between Lily and the man play out. But when Garrett saw the anger on her face, heard her screech when the man pulled on her arm, he couldn't stand by any longer. The skinny man let go of Lily as soon as he saw Garrett coming, but it didn't calm him down at all. He grabbed the front of the man's jacket and shoved him against the door frame, his chest landing with a thump on the other man's as they collided. Garrett just breathed and enjoyed the play of fear and apology on the guy's face.

"You were just leaving," he finally grumbled, satisfied that the man's limbs had gone soft and submissive.

A gentle touch on his lower back told him Lily was there. He could smell her perfume, feel her presence, and it was a small comfort to the rage.

"Garrett, it's okay. Let him go."

He pressed against the man's chest with his forearms, hard, before jerking back and releasing his coat.

"Rob, you'd better go," Lily said, standing half behind Garrett, close enough that her shirt brushed against his arm.

Garrett willed his breathing to settle. He got worked up, sure, but never over a woman and never quite like this. It was more than a protective instinct…it was staking a claim. He gestured with his head that Rob should leave, but the man didn't move. Instead, he put his hands out, palms up.

"Look, I'm here all week. If you find what I asked for…"

She nodded, her arms tightly crossed. "I'll text you if I find it and you can pick it up from Doug at the office."

Rob stared at her a moment before ducking his head and walking out the door. Garrett turned and took Lily in his arms. She held him tight. He closed his eyes, relishing the feel of her. The anger was slow to leave, but it finally started to, leaving behind a simmer of desire.

"Don't say anything," she said as she pulled away. Her expression was guarded, bringing him back to the reality that they needed to talk…that he was on the brink of demanding to know what the hell had just happened here.

"But—"

"Shh."

He looked to the ceiling. "Not again with the silence thing, Lily."

She tilted her head, a cute frown on her face. "You don't listen so well. Look, I know you probably have questions, but I'd rather not do this here. Can we go somewhere private?"

For the first time, Garrett was aware that bar patrons were staring at them, murmuring and chatting about what had just gone down. Lily's cheeks pinked. She didn't have to ask twice.

Garrett grabbed her hand and led her through the room, slowed momentarily at the bar where Mikey waited with one elbow propped on the edge. Garrett gave him a scowl that begged Mikey not to stop them.

"I'm Mikey."

Dammit. Lily paused as Mikey thrust out a hand, forcing Garrett to stop. He grumbled, shooting darts at his friend, who only grinned in response. "Mikey Cain. And you are?"

"Lily Ashden. Nice to meet you." Garrett tugged on her hand again, but she held back. "Wait, are you Bodie's brother? The metal artist?"

"Yes, ma'am."

Garrett mumbled a curse when Lily held a finger up to him, indicating she wanted a moment. Lily slipped the canvas bag from her shoulder and produced a long, narrow box. She lifted off the cover and extended it to Mikey.

"I found these today. I thought maybe Bodie could use them."

Garrett peeked over her shoulder at the box of skeleton keys. He smiled at her thoughtfulness and gave her arm a gentle squeeze. Mikey poked at the keys, and Garrett knew his friend well enough to know he was having trouble finding the right words.

"Have you ever taken him to the junk fair in Picard?" Lily asked. "It's held once a month and it's huge. It's an artists' paradise, really."

Mikey gave a lopsided grin and brushed his hair out of his eyes. "I've heard of it, but, no, we've never gone. Lots of this kind of stuff, huh? Bodie would love that." He gave the box a little shake.

"Oh, yeah. Last time I went, I found a—"

Garrett cleared his throat and tugged on Lily's hand. Any more of this and he was going to explode. Patience had never been one of his virtues—not that he had many to begin with. Besides, his inner coward was making a very rare appearance, and if he didn't do this now, he might opt for that whole lying thing after all.

"You guys can take this up later. Lily, we need to talk. Mikey, interrupt me and I'll kill you." He pulled Lily along with him to the office and shut and locked the door behind them. She spun, eyes questioning, and leaned back against the door.

"Caveman much?"

Garrett ran a hand over his mouth, his other hand resting on his hip. The anxiety inside was a blend of the conversation they were about to have and the aftereffects of seeing another man with his hands on Lily. When he'd thought that guy was kissing her...

"Who was that guy?"

She crossed her arms, eyebrows coming together in a slight frown. "Ex-fiancé. Garrett, what's wrong?"

He turned his back to her and walked to the desk, fiddled with something, anything. "The one who never bought you flowers? I knew I should have rearranged his face."

"It's okay. He took something I wanted to get rid of."

Her footfalls padded behind him. The touch of her hand on his shoulder gave him a warm shiver. Garrett looked over his shoulder at her.

"Oh, yeah?"

"His glass."

He turned then with a light chuckle. "Really? I'm glad.... That's good, Lil." He gestured for her to have a seat as he leaned his butt against the edge of the desk and slid his hands into his front pockets. Concern was clear on her face, and it pulled his heart. He'd been dreading this, yet also longing for it. As much as he wanted Lily to know the truth, he also knew revealing it was the perfect way to keep his heart in check. If she hated him, she wouldn't want more from him and his heart would be safe. It sounded good in his head.

"Lil, did a member of the fire department ever

get in touch with you or your family to explain
what happened the night your sister died?"

Her hands gripped the sides of the chair. Garrett knew his question had blindsided her, but he
had to start somewhere. Besides, he suspected
from their previous conversations that she didn't
have the information she deserved.

"Um, no. We never heard from anyone except a
police officer telling us Katja hadn't made it out."

"Jesus."

She'd had no closure. None. Anytime there was
a fire-related death in Danbury, their fire chief
spoke to the victim's family and answered whatever questions he could. Not all departments did,
but he felt it was the least he could do to help the
family heal. All this time, Lily and her family had
been left with a blank page, where a few words of
explanation and condolences might have helped.

"How much do you remember?"

Lily spread her hands. "Why are we talking
about this?"

Garrett shifted his position against the desk.
"Can I just ask you to trust me for a minute? I
just… I'd like to know how much you remember
because I think I might be able to help with some
of the questions that weren't answered for you."

She rose from the chair. "Did you talk to my
friend Macy?"

He shook his head, his heart rate ticking up.

He hoped he wasn't scaring her off already, because even though this was going to hurt, maybe he could give her comfort, too.

"She seemed to think that maybe I should talk to you," Lily explained. "That maybe you'd have some perspective."

He liked Macy already. "Maybe she's right." After what he and Lily had shared, it was important to help if he could. He wanted that more than anything.

She gripped the back of the chair and looked down, her hair falling like a curtain around her face.

"I went to Katja's to spend the night. We did that often—met at one another's apartments and stayed up watching scary movies and whatnot. It happened to be my turn at her place. We stayed up until about three o'clock, and I finally fell asleep. I kept hearing noises, but I thought I was dreaming, you know, that in-between where you're not really awake and not really sleeping? Finally, there was a loud knock on the door and I knew something was wrong. Smoke was coming under the door, and when I opened it, a huge wave of it came inside."

Garrett's heart raced against his breastbone. He knew how this story ended, but the beginning and middle were a mystery. Now that he was on the verge of getting the whole picture, he wasn't sure he wanted to know.

"By the time we went out into the hallway, the flames were already huge. We could see them hovering around the ceiling at the far end of the hall. People were spilling out of the stairwells. Katja and I ran out, tried to follow everyone, but the smoke was so thick. It was in my throat and my eyes. Next thing I knew, Katja was running away from me, saying she had to get something from the apartment. What that was, I'll never know. I tried screaming for her, but the smoke...

"God, I think I passed out. Either I managed to get to the fire escape or someone pulled me over there because I vaguely remember fresh air hitting my face. I woke up on the grass and looked over and watched the building just disappear behind a wall of fire."

In his mind's eye, Garrett recalled exactly how that building had looked. He remembered the injured being taken to staging areas on a lawn across the street. Ambulances had been lined up, taking the most critically injured first while those who could wait longer did. Lily had been there, on that grass, waiting for her turn while she watched the building burn with her sister inside.

Lily turned slightly toward him, her voice soft and thick.

"I saw all the firemen just standing around.

Some had hoses and were spraying water, but the rest of them had come away from the building. Even though they knew people were still trapped inside, they just stopped trying to get them out. I can't imagine... I can't grasp *why*. Why? What would your department have done?"

She might as well have driven a knife in his chest. He wanted to look away, but he couldn't feed the coward. He caught her eyes and pushed past the anguish he saw there.

"Five hundred and twenty-five degrees, Lily. That was the last Fahrenheit measurement we had on your sister's building before we were called off." He swore he heard her heart kick up a notch.

Her mouth fell open. "Wh-what?"

"I was there, Lil. Originally, I was part of a teardown team that went in and started to pull away falling debris to try to slow the fire down. But it got too hot."

The chair clanked against the floor as she pushed away from it. "What...wait...what?" Ah, damn. Her face... "You were *there?* Inside the building?"

"We were called for mutual aid and arrived as the second department on scene. By the time we got there, the fire was already out of control. There wasn't much we could do except for contain it."

"But you were inside? Did you...did you look

for anyone? I mean, did you go through the building and *look?*"

Garrett could explain how search and rescue worked, or he could let her think he was a piece of shit who hadn't done a damn thing. What was worse? Telling her he hadn't personally gone on recon? Or that the team before him had located two deceased victims but had been unable to recover their bodies because it was too dangerous? He'd known from the beginning that he wouldn't come out of this conversation unscathed.

His pulse thrummed with pain and sympathy for her. "No."

"Did you know there were people still inside?"

"Yes."

It was personal now. Even if he could explain all of it, Lily wouldn't really listen or hear him. Grief was going to block out rational thought and cling to what it wanted to hear.

"You knew people were inside, but instead of getting them out, you just left?"

"I was called off. Lily, it was no longer safe for firemen to be inside—"

"I thought that was your job! To keep going… to keep looking, no matter what."

No fireman wanted to die on the job, but if it happened, it happened. Going down with honor was always a possibility, but none of them pushed that risk further than they had to if they could help it.

"There wasn't a firefighter there who wouldn't have gotten Katja out if he could have."

Lily's shoulders trembled with a chill that seemed to come from deep inside. Garrett wanted to pull her into his arms, but he knew better. There was no warmth he could offer right now that she'd accept.

Her eyes were glistening with tears she didn't let fall. "How long have you known?"

He wiped a palm over his mouth. "Since Wednesday, after I left your place. It kind of all came rushing back to me. I didn't…I didn't want this hanging between us, Lily."

She put a hand to her forehead and turned away, silent. Garrett couldn't stay by the desk anymore. He moved up behind her, staying just far enough that he wouldn't touch her.

"You saw my father's helmet at the bar, Lil. The fire that killed Katja was the same. Too hot, too strong for anyone to get inside. I'm afraid there isn't anything that would have saved her."

That wasn't completely true. If Katja had continued leaving the building with Lily instead of going back to the apartment, she'd probably be alive today. But Garrett wasn't a big enough asshole to make that point. Deep down, Lily had probably already considered that a million times over.

Survivors of tragedy often suffered from a lot of things: guilt over being the one who made it out alive, rage at the person who didn't make it, a constant game of what-if. He wouldn't be surprised if Lily struggled with all of that.

She finally turned to look at him, her mouth in a tight line. She was probably already cutting down any feelings she might have grown for him. Good. That would be good. Because he'd hurt her enough and the thought of letting her love him, and loving her in return, only to lose it all, was a pain he could avoid. And he would.

For her sake.

"Thank you for being honest with me." She headed to the door, but he caught up with her before she could unlock it. His hands found her shoulders; the warmth of her skin and the way she jumped at his touch pulled him in two different directions.

"Lily."

She shrugged him off and unlocked the door. "I have to go."

Lily opened the door and slipped into the hall. He forced himself not to watch her walk away, not to feel guilty about being honest. Both were easier than convincing himself the ache in his chest was a by-product of too little sleep and too much adrenaline.

"Garrett, we gotta go!" Mikey's voice sounded

before he slid to a stop in front of the office door. "Double house fire on Sixth and Main!"

Looked like work was starting early and that was good. That was great. Anything to take his mind off the knowledge that he'd just lost something important.

CHAPTER TEN

THE WIND WAS working against them. Garrett wished the storm system brewing overhead would just freaking bust open already. It would make his job a hell of a lot easier if it would just rain. House fires were always unpredictable, and this one was a raging beast, attempting to consume the house next to it thanks to the wind. They'd needed every available man on their department to fight it. Garrett gritted his teeth and ignored the sweat running between his eyes. Exhaustion was no longer an option.

"More hose!" Garrett shouted to the men on the water tanker behind him. They'd already tapped into the hydrants and had a portable water reservoir filled and ready to go.

He was in command of the scene, standing back and keeping everything organized while his men did the dirty work. He cursed Chief Grail for being gone, told himself this was part of his duty as assistant chief, nerves and all. It didn't matter how many fires he'd worked, or how many still lay ahead of him, nerves were part of the deal.

Good thing the adrenaline high overrode nervousness every time and helped him focus.

He'd already had the neighboring house evacuated, with a crew hosing it down in an attempt to keep the fire from taking hold. Right now, they were using every available resource, and as the sun started to set, it was hard to tell what was daylight and what was refracted light from the flames.

"Shit, Garrett, I'm going into the cold house." Mikey's voice came over Garrett's radio. "The homeowner's dog is still inside. Copy?"

Garrett scanned both houses, satisfied the unaffected "cold" house had been watered down enough to be safe. For now. Flames reached with desperate arms, wavering around the streams of water his men shot at the siding, just looking for a place to catch on.

"Copy, Eighteen," he replied, using Mikey's firefighter number. "Take Thirty-One with you."

He made a mental note of where his men were—some working the flames, some getting equipment, some on rip crew and some on the wet house and, now, two going inside for a dog. "Ten minutes. No more."

"Copy."

Garrett checked the time on his handheld radio. They'd been at this for three hours already, and he'd rotated men in and out of the fire twice. The local ambulance had come to keep an eye on the firemen, ready in case anything happened.

He called over the radio for a switch, took the grumbling and swearing from the men he was pulling out of the action with a steeled jaw and sent a rested crew in.

They were all exhausted, to the point where rotations wouldn't refresh them much anymore. Refreshed or not, it didn't matter. There wasn't a man on this crew who wanted to be pulled from the action and forced to sit it out awhile, Garrett included. These men had other jobs, families, reasons to be up late and get too little sleep. When the pager went off in the wee hours of the morning, it affected them all.

Garrett glanced up at the sky again. "Just rain already, you bastard."

The humidity was stifling, the green swirls in sky still visible in the waning sunlight. A loud pop drew him back.

Window glass exploded in a quick series, from the top floor to the bottom, shooting shrapnel into the air. They'd broken what windows they could safely reach when they'd arrived, but the fire had already been so hot, so fierce, it hadn't been safe to go for them all. The last window shattered as a huge gust of wind fed the flames, whipping them like a mushroom cloud into the sky. It flashed high and quick, settling down with a roar that consumed the atmosphere.

In the next breath, the windows began to pop on the cold house, the glass shattering beneath the force of the heat and explosion in the house next to it. The smoke cleared just enough for Garrett to see flames shooting out of the wrecked window on the house that until now had been flame-free. One house fire had become two.

"Report, now!" Garrett yelled into the radio. Almost instantly, a series of numbers came through the radio as his men responded. Garrett went through the list in his head—he knew them by heart. All accounted for.

Except for Mikey and Roan.

Garrett turned to the cold house. It was surrounded by black smoke that streams of water did nothing to dissipate. A streak of orange flashed from the back of the house, wrapping around to the side. It wiggled through the smoke and water, taunting them. Like a little kid sticking out his tongue after taking something he wasn't supposed to have.

Garrett's heart flipped as he pressed the button on his mic, never taking his eyes off the flame. In a matter of seconds, the flames could completely light the house up. With his men inside.

"Eighteen, Thirty-One, report." He turned to the men behind him, waved to get their attention and pointed to the flames. He jerked his thumb into the air with an upward motion. *Another hose, more water.*

"Eighteen and Thirty-One, report *right now.*" Garrett moved down the sidewalk, trying to see more clearly through the jet-black smoke.

Static was the only response through his radio. He didn't get rattled too easily when his men didn't report back instantly. He knew it sometimes took a minute to maneuver the mic with bulky gloves on.

But it didn't stop him from worrying about them all—especially Mikey, who was not only his best friend, but who had Bodie counting on him. Losing Mikey would be a pain he'd never overcome.

How Lily surely felt about losing her sister.

Garrett punched a fist into the air, frustration pouring out of him. He couldn't think about that right now. Closing his eyes, he pressed his mic button one more time.

"Mikey, Roan. *Report.*"

He moved as close to the house as he dared, scanning what windows he could see for any movement. He braced himself for the screech of an alarm—the panic button that each fireman wore that would be triggered if he remained stationary too long. A stationary firefighter was a man in trouble or injured. Or worse.

A scratch of static came through his radio. Followed by what sounded like…a bark. Garrett held his breath, his thumb hovering over the talk button on his radio.

"Ten-two. We're ten-two." Mikey's voice came through. *We're fine.* "Coming out the front door, with one rescue."

Garrett tilted his head to the side and let out a relieved breath.

"Flames on the top floor."

"I see 'em. Come on, Mikey, get out of there." *I don't have the energy to worry about you right now, and Lily, too.*

Garrett backhanded sweat off the bridge of his nose. But he did worry about them, because they were important—Mikey was like family. And Lily… Losing either of them would rip him wide-open. He cared about them both.

A lot.

Cared about Lily a lot.

Garrett faltered, nearly crashing into a hydrant. A chill washed over him. He started barking orders into the radio. He'd gone years without ever feeling this way about a woman. Years… Was it more than just caring…like a precursor to something *more?* He cursed at himself. It was stupid to even consider it, and this wasn't the time.

He'd done what he could to try to make her understand what had happened the night of the fire. What he was feeling was nothing more than a misplaced sense of responsibility or something. He wrinkled his nose at the thought. That wasn't right, but it was the closest explanation he could come up with for why he was so invested in her.

And why it cut him to the bone to think that he'd hurt her tonight more than he'd helped. And why he never stopped thinking about her. None of these fluffy feelings were going to lead anywhere, but it seemed he couldn't stop them.

A loud crack snapped him back to the house Mikey and Roan should have been exiting. A well of smoke came out of the open front door, followed by far-reaching arms of flame. Shouts erupted around him as a team hustled to get water on this new fire.

Garrett shouted to Mikey over his mic, waiting with every muscle in his neck and shoulders tight to see his men come outside.

From the sound of it, something had cracked or fallen inside the house and his mind raced with all the potential pitfalls. Dread filled every crevice in his chest—that familiar, sticky sensation that reminded him how quickly bad things could happen.

After a minute of straight water dousing the interior, Garrett was ready to burst with anticipation. He called Mikey a few times on the mic without getting a response, sending that damn sense of impending doom into overdrive. He was just about to send a team inside to search for the men when a figure moved through the weakened smoke that still hovered around the front door. Mikey crossed the porch, a dog under one arm, his other around a limping Roan.

Relief smacked Garrett to the point where had he been more in touch with his feminine side, he might have gotten tears in his eyes.

"We're fine, we're fine," Mikey reassured him as Garrett rushed to them. "Roan tripped and we had to wait for the flames to settle a bit before we could see out."

Garrett patted Mikey's helmet and moved to take Roan's other side as he hopped to the fire truck.

Tonight, like any night, had been a close call. Too close.

THE NEIGHBORHOOD HADN'T changed much in the past year, but the space where Katja's apartment building used to be had. Everything else was so similar that Lily had a hard time processing the manicured lot in front of her. A bright square in the middle of a block that housed brown apartment complexes, brick townhomes and gray sidewalks. It reminded her of an eccentric square in a mundane quilt, so foreign to what she remembered about this place, and it took her brain a full minute at least to comprehend what she was looking at. And, honestly, why she'd come here at all.

The past twenty-four hours had found her working furiously in an attempt to forget about what Garrett had told her. She'd finished his proposal, determined to complete her obligation to him and be done with him for good.

But every burst of anger soon ran out of steam, leaving her mentally exhausted but not untouched. Every time she thought about his confession, her chest tightened and she felt on the verge of a full-blown panic attack. He'd reminded her of Katja's death before, and now...he was a tangible link to that night.

He'd probably stood here, on this very sidewalk where so many of the other firemen had been, watching the apartment complex that used to stand where grass now sat as it burned. How far away from her had he been? For all she knew, he could have been right next to her.

Lily turned to the lawn where she'd lain down and fallen apart. Her throat and lungs had ached, her chest on fire from trying to cough out the soot she'd inhaled. And all the while, she'd hoped... prayed that her sister had found a way out.

Lily tugged on her lower lip as she left the sidewalk and moved to the open lot where the apartment building had been. A chain-link fence had been put up around the lot, and large, bright orange X's marked areas in the middle. She stopped by a small sign that showed a diagram of play equipment. Future Home of West Oaks Playground.

Her vision blurred as she read the sign again and again. She couldn't focus on anything just then except the knowledge that something wonderful was soon going to stand where a tragedy had occurred. Children would play here, covering the residue of tragedy with laughter and giggles and excited energy. In its own way, the city of Barron had let go and, in the process, was doing something good to heal the wound.

Lily leaned against the fence, noticing for the first time the warmth of the sun on her bare arms and the smell of something sweet in the air.

Katja had loved this little town because it was close to Danbury yet just far enough away that she had her independence. She'd loved the old-fashioned shops, the flower-lined main street, and she would have loved the idea of a park right here. A warm tear rolled down Lily's cheek. Yeah, she would have loved it.

She stood there awhile, blending thoughts of what Garrett had said with memories of spending time here with her sister. He'd said she had never had closure, and he'd been right. But she'd never expected to have closure. Not completely anyway, given that they'd never know why Katja had gone back inside the apartment or why the fire had started in the first place.

Yet of all those loose ends, she'd chosen to focus on the firemen and what they had and hadn't done. None of the other questions had seemed nearly as important as why they weren't trying to get Katja out.

Now she knew. They'd been trying to prevent more melted helmets. What if Garrett had gone inside…died trying to rescue the victims? Then she'd never have known him. That invisible wheel of fate would have turned around and around, and she'd never have known otherwise.

But she did know him. She knew the sound of his voice and the scent of his skin, how his lips tasted and what he was afraid of. Lily recognized the woman she was when she was around him—how good he made her feel. He'd been here with her that night, a silent sentinel in her worst time. One who had come back to empathize with her pain and pull her up.

Because she finally had the answer to that *why* that kept bugging her in her dreams.

The realization left her knees wobbly. Lily sank down against the fence and covered her mouth. She had the answer to the question her subconscious kept rolling around: why the firemen hadn't done anything. Her subconscious must be satisfied, because she hadn't dreamed about it last night after Garrett told her the other side of the story. A big part of her wanted to accept the peace that Garrett's revelation offered. Yet a residue remained, because each time she looked at his face or heard his voice, she'd remember the night Katja died. He was a living, breathing reminder, and Lily had no idea how to make that better.

A cloud drifted, allowing a fresh spill of golden light to spread out over the grass. The street was quiet with soft sounds of the neighborhood swirling in the air.

Maybe Katja's ghost had been nudging her while she slept, pushing her toward Garrett and the information he could provide. Though there could never be a future for them, Lily wouldn't change the moments she'd shared with him. In many ways, he had changed and enriched her life. And she couldn't be angry at him, even if she wanted to be anymore.

She sank all the way to the ground and clasped her arms around her bent knees. She wanted to grieve, but she also wanted to let go. So she sat a bit and did both.

LILY HAD DRIVEN around the block three times to avoid going inside the fire station, feeling stupid and hoping Garrett wouldn't see her as she passed by again and again.

Finally, at the end of the third rotation, she forced herself to park in the lot. Garrett's paperwork sat in her bag, the reason she'd come. But despite her visit being totally professional, there wasn't a way to keep her personal feelings out of it. And here she sat, torn between wanting to see Garrett and anxious at the thought of actually doing so. It would have been easier to send one of her employees to deliver his proposal, but that would have been a blatant cop-out, and she'd never been one to leave her work undone.

One big garage door opened, revealing the fire engine sitting behind it. Two men walked around the side of the truck. It only took a second for Lily to recognize Garrett. He had his hand on another man's shoulder, laughed at something before tousling the shorter man's hair. Three men got out of a vehicle parked two down from hers, two of them wearing some kind of helmet. Garrett waved to them with a huge smile on his face. The men crossed to Garrett and the entire group took turns giving short man-hugs and pats on the shoulders.

Lily contemplated leaving and coming back another time. Garrett was clearly busy. A few more men came out to stand by the engine. This wasn't really the place to bring up anything personal. She'd catch him for a minute about the proposal and leave.

She was still hedging when Garrett spotted her, looked straight at her and didn't hesitate a lick before jogging her way. No turning back now. She'd just opened her door when Garrett was at her side.

"Hi," he said quietly. "What are you doing here?"

The beautiful lines of his face struck her stupid, almost as if she was seeing him for the first time. In a way, she kind of was. She was seeing the Garrett she knew and cared about instead of the man she'd assumed he was. Bittersweet longing filled her. Yep, she'd made a mistake by coming here herself.

"I called the bar, but they said you were here. I have your proposal. You seem busy, though, so I can come back."

Garrett glanced back at the crowd by the truck.

"No, no. You're just in time. Dinner is almost ready." His smiled and opened her door. "I'm really glad to see you."

Lily hesitated before getting out. She'd planned on dropping off his papers and leaving. She gave a resolute sigh. When did anything with Garrett turn out the way she'd intended? Especially when he was more of a reminder of her pain than he'd been before?

They crossed the street and she focused on the group of men to keep her composure. It was hard when she wanted to cry and laugh at the same time. Her emotions were a mess and looking for a way to escape. Lily was sure it wouldn't be pretty when it happened.

She recognized Mikey as they approached. He gave her a crooked grin, his elbow bumping into the man next to him. It only took a flash for her to realize it was Mikey's brother, Bodie. They looked alike—the same dark chocolate hair, the same rounded chin and narrow, heavily lashed eyes.

"Bodie, this is the lady who sent you the keys. Lily Ashden."

Mikey spoke quietly and evenly, and after a second, Bodie gave a nod. He reached out a hand but made no move to actually grasp hers when Lily took it.

Undeniable grief welled inside her when she saw the arm braces he wore. The right side of his head was misshapen just above his ear, like a lump of Play-Doh had been poked and molded into an oddly shaped ball. His right eye was nearly closed; his cheekbone and jaw were slightly sunken. He smiled—a smile that lit his entire face and showed the handsome lines of the man underneath the injuries—as he eyed what could be seen of her tattoo beneath the flutter sleeve of her top.

"Wicked ink." His words were slightly slurred,

but she understood. As much as she wanted to come back with something witty, the lump in her throat wouldn't allow it, so she nodded with a smile instead.

"Oh, here we go. He's a tattoo freak." Mikey gave him a light punch on the shoulder. "That doesn't mean you can whip off your shirt and show her yours. Deal?"

Bodie grinned and leaned away, clearly enjoying the attention. Bodie would have been Mikey's height, Lily figured, but his back was slightly bent, making him appear smaller. His frame spoke of past strength, but he was now lean, even his hands gaunt.

She recognized the look of his hands—long fingers, big knuckles, the slight appearance of bone beneath tight skin. They were the hands of a man who never stopped tinkering—the hands of a builder, a maker, one who worked his art with a feverish pace. She'd seen hands like that before on some of the painters, carpenters and metalsmiths she'd worked with over the years.

Bodie had beautiful hands.

Lily realized she'd been staring and quickly looked away. The group was talking softly. Garrett put one big hand on her shoulder and pulled her closer.

"Once a month, we have Bodie's friends by for dinner, and they help us check equipment

254 THE FIREFIGHTER'S APPEAL

and whatnot. These boys here are former marine and army, like Bodie. Derek and Rod." He indicated to the two men wearing the special helmets. "They're part of the traumatic-brain-injury support group Bodie and Mikey go to."

Bodie tapped Lily's arm with the back of his hand. "Hey. I have things for you."

Just then a booming voice came over an intercom loud enough to resonate outside. "Hey, jackasses, come and eat."

Bodie made a happy fist pump and hurried off, pulling Mikey behind. The group drifted inside, but Garrett held Lily back.

His eyes were searching when he turned to her, smoothing his palm down her upper arm. She waited for him to speak, but he didn't, just gave a nod with his head for her to follow him. He crossed the threshold and went inside the garage.

Lily hesitated, her heart pounding. The awkwardness between them was almost painful, but she understood. Things might never be the same, but she hoped they could find peace together, if nothing else, before she left town. He glanced back, then turned and walked to her with concern.

Before she could think of anything to say, Garrett gathered her in his arms and held her tight. There was no fight, no resistance, just a flood of relief that she'd get a chance to say her piece and they'd part on good terms. Lily pressed against his chest, his warmth wrapping her in comfort and memories. The muscles of his chest relaxed as he slowly exhaled.

"You're not mad at me?"

"You were right," she said against his uniform shirt. Garrett stroked her hair and made no move to pull back. "There was nothing anyone could do for my sister. She made her choice to go back and she paid the price for that."

Yes, he was right, but it didn't make the hurt feel better.

His voice was heavy when he spoke against her hair. "I'm sorry, Lily."

"Don't be." She pulled back enough to look at him. "I needed to hear the truth. I mean, I think I already knew, but I just needed to hear it."

It had taken a lot for Garrett to give her that truth; it had cost him, too, and she hoped to set his mind at ease. Garrett touched her cheek and leaned in as if he was going to kiss her. Lily tipped her head in response—it was so automatic to want his touch—but he stepped back.

She swallowed her disappointment. It was better this way.

"Hungry?"

No. "Sure."

"Yeah? Follow me. We'll look at those papers when we're done, all right?"

He took her hand again and held it gently while leading her down a hallway and into a big open room. A long metal table sat in the middle with folding chairs all around. A small commercial-style kitchen was visible on the far end; the other end boasted a wide-screen television and several leather recliners.

Most of the chairs were already taken, but Bodie pointed to a couple of empty ones by him and gave a shout. Garrett made introductions as he and Lily made their way over. She barely heard him over the noisy banter and chatter. A radio blasted country music from somewhere in the room, and the television was on. Despite the activity, the chaos wasn't overwhelming. The men were so comfortable with each other, and with being in this place, that it was akin to being plopped down in the middle of a loving family.

Lily sat next to Bodie, who immediately started rattling off something she couldn't understand. She tried to pull conversation out of what he was saying, but Bodie barely took a breath and mumbled more to himself than to her. Luckily, he didn't seem too concerned that she wasn't giving any kind of response.

Mikey leaned back in his chair and shook his head. "I swear he never talks this much. He's got a mumbling problem sometimes. The mouth and brain don't always connect." He slapped Bodie on the back. "Bode, maybe you should stop talking Lily's ear off. You're going to scare her away."

Bodie looked at him, silent and expressionless. Then his face lit up, and his words came out crystal clear. "Maybe your girlie hair is going to...to scare her off."

A roar went up from the table. Mikey crossed his hands over his middle. "That the best you got, little brother?"

"I'm pretty sure hair that long is against the dress code. Anyone got scissors?" someone offered up from down the table.

The sudden volume of conversation made it impossible for Lily to tell who was saying what. The men were laughing and poking fun at each other and she lost herself in the hominess of it. She looked around, realizing for the first time that Garrett was nowhere in sight.

"I'll be right back," Bodie said. His head bobbed as if it were too heavy for his neck all of a sudden. The finger he pointed at Mikey was as steady as a beam. "Don't eat my wings."

Mikey gave a noncommittal shrug. "Well, then, don't drag ass and get back here."

His words died off as Garrett appeared with another man beside him, both carrying big silver trays of wings and fries. The chatter gave way to the clink of plates and forks.

"God, I love wings," Mikey said as he piled

his plate high. He turned a pair of chicken-filled tongs her way. He frowned when she put up a hand. "You don't eat chicken?"

"No. But I'll eat the fries," she replied.

Garrett sat beside her, digging in like the rest of them. She was pulled into conversation with the firemen, whose names she couldn't remember, soaking up the moment with an ease she'd never thought possible. She thought about what Garrett had said at the Pit, about every man on his squad carrying around emotional baggage caused by their firefighting work.

She'd been selfish to think any of their lives were worth less than her sister's or anyone else's. In that perspective, no life was worth more than another, but she realized now that any one of these men would have tempted fate to get her sister out had they had the chance. She'd just taken a drink of water to wash down those thoughts when a small box plopped on top of her plate, sending her food flying.

"Easy, Bodie!" Mikey's hands went wide as a fry made a double backflip into his glass of root beer.

Bodie blushed. "Sorry." He nudged Lily with a hand. "Open it, okay?"

Garrett gathered up Lily's plate, trying to hold back a snicker and failing miserably. Lily slid the box closer and lifted the top. Everyone leaned in, crowding her like a pile of kids at a birthday party. She pulled aside crumpled pieces of newspaper, her heart flipping at what lay beneath.

A string of glittery crystal beads ended with a skeleton key attached to the bottom. Hand-pounded copper and brass disks were fastened to the opening in the top of the key and hung down like eclectic earrings. A bit lower than the circles hung a tiny square picture frame.

"See?" Bodie opened his left hand, showing her a similar ornament. Inside the picture frame was the face of a smiling man in a marine's uniform.

Garrett rubbed the back of Bodie's neck. "Is that Zach?"

Bodie didn't reply right away, and Lily couldn't tell if it was because of emotion or inability. "Yeah. For his mom."

"God, Bodie. It's beautiful." Garrett's voice was thick. He turned to Lily and gave her a wan smile. "Zach was killed in the same blast that injured Bodie."

Bodie blinked rapidly, staring at Lily. "It's a key to heaven."

Lily flipped the ornament, fingered the disks with their decorative stamped edges. When she held it by the top of the string, the disks jingled like a chime. She gave a small smile, the best she could manage through the maelstrom of emotion inside. How did Bodie know that she'd have a picture to put inside? And how could she have misjudged this entire department so badly?

Bodie mumbled, but Lily understood him. "Everyone has someone in heaven, right? Thanks for the keys. Hey, where's my food?" He moved off to his seat. Moment over.

Garrett watched her closely as she put the ornament inside the box. She hadn't even said thank-you, but Bodie didn't seem to care. Her mouth formed the words, but sound didn't quite make it out.

Each second that she was inside this fire station, she forgot her pain a little more. Garrett did more for others than he probably did for himself. Mikey's dedication to his brother went beyond the duty of a brother and the honor of a fireman. These men—they loved each other in the quiet way that men do, and it spilled over, filling the room, filling her.

Lily fingered the top of the box as she caught Garrett's eye. He was everything she wanted in a man—was everything she'd convinced herself she'd never have. He'd been off-limits because he was a fireman, but hell, how could she overlook the person he was? It spoke louder than her insistence he could never be right for her. She wanted to hang on instead of let go. Not just for right now, but longer. Tomorrow, the next day, the day after that. She wanted to keep hanging on. She was slipping…falling…so deeply into him, and she didn't want to hold it back.

But she had to hold back, because he didn't do relationships. More than that, Garrett represented the worst day of her life. It wasn't fair to him that she couldn't forget—wasn't fair at all. But she couldn't stop it.

Overwhelmed by her thoughts, Lily pushed her plate to the side. Her appetite for food was gone, but not her hunger for something else. She needed to get out of here before she burst into tears or jumped Garrett on the dinner table. Lily stood quickly, almost knocking over her chair. Luckily, everyone was too busy eating to notice. Except Garrett.

She gave a tight smile. "I'd better get going."

Garrett stood with her, his eyes questioning, but he didn't ask. A few minutes later, she said her goodbyes and gathered her things. Garrett walked her to the parking lot, his stride easy and slow. She was nearly frustrated with his pace, but she took a breath and fell into step beside him. The way her heart was racing and the deep lull of desire pulsing in her blood made leaving more urgent. Because dragging this out any longer would be foolish.

She fished the packet of papers from her bag as they stopped at her car. "Here you go. There's one proposal for the bar renovations and the lot development and one just for the bar, in case. Look them over and let Doug know if you have any questions. If not, feel free to sign them and drop them off at the office."

He clasped her upper arm gently. "Are you cutting me out, Lily? I have to deal with Doug now?"

She shrugged and tamped down the ache in her chest. "There's no reason he can't help you from here on."

Garrett was shaking his head before she'd finished her sentence. "That's not an answer."

"I don't know what you want me to say."

"Say I can see you before you leave for Nashville. Dinner, a walk, something."

"Sounds a lot like a date, Mateo," she teased. "Stepping out of your comfort zone?"

It would be good for him, she'd bet, to step out of his no-dating, no-relationships box. While they'd never spoken about his reasons, Lily suspected he suffered from a hefty dose of the same thing she'd had all this time: fear of facing the truth for what it was. Something must have happened to make him so reluctant to have a relationship and he probably hadn't faced it, though he'd been great at pushing her into doing just that with her own problems. His father's death, if she had to guess.

He didn't answer directly, just leaned in until

his lips nearly touched her cheek. "Can I see you tomorrow?" he asked.

Tomorrow was another obstacle to get through, one she didn't want Garrett to witness her struggling with. There would be nothing easy about getting through the first anniversary of Katja's death.

"Tomorrow isn't a good day." She didn't want to elaborate and was glad when he didn't push.

"Well, then, I'm off in three hours. Drinks at your place?"

That boyish twinkle in his eye and the sensual outline of his lips made it very hard to say no.

"I think you're awfully cute when you're being stubborn," he quipped when she slipped into the car and started it without a response.

"And I think you need to stop being so damn wonderful." Lily pulled the car door shut and pulled away with a wave. She'd just rounded the block and stopped at a stop sign when her cell beeped. She flipped it open while she waited for traffic, a message from Garrett filling the screen.

Hey, Ashden, I'm taking that as a compliment. I'll be there about eight.

GARRETT HAD STARED at his cell phone a long time, knowing Lily wouldn't likely text back since she was driving.

He'd resolved to give her a few days to process the information he'd shared about the fire and maybe settle her feelings about it. Seeing her at the fire station had been a pleasant shock. No matter how many times he'd told himself that Lily would probably never get over being angry at him, Garrett hoped that she would. He'd missed her, and seeing her today brought that hope to fruition. She wasn't mad, and that meant there was a chance for them, right? If he wanted one; if he was ready for one.

Garrett cleared the steps on Brad's front porch, a manila envelope tucked under his arm. He had some time after his shift before heading to Lily's to see Brad. Garrett figured the phone call he'd just taken would bring a huge smile to his uncle's face, and was too important to wait. His ten-year-old cousin, Brittany, met him excitedly at the door and pulled him inside. She was a mini-Brad with the trademark blond hair, blue eyes Mateo coloring.

"We were just laughing at pictures of you!" Brittany giggled as she tugged him along to the family room.

Eight-year-old Andrea looked up from her dad's lap on the couch and made a disgusted face. "We just saw you naked in the bathtub!"

Garrett tugged on Andie's braid before shaking

his uncle's hand. "Traumatizing your girls with my chunky baby bottom?"

He took a seat next to Brad and warmed inside to see the color in the older man's face today. A stack of photo albums sat near Brad's feet, one open on his lap with Andie. Garrett recognized the pea-green leather album as the one filled with pictures of him, Cash and Sawyer as kids. It had been a very long time since he'd seen it.

"You were a pretty chunky kid," Brad joked. "Good think you figured out that whole exercise thing, or you'd still be soft."

They flipped through a few pages, making the girls giggle and squirm with photo after photo of naked or half-naked little boys on the beach, in the water, in the tub, playing in the backyard.

"It's hot in Hawaii," Garrett explained. "Clothing is definitely optional when you're two."

"'Nuff naked boys," Andie said and placed a red album on top of the green one. "My dance pictures are in this one."

Garrett's vision was immediately filled with images of the girls in colorful ballet costumes, making pretty poses against artful backdrops. He smiled, remembering many of the costumes from their recitals that he'd attended.

The girls chattered excitedly about each picture, filling the living room with sparkly energy. Brad's expression changed from a smile to something more serious as the girls flipped pages. Bags filled the space under Brad's eyes. His cheeks were slightly hollow, though not as gaunt as they'd been just a few months ago. He'd lost almost thirty pounds during chemotherapy, and Garrett found it encouraging that Brad was gaining a little of that back and keeping it on.

Maybe there was hope. Brad snuggled both girls close, laughing with them in a moment that robbed the sadness away from his expression.

Before he'd gotten sick, Brad had worked countless hours at the bar, getting home well after the girls had gone to bed. Since he'd been forced to slow down, he'd transformed into a man who spent every available moment with his family. The risk of death did that to a person, Garrett supposed. Made you reprioritize your life, and though Brad had pretty much been forced to change, he seemed...content.

Would Brad have changed his mind about having a family if he'd known he was going to get cancer? It was a question Garrett had been tossing around for a while. Despite the obvious struggle they were going through with his illness, Brad's family had never seemed closer in Garrett's eyes.

He related that a lot to Mikey and Bodie. Before Bodie had left for Iraq, he and Mikey hadn't been close, and now...they were almost inseparable. Garrett cupped his hands together and focused on them. Bad things had happened to the people he loved, but they'd found a way around the tragedy—found a way to be happy again.

Brad gave each of the girls a kiss and shooed them out of the room to go help their mom in the kitchen. The tenderness he gave each daughter told Garrett there was no way in hell Brad would have not had his family if he'd known what lay ahead.

Garrett slipped the envelope onto his lap with the very strong sense that maybe he was a coward after all.

"Here." He pulled the proposal from the envelope and handed it to Brad. The numbers were right. The project descriptions were right and the time frame for getting started was perfect, too. Brad made a few comments as he looked it over, but Garrett already knew he'd be pleased.

"This is the proposal that includes the lot." Brad's brows knit together. "You haven't heard back on that yet."

Garrett reached inside the envelope and pulled out a half-folded sheet of paper and handed it to Brad with an innocent-sounding whistle. Brad looked at it. A moment later, he cleared his throat and rubbed a thumb over his eyes.

"Sylvia sold. Amazing."

Sylvia had called him earlier, ready to sell.

Garrett hadn't wasted any time getting to her office with a check and a pen to sign the contract. Terrified she was going to change her mind the entire time, he'd quickly signed the paperwork, half expecting to find out he was being pranked at any moment. But she'd settled up with a smile and a handshake and that was that. He couldn't wait to share the news with Lily, too.

"She liked Lily. A lot. I think that's the only reason she finally gave in."

"Got a pen?" Brad asked softly, his voice thick with emotion. Garrett handed one over, watched silently as Brad signed his name. "You know, when I asked you to come to Kansas to help me out, I never expected you to hang around this long, Garrett. I can't thank you enough for all you've done. I'll rest better knowing the bar will be tip-top."

Garrett took the paper and signed it, too, before putting it away.

"Lily did a great job on the proposal. You should be thanking her for giving us what we needed."

Brad patted his knee, then turned his head away as he blinked a few times. Garrett tugged Brad's sleeve until his uncle faced him again and embraced him for all it was worth.

"We got this, Brad. Together. I'm not going anywhere."

Brad's hand dug into the back of Garrett's shirt. "Your dad would be proud of you, son."

They were silent for a long time until the sound of little feet raced into the room and stopped dead, followed by an "ewww" and Andie running back to the kitchen shouting, "Mom, Uncle Garrett and Dad are acting weird!"

They broke apart and Brad rolled his eyes with a nod in his daughter's direction. "Time for you to settle down and have a few of your own so you can enjoy the madness, too."

Garrett smiled and wiped his eyes. The thought wasn't so foreign anymore. "Yeah. Maybe."

CHAPTER ELEVEN

"DEVON IS GONE." Macy held out a shirt and studied it a moment before throwing it into a pile at her feet.

"How do you know?" Lily retrieved the shirt Macy had put in the "gross and ugly" pile and tossed it on her bed.

Macy had shown up unexpectedly after Lily had gotten home. Figuring she had time before Garrett arrived, she put Macy to work helping her look for the misplaced engagement ring. Finally, after tearing apart her walk-in closet, they'd found it in a hospital bag she had hanging up in the back, along with a few other things she'd forgotten about: a watch, a pair of earrings and a half-empty box of Tic Tacs. All the things she'd had on her when she'd been taken by ambulance to the hospital the night of the fire. Overwhelmed with grief over her sister, Lily had simply forgotten that bag existed.

"A mutual friend told me. Said Devon wanted to get settled into his new apartment before college starts, so that's that." She brushed her hands together. "I'm done with him. The same way you're done with this skirt. Are you secretly a hippie?"

Macy held the multicolored gauzy skirt to her waist, all but drowning in the length. Apparently now was a great time to clean up her wardrobe, since Macy had practically destroyed the closet.

"I have no idea where that came from." Lily laughed, grabbing the skirt and tossing it into the ugly pile. "I think it was here when I moved in."

They continued sorting, laughing and horsing around the way they usually did. Some of that had been missing from their relationship in the past months, and Lily realized that had a lot to do with her. But her spirit was lighter today. She'd been sleeping without nightmares, and when she woke, her outlook on the day ahead was brighter.

"Oh, my God!" Macy turned with a black corset pressed against her torso. "Where did you get this?"

The corset had been specially made to fit Lily's body, the boning fine and elegant, the black satin shining in the light. Lily peeked inside the closet and pulled out a burgundy skirt and white blouson shirt with a velveteen bolero jacket and laid them on the bed.

"I went to a steampunk convention a couple years ago with Katja. It was really fun." She dug a little more and found the finishing piece. "See? A fascinator."

She plopped the tiny black top hat on her head. Macy went crazy with laughter. When she finally recovered, she headed for the bedroom door, thrusting the corset at Lily.

"You wore that, but you had a fit about the coconut bra? Really? I need a drink."

Lily pressed the corset against herself—she'd forgotten just how sexy it was—and followed Macy just as a knock sounded on the door.

"Got it." Macy undid the lock and opened the door. Goose bumps lit on Lily's skin when she realized what time it was.

"Well, look at you," she heard Macy say. "You're not here to put out a fire by chance, are you? Because I think there's one right over there."

Macy swung the door wide and pointed at her. Garrett stood at the threshold, looking amused at first. And then his eyes went huge and Lily realized she was still holding the corset against her breasts. She let the corset drop, taking in his fire uniform and the bottle of wine in his hand.

"Pretty hot, right?" Macy stepped aside so Garrett could come in.

He did and held a hand out. "Garrett. I remember you from the fund-raiser, but I don't think we officially met." He flashed that trademark smile, and Lily was sure she heard Macy's blood sizzle.

"Macy. Nice to meet you. You don't happen to have a brother…" She winked.

Lily rolled her eyes. Garrett set the bag on the coffee table and shrugged out of his jacket. "Two, actually. One is crabby as hell and the other is a hermit, so I'm afraid they aren't fit for polite company."

Macy waved a dismissive hand. "Right, but do either of them look like you?"

Garrett grinned and looked down. "Um, a little, I suppose."

"That's all that matters."

"Welcome to the Macy Experience," Lily said, tossing the corset onto the couch.

Macy retrieved her purse from the kitchen counter and dug out her keys. "That's my cue. Lily, will you drop Adam off at my place tomorrow?"

As if sensing he was being talked about, the cat peeked out from where he was curled up on the recliner. He had no idea what he was in for at Macy's apartment where he'd be staying while Lily was in Nashville. Her shimmery curtains and fluffy couch pillows were going to be the joys of his life.

"I will." Lily walked Macy to the door and closed it softly after her friend had left. A small silence stretched, reminding her that she and

Garrett were alone. "I'm frequently exhausted and bewildered after she leaves," Lily teased.

"I can see why." He handed her a manila envelope. "Sylvia sold me the lot."

A tingle raced down Lily's spine as she took the envelope. "That's wonderful! I'm so glad."

All his chips were falling into place. Her heart swelled for him and all that was to come for his family, for Mikey and Bodie, thanks to that empty lot.

"All the appropriate paperwork is signed. I couldn't have done it without you, Lily."

She waved him off. "I just…well, I know it'll be amazing."

He grasped her hand.

"I wish you'd be here to see it through, so you can enjoy it when it's completed."

Hmm, there was a touch of longing in his expression, and the longer he looked at her, the more blatant it became. She still had no idea what the future was really going to hold for her—whether she'd stay here or Nashville, but the look in his eyes made her think he was rooting for Danbury. And it made her ache with the desire to give him everything, but not being able to. Wanting him almost hurt more than the memories he conjured in her, because with Garrett, she'd always want more.

"I'll see it. Don't worry," she replied.

Lily turned to the couch, pulling him down to sit with her. She'd intended to get her thoughts in order, to find the right way to bring up what was between them, but the moment his weight sank on the cushion next to her, Lily forgot.

Maybe she reached for him first, or maybe he'd reached for her as she slid onto his lap and found her lips meshed with his. The kiss was demanding and giving, pulling her into the tingly daze only Garrett had ever been able to inspire. His big hands were in her hair, holding her at just the right angle, their chests pressed together so his heart beat against hers. It made her forget, blissfully.

She absently found the buttons on his uniform shirt and began popping them, getting to the third one before she realized what she was doing.

Garrett took her face between his hands and looked at her. "Sex isn't why I came over tonight. I want you to know that."

She pressed her hands against the sculpted hardness of his chest, finding it hard to breathe enough to get words out. "Why did you, then?"

He kissed her again, giving her the impression that he was stalling.

"Garrett."

She pulled away and there it was, that deepness in his expression that she wanted to understand. He always wiggled information out of her, and it was her turn to do the same to him. She slid off his lap and crossed her arms. There were things she wanted to hear him say, and things she probably wouldn't like hearing. Either way, it was time.

"Start talking."

GARRETT STOOD TO give himself some space. He needed it if there was any chance of making sense of the thoughts in his head. This was a completely foreign place for him to be, and his entire body recognized that. He didn't know what to do with his hands, so he put them in his pockets. His legs were restless, so he started a slow pace around the living room.

And then he found that, as much as he thought he'd needed space, being separated from Lily's touch left him empty. He went back to where she sat and crouched down, putting one hand on each of her knees. She waited expectantly, patiently, and he was glad he had a second to get it together.

"All right, here it is, Lily. I want…I want to see if there could be an *us*. But I don't know if I can."

The confession didn't leave an acid trail in his mouth the way he'd feared it would. But it did make his lips tingle and his scalp burn, because this was as far to entering a relationship as he'd ever gone. How did some men do this over and over? The sex, sure, he could see that. But the admitting feelings and wanting more… No, this was a onetime thing, and if she said no…if it didn't work out, he'd happily never go down this road again.

What if it all went wrong—if fate chose him? Or worse, chose her?

Lily reached out and smoothed his hair behind his ear. "Why don't you think you can?"

Her thighs were warm through her jeans as he braced his hands there. Touching her gave him the courage to talk about this, so he lightly ran his hands up the length of her legs to her hips, his fingers kneading through the denim. And then she stole his breath away by leaning forward and reaching for the buttons on his shirt to finish what she'd started earlier.

"Talk to me," she said encouragingly, finishing off the rest of the buttons.

She spread his shirt open with her hands, her palms rubbing against his chest and shoulders as she whisked the fabric away. Garrett shrugged and the shirt slipped down his back. Lily looked over his bare skin, a little moan coming from deep in her throat.

It was instant, fast and hot, this reaction he always had to her. Fast and wonderful. Garrett's hands moved across her middle and came to rest on the button of her jeans. His eyes caught hers as he slowly worked it free.

Garrett pulled her zipper down slowly, noting each flicker of expression on her face. "You know that my father died in the line of duty."

Lily's breath hitched as he opened her fly. He leaned into her, pressed a kiss to the exposed skin over her belly. The lavender scent of her skin threatened to drive him completely out of his mind.

"My mother never fully recovered from losing him. I can't…"

He edged up the hem of her shirt, his tongue making a little swirl around her belly button.

"I don't know if I can ask any woman to risk going through the same thing."

Garrett kissed down to the edge of her panties. Lily's hips tilted up in response, her fingers in his hair digging and kneading deep.

"It's not a blind risk, Garrett. I… Oh." Her fingernails pricked into his scalp. "I'm aware that it's a dangerous job."

Her breath came out in desperate pants. Garrett grasped the waist of her jeans and leaned back on his haunches as he urged her hips up and pulled the denim down. Her lower half bared to him, Garrett took in Lily's long, tanned legs and the smooth, slightly rounded rise of her belly. Taking this slow, letting it tiptoe through time was as tempting as throwing her down on the couch and loving her hard and fast. Slow would have to win, because he wasn't done talking.

"I've seen things on the job and off that make it hard, Lil." He kissed the inside of her knee, relishing the soft moan that fluttered from her lips. "My dad and uncle used to swap horror stories when they thought we were in bed. But I heard—all the bad things…"

Lily cupped his chin and took a heavy breath. "Garrett…" The soothing tone in her voice riled up the part of him that really didn't want to be having this conversation. The shift was sudden and unexpected. He didn't want to be placated. He wanted her to understand that this risk was real. Maybe she wouldn't ever be able to understand the fear he carried around.

"What happens if you're driving home from work with the kids and a semi takes you out?" He gripped her hips, the satin of her panties a delicious treat against his rough hands. "What if I get nailed by a house collapse, or lose my mask and suffocate? What then, Lily?"

He grabbed her thong on either side and yanked it down over her soft hips. Lily gasped and shifted her body to allow the material to slide down her legs. And then she just looked at him as her thumb caressed his cheek.

"What if every time I look at you, I'm reminded of how much I have to lose? Because that's what love is, Lily. A constant reminder of how much can go wrong."

Her hand jerked away from his face. "What did you say?"

The sudden stillness of her body made his breath hitch. A moment passed before he could process her question.

"I don't know how to move past that hang-up, Lily." It was all he could think of to say, because it was the hands-down truth. He'd been able to overcome hundreds of obstacles in his life, but never the fear.

Warmth from Lily's palms pressed into the sides of his face. With her eyes tightly closed, she lowered her forehead to his.

"Neither do I. Everyone takes a risk when they fall in love, Garrett. Besides, it doesn't seem fair."

Needing the distraction of her body to keep going with this conversation, Garrett slowly ran his hands over the insides of her thighs. "What's not fair?"

"Denying someone the chance to love you. Denying yourself that chance in return. Love is a part of life, but so is all the other stuff, right?"

Deep down, he'd known she would understand. They had a shared connection that linked them to the worst tragedy of Lily's life. They'd been brought together then, and again a year later.

Maybe…this was exactly where he was supposed to be—taking a chance with this woman.

"Are you saying that you're willing to be more with me?"

LILY'S HEAD TIPPED back against the couch, her mind clouded with the sensations Garrett's mouth caused. "I don't know." All that mattered just then was this closeness they shared. Right now, it was enough, because his touch helped her imagine that more was possible.

Before Lily could think of another way to explain, Garrett pushed her legs apart and leaned in; the heat of his breath on her sensitive skin made her squirm with anticipation.

He descended closer…a little closer, pulling her right thigh over his shoulder, and then the left. Her bottom rose off the cushions, and the vulnerability of this position hit her hard and fast. Lily squirmed, but his hands grabbed her hips. Garrett turned his face and kissed the inside of her thigh. The bud of heat from that imprint sent shocks through her. He was so close to where her body wanted him, yet not close enough. As much as she longed for it, the sensation of being completely out of control in this position was almost overwhelming.

Garrett caressed the outside of her thighs as he dotted kisses along the tender insides. Her spine arched, her head back against the cushions, though awkward, wasn't uncomfortable. A warm stream of breath washed over her center, making her arch up.

And then he placed a kiss on her center, pulling her closer to meet his mouth, holding her with a firmness that left no escape—no doubt. The tip of his tongue parted her and stole away any inclination to resist. He sent her into an immediate spiral, overwhelming her senses with his touch. The roughness of the stubble on his jaw rubbed against her thighs and made a startling contrast to the pleasure he was sending right through the heart of her.

"God, you're beautiful," he murmured with a tone so pure, it gave her another push closer to the edge—the edge she could jump off and fall straight down into love with this man. But she wouldn't. She'd let him push her into a spiral of release, but the rest could wait until they'd figured out this thing between them.

She hoped.

Garrett pulled back, gently lowering her legs and supporting her with an arm around her lower back. He pulled her onto the carpet, his hands stroking her belly and the sensitive skin over her ribs before resuming the wicked play between her legs. She squeezed her eyes shut, afraid if she opened them, everything would dissipate...

be just a dream. The sound of his zipper, the rustle of fabric, a frustrated curse under his breath. And then a warm kiss on her lips…another as he touched her in the way she needed the most.

Lily arched her back as velvet heat uncurled at a dizzying pace. The warmth of Garrett's body hovered over hers as he moved between her legs. He pulled her back just slightly and slid inside with a hard, insistent thrust that sent her into release. Each stroke prolonged the pleasure, fanned it, flamed it. Time ran away, leaving nothing but the sensation of him moving in and out of her, his fingers digging into her hips and the seductive sounds coming from low in his throat.

Garrett growled her name, one arm looping under her back as he covered her with his body and shuddered. The hardness of his body was a comfortable weight as he relaxed, her arms holding him tight as their breathing slowed.

Awareness returned slowly. Her skin cooled, making her shiver. Garrett rolled to his side, pulling her close to his body heat. His lips lazily traveled her neck before he angled her head to the side and met her lips. Lily managed to twist in his arms so they were face-to-face, her leg around his hips, his hands in her hair. The kisses turned leisurely, soft, each one wrapping her in the warmth of being cherished.

In between kisses, reality seeped in. She was

leaving town soon, and now instead of filling her with excitement, she was a little hesitant about it. In the matter of the past half hour, her perspective had shifted and her future was more undecided than ever.

Garrett raked a hand through his hair, his face tilted to the soft light in a way that made her breath hitch. There really wasn't an angle from which he didn't look drop-dead gorgeous. And as much as Lily didn't know what to do about Garrett, she knew she didn't want him to leave just yet.

"Come to bed with me."

He smiled sweetly. "I have to work early in the morning."

"You can leave whenever you want. Sneak out in the middle of the night if you want. I just...I don't want you to go right now."

The intensity of his expression looked the way she imagined love might. He stood and pulled her up, swept her right into his arms. He started to walk away, but then he side eyed the couch with a wicked grin.

"It's a shame to just leave that there, don't you think? We could put it to good use."

He'd spotted the corset where she'd tossed it on the end of the sofa. Lily laughed and rolled her eyes.

"Coconut bra is in my closet."

He whisked her into the bedroom with a wag of his eyebrows, the lines of his face as relaxed as Lily could ever recall. Maybe life would begin to smooth out for them both—take some of the weight of responsibility off Garrett's shoulders and finally give her the chance to make amends with the painful parts of her life.

A pile of clothes still lay on the edge of her bed, and things were scattered around the floor from the closet-cleaning fiasco. Garrett gave her a quizzical glance, but he shoved the clothes onto the floor and tossed her on the bed. Lily scooted back at the same time Garrett put his knees on the mattress and made a slow crawl over her body. The blue of his eyes was intense as he hovered over her, the ends of his hair curling around his face. He dropped a lush kiss on her mouth before rolling to his side and pulling her close.

As her body relished his warmth and strong embrace, Lily's mind slid to tomorrow. The anniversary of Katja's death. As hard as she tried to push the thought away, a potent reminder was wrapped around her. The even pace of Garrett's breathing taunted her, reminded her of why this thing between them couldn't continue, even as she clung to him, reluctant to let go.

"Garrett?"

"Yeah?"

Lily swallowed hard, hating the bitter words that were forming in her throat.

"I can't be more with you."

He didn't say anything at first, just tightened his arms around her.

"That's okay, because I don't know how to be more for you. Maybe when you get back from Nashville, we can try to figure it out."

Maybe. Because this felt a lot like goodbye.

LILY SET THE small plastic bag on Doug's desk and a take-out coffee cup next to it. He didn't look at her, but he gave a sideways glance to the things she put down.

They weren't usually chatty in the mornings, or any other time for that matter, but Doug had *sour mood* written all over him. It was almost palpable in the air. Lily had expected this. She felt the same but was determined to deal with her emotions today —all of them—instead of letting them consume her. Today was the day Katja had died a year ago, and combined with her evening with Garrett last night and her trip to Nashville tomorrow, Lily's nerves hummed with hyperenergy.

She'd delivered her cat to Macy early that morning and been coerced into spilling everything that had happened between her and Garrett last night. All the wonderful details came back in a rush, filling her once again with the bittersweet pull. Garrett had left in the night without waking her to say goodbye. She could read into that or just accept that it was better that way. Both sucked.

"Rob will be by later today for that." She flicked the plastic bag with her middle finger and thumb, glad to be tying up that loose end. It was pretty amazing that she'd never once thought to look for that ring after she returned home from the hospital, even before Rob had left. It was a loud testament to her true feelings all this time.

"Rob?" Doug pulled his reading glasses off and squinted. "What's that bastard doing in town?"

Bastard? That was a first. Doug had always remained neutral on the whole Rob issue.

"Um, coming for the ring. He's getting married, apparently."

And she couldn't care less. It felt amazing not to waste any more energy or precious time on him. She cleared her throat and hurried on before Doug could start a grand inquisition.

"The Mateos agreed to the proposal. So you're welcome." She pulled an envelope with the contract inside from beneath her arm and set it on his desk.

Doug stared at her and rubbed his chin with a thumb, the rough stubble of his day-old beard making a scratching sound.

"What?" Lily asked, taking a seat in the chair

opposite him when he didn't say anything. She took a sip from her coffee and crossed her legs.

"You did good, girlie."

Lily leaned forward in her chair, a suspicious tilt to her head. "What kind of happy pills are you taking, Doug? Wait, did you go to the doctor and finally get something for your severe case of asshole-itis?"

"That's enough. Funny. Har-de-har." He propped his chin in one hand and closed his eyes just a moment before looking down.

Lily leaned her forearms on the desk, hoping against hope that he'd say it. Bring it up. Let it out. Today was a day of loss—a reminder, a painful shadow lifted to reveal the truth they couldn't get away from. She needed his commiseration, on some level, just to know she wasn't alone. But as several seconds passed and he did nothing but stare at the top of the desk, Lily knew she'd get no more out of him than she had before.

"They're making a playground out of the lot where the apartments were."

He didn't respond.

"It's quite beautiful, actually. The grass is a really bright green and there are little patches of flowers already growing. And there's a diagram of all the play equipment that's going in—"

"So what?" He riffled through the manila envelope and pulled out the contracts. She wasn't going to let his indifference prickle her. Not today.

"So it's a wonderful use of that space, and I know Katja would be happy about it. I just thought you'd like to know."

"Katja's dead, Lily. I don't think she really cares about some stupid playground."

The deep gravel of his voice dripped distress, but his face didn't show it. Sarcasm was a great shield, but she'd learned to poke holes in it, and every once in a while, the real Doug Ashden would show through. Sometimes he actually cared, and she knew that today, of all days, he did but had no tools for breaking free of his shield and showing it.

Lily slid her hand on top of his, thinking he'd pull away. But he didn't. "Dad."

He looked up. She rarely called him by what she'd come to consider a title of affection, because there wasn't really affection between them. Right now, her heart was full for her father and it was a say-it-or-explode type of situation.

"Dad, I miss her, too. It's okay to miss her, and I think today is a perfect time to talk about it."

Doug looked out the side window. "Let's not do this, Lily."

She bristled. "Why not? We both miss her."

He continued to shuffle through the papers in

his hands, hoping, Lily was sure, that she'd give up and go away.

"I met a fireman who was at the fire that night. You might know him—Garrett Mateo." That drew Doug's attention, even if it was just a quick look before he pushed his glasses higher on his nose.

Antsy, Lily stood. "I spoke to him about the fire, and he helped me see what happened in a different light. And then I went to Barron and saw the playground being put up on that lot, and…it helped, too, Dad. It did. Garrett… He reminds me of her, you know? But I want to get over that, Dad."

He put the contracts down and placed his forearms on the desk, his index fingers coming together to make a point. "Sit down, Lily."

She did and put her hands on the desk. "Don't you have anything to say about any of this?"

"You're not going to Nashville."

Dumbstruck by the change in topic, and again by what he'd actually said, she had a hard time making her lips work. "Wh-what?"

Doug leaned back in his chair. "Lincoln got a call yesterday and has a very sudden meeting with a major development firm in New Orleans. I'm heading out the day after tomorrow to meet him there. I need you to stay here and hold down the fort."

Every fiber in Lily's body felt like stone. Tension crept up her spine, wrenching the muscles in her back on the way to her neck, her jaw, even the top of her head. She breathed shallowly through her nose, her lips too numb to open up and allow air through.

All this time, Doug had known how much she wanted to explore whether Nashville would be a good change for her. She'd briefly thought about dropping that opportunity after what she and Garrett had shared last night, but no way. She was doing this for herself, not anyone else.

"I *am* going. Your blessing is no longer needed." She tried to rise, faltered, took a breath and managed to stand. Doug could be pretty crappy sometimes, but this was a new level of low for him.

"Lily."

"You have good employees who are capable of running this business while we're both gone. I *am* going to Nashville. I'll meet up with Linc when he gets back to town."

Doug rose, his leather chair rolling back against the wall. He slammed a hand on the desk, clenching his jaw tight.

"I need you here."

She laughed, a tight, sarcastic sound. "What *you* need—what *you* want—doesn't mean shit to me, Doug. Not anymore."

The only reason she'd worked with Garrett was the contract; she'd gone against her conviction to never, ever get involved with a fireman for the sake of this company. Yes, it had turned into something more meaningful, but the point was that she'd laid her moral fiber on the line for Doug and for this company only to have him still deny her what she needed and wanted the most.

"Dammit, Lily. Listen—"

She pointed a finger at him, poked it in the air a couple of times. Doing something with her hand helped hold back tears.

"You are welcome to rot here, alone, into a pile of miserable dust. Because I'm done."

Doug was out of his chair and at her side before Lily could reach the door. He didn't touch her; the energy crackling off him was enough. The way his shoulders slumped and his spine arched screamed defeat to her, but Doug Ashden had never been defeated.

"I can't talk about her, Lily."

Lily tasted salt on her tongue and wiped her face, aware for the first time that tears had started streaming down her cheeks.

"In my mind, if I don't think about that day, I can almost convince myself that she's going to walk through that door any minute. Do you get that? Do you understand that?" Doug wiped his mouth with a palm and took a step back.

"I expect her to call. Sometimes I look at my cell and wonder why the hell I haven't heard from my daughter in so damn long. And then I remember why. And inside me comes this rage so dang powerful that I have to shut it down. I have to just shut it down or I'll explode."

Lily's chest heaved as every nerve hung on edge waiting for what he would say next. This was the first time he'd ever acknowledged Katja's death. She wanted to comfort him, but it was a passing inclination because she knew better than to risk her heart that way.

"And I see you. *Every day.* And it reminds me that Katja's never coming back."

You'll never be good enough. It wasn't what he said, not exactly, but it was what she heard behind his words. So was that what this was? He'd lost his favorite daughter and was forced to put up with the second best? Shame filled her along with a sense of loss that was all too familiar. Her entire life had been spent wishing for her father's love when, really, he'd reserved it all for only one daughter.

Lily edged to the door, too broken to say anything. What was there to say? As angry and hurt as she was just then, she had a profound sense of pity for her dad, too. At least she'd started to let go of some of the gunk inside her soul. Doug hadn't been so lucky. The emotional turmoil he was in couldn't be soothed until he was ready, but she was done being his punching bag until then.

Lily wiped her eyes before crossing the threshold with an ungraceful wobble. The short distance she'd put between them gave her strength. She straightened her spine and held down the clog of sorrow in her chest. Lily walked straight out the Ashden building, not knowing—not caring—if she'd ever set foot back inside it again.

Lily didn't allow herself time to cry as she slipped into her vehicle. Half expecting Doug to come after her, and feeling more foolish than ever for even considering that he would, Lily pulled out of the lot and drove. Once she was around a corner, she parked on a side street. In the distance, the sound of an emergency siren blared. Garrett out on a call? She slumped in her seat as his name came to mind.

He'd helped her so much. She'd be a fool not to recognize that. Their connection went so much deeper than two people being present at the same tragedy. His fears were her fears; his reservations matched her own. How could they ever move past that shared fear?

Lily grabbed her cell and called Lincoln, relieved when he answered on the second ring. He'd been on her mind all day and she'd intended to call him, knowing he'd also be grieving. But she'd foolishly waited to speak to Doug first.

"I'm coming tomorrow," Lily rushed before he even said hello. "I'm leaving at daybreak and I'll call you when I get close."

Lincoln made an indecisive sound. "Wait, I thought Dad said you were staying in Danbury?"

"No." She looked at her lap. "I can't...I can't stay with him anymore, Linc. I need space."

Lincoln didn't even pause.

"Okay, good. Come, please. You can stay at my place since Dad and I will be gone anyway. It'll be a minivacation for you until I get back."

She tried to respond, but the tears came, fast and hot and relentless. Lincoln's voice dropped. "What's the first thing you're going to do in Nashville, sis?"

She leaned back against the seat. "I'm going to Killer Dan's and getting Katja's name tattooed on my left arm."

Lincoln gave an appreciative chuckle, but the sound got lower...deeper still until the next breath he took came out in a shudder. Six-four and built like a linebacker, yet Lincoln Ashden had never been one to hide from his emotions.

"Goddamn good plan, Lil."

"Yeah?"

"Yeah."

"You have time to talk a bit?" She found a tissue in the glove box and dabbed her eyes.

"Time for my best girl? Always, Lily. Always."

CHAPTER TWELVE

WHAT THE HELL was that noise? Garrett's arms came out to steady himself. He was falling... Wasn't he? A steady, loud beeping cut through his mind. He groaned and rolled onto his side, the tug of sleep slow to leave. Maybe it was Lily.

Lily. He groaned again and ran a hand over his face. He'd called her last night, just because. Mostly because he knew she was leaving this morning and it was killing him. The way they'd left things the other night—no commitment, but the promise of trying to figure this out, whatever this was—was driving him crazy. Because he wanted her, and Garrett was pretty sure Lily felt the same way about him. But they were both too scared to do anything more about it.

She'd said she was packed and ready to go, would be heading out at dawn for the long drive. And she'd sounded happy, almost, and he was glad for her. Or tried to be. What time was it anyway? Maybe something had happened—

He shot up and realized he was on his couch. He looked down. His cell phone was lying in his lap and ringing like mad. He grabbed it and looked around as the groggy sleep confusion began to fade away.

God, what time was it? He grappled to flip his cell open.

"What?" he roared into the phone. His fire pager was screeching from the kitchen table. That must have been what had woken him in the first place. Scrambling to his feet, Garrett stumbled to reach it.

"Garrett?" An unfamiliar male voice burst through the line.

"Yeah." He grabbed the pager, pressed the silence button. But there was another noise that refused to die, revolving in crescendo and decrescendo through the house. It was the sound of storm sirens coming from the city watchtower. They gave off a loud, insistent wail anytime a severe storm or tornado was approaching Danbury. He ran to his kitchen window and looked out. The morning was hazy but filled with sunlight. The insta-dread he always felt when the sirens went off melted away. Probably just heavy rain headed their way or something.

"Where the hell is my daughter?"

"Ah, who is this?" Garrett hit a button on his fire pager to see what the call had been. He wasn't on duty today, but if it was bad enough, he'd go help. Nothing but static replayed back.

The voice barked at him. "What do you mean, who is this? It's Doug Ashden."

Garrett slid the pager into his pocket. "Mr. Ashden. Why are you asking me where Lily is?" An irritated grunt came over the line.

"I've been calling her since six and she won't answer. I figured she might be with you."

Garrett glanced at his cell. Nine o'clock. Exhaustion took him down a few IQ levels. He sighed and ran his knuckles over his forehead to try to wake up.

"She was heading out early this morning for Nashville.... Why don't you just drive over and see if she's home?"

"Because I'm in jail."

Garrett looked at the ceiling as that little nugget sunk in. "Why the hell are you in jail? And how'd you get my number?"

"You're still talking when you should be getting down here and posting bail, seeing as how I can't get hold of my daughter."

Now Garrett knew were Lily's abrasive streak came from. He made a dismissive sound and waited.

Doug scoffed. "Lily added your cell number to your contract. I put it in my cell in case I needed to talk business with you."

The contract. The thing that had brought him and Lily together in the first place. No sense in thinking about that right now, because it just made him queasy inside.

No, right now he needed some jeans and extrablack coffee with a little whiskey thrown in to help him deal with Doug Ashden. He found jeans, his chest squeezing every time he thought of last night...and the fact that Lily was gone. He'd finally allowed himself to fall for a woman and he didn't know if she was going to stick around. Irony, that.

Hopefully, Doug hadn't done anything that would jeopardize the construction project. God, these Ashdens were going to be the death of him.

"Okay, okay, I'll be right there."

Garrett was met with the blare of the storm sirens after he cleaned up and stepped outside. The sky was bright, though a greenish haze was working its way like a toxic fog over the sunshine. The air was sticky and heavy, making him glad to slide into his air-conditioned truck. Flipping to the local radio station, he listened as a severe-storm warning came through. Hail, rain and high winds were headed this way, although the weatherman said it might blow to the north and bypass them all together. Wind, like fire, was an unpredictable beast and could either save them from the storm or bring it clear down on top of them.

It took fifteen minutes to get downtown and another forty to get Doug's bail posted at the jail. Disorderly conduct. *Huh.* Garrett didn't have much time to ponder exactly what that might mean when Doug was brought up front, looking ornery enough for a repeat performance.

The drab gray of the older man's T-shirt and his more-salt-than-pepper buzz cut made him fit right in with the severe gray-blue of the jail walls. He was built like a WWE wrestler who was slow to leave his prime, and if the glower was any indication, he was used to intimidating people into a puddle on the floor.

Garrett half waved as the warden brought Doug up to the counter and uncuffed him so he could fill out paperwork served by a woman behind a barred cubical. The warden handed Doug a cell phone, prompting Doug to give him a nod of appreciation. "Thanks for the extra phone time."

"Want to tell me what happened?" Garrett rested an elbow on the counter. Doug didn't look up from the paperwork.

"I don't answer to you, son."

Garrett tapped his wallet in his palm. It was a hell of a lot lighter than it had been earlier. "You do when I just posted eight hundred and fifty for your bail."

Intimidation had never been Garrett's thing. He wasn't moved by the aggression of other men and didn't back down without good cause. When Doug made a slow turn toward him, Garrett held his ground, relaxed, giving nothing away. He'd faced walls of fire and car accidents slicked with so much blood and body fluid it took months to get the stains off the road. It was going to take a hell of a lot more than a sour look and some biceps bulging to throw him off balance.

"You hear from Lily yet?" The concern in the older man's voice rubbed Garrett raw.

"Don't avoid the question."

Deflection was Garrett's card, and he knew how to play it. Doug signed the paper in front of him with more flourish than was probably necessary. The woman behind the box handed Doug a paper bag and wished him well.

Doug gathered up his things. "I hit the bastard, that's what happened. And I put five years of frustration and dislike into that punch, and I'd do it again in an instant."

A scratchy dispatch came through the base scanner unit somewhere inside the closed-off cubicle, followed by a series of high and low tones. Storm tones. Garrett put a hand to his hip, expecting to feel his fire pager there, then remembered he'd left it in the truck.

"Who pissed you off for five years?" He decided to press his luck. Doug's eyes narrowed.

"Lily's ex." He fished his wallet out of the paper bag, along with some keys and change. "I always hated that little shit. What she saw in him,

I'll never know. I stayed out of it. Let her live her life. The day she came home and found all his stuff gone…I almost lost it. He'd moved out without a word." Doug shoved his wallet into his back pocket. "Bastard left a note, though. How nice of him."

Garrett rubbed his brow with a thumb and forefinger. Doug crumpled the bag and tossed it in a trash can as they headed out of the jail.

"Rob was Lily's first…everything. I didn't want to interfere with all that first-love bullshit. She and I, God, we butt heads, but I couldn't let him get away with hurting her like that. When Lily dropped the ring off with me yesterday, it gave me something to look forward to—having Rob come in and ask for it. He called this morning. I met him at the coffeehouse, and, dammit, couldn't help myself. I nailed him."

"Ring?" He thought back to the day she'd run into Rob at the bar. Rob had asked her for something, but Garrett had never pressed for information.

Garrett held the door for Doug, who surprised him by actually providing details. "Lily still had the engagement ring Rob had given her. He came to ask for it back so he can marry someone else. The father in me didn't take too kindly to that."

They crossed the parking lot to the tune of the sirens. Humidity laid an immediate blanket over their skin. "Which leads me to this question. How long have you been sleeping with my daughter?"

Garrett was pretty sure a giant red X had just formed on his forehead as the perfect mark for Doug to aim for. He knew Lily's relationship with her father was tense, and, truth be told, he was surprised Doug had shared so much with him just now. He was a client of Doug's after all, not just the guy who was involved with his daughter. It added a complicated layer.

If he wasn't already in love with her, he was damn close. But that wasn't something he wanted to think about right now.

"Lily's a big girl."

Doug stopped on the passenger side of Garrett's truck and glared. "That wasn't an answer to my question, son."

Pushing his luck but protective of Lily's privacy, Garrett shrugged and tossed the older man's words back at him. "I don't answer to you, Doug. You want a ride or not?"

Doug wasn't looking at him any longer; instead, he was staring up at the sky, his expression concerned. "Look at that."

Doug pointed up. Before Garrett's gaze could follow suit, the storm siren started a new kind of wail, the ear-bending one that said this storm was now something else.

It was the tone for a tornado.

The wind had shifted, all right, but in the wrong direction. A wall of deep gray clouds hovered in all directions like an ominous spaceship covering the sky. The wind was coming from the east, seemed to be picking up speed as they stood there. Garrett thought back to the structure fire last night and how the wind had seemed to change direction constantly, making the fire a hundred times more difficult to put out.

He wrenched open his truck door and grabbed his pager. The red light on top was blinking, indicating a page had gone through. Nothing but static came back at him when he pressed the repeat button.

Frustrated, he grabbed his handheld radio and shoved it in his back pocket. It was more reliable and allowed him to talk back and forth rather than just listen to what went out over the emergency frequencies.

"Shit." Garrett pulled back from the truck and reached for his cell phone. Three missed calls. The air settled around his skin like a weight, his ears filling with a slight pressure.

"Double shit."

Garrett looked up at the wavering tone of Doug's voice. His eyes latched on to movement from the east, but his brain didn't want to register what he was seeing. "Funnel cloud."

"Yep."

Garrett slowly looked around. A few pedestrians on the sidewalk were already racing inside the nearest buildings. A lone bicyclist pumped frantically down the street. Cars were turning around at or flying through the intersection, trying to get out of the way. The siren filled his head, the pressure increasing like a slowly expanding balloon. The lid of a trash can skidded through the parking lot, pulling his attention.

"Back inside the jail, Doug."

The wall of clouds above them made a slow descent, moving horizontally as if to squish everything below. Garrett had experienced a lot of storms in his almost five years here, but he had never seen anything quite like this. All the hairs stood up on his arms and the back of his neck. In the distance, the squiggly dance of the barely visible funnel cloud came closer. By its position, the tornado looked as though it was ripping through the center of town, the way he'd come that morning.

"Doug, we have to get inside." Garrett ran around the front of his truck and grabbed Doug's arm, but Doug was fixed on the tornado. Wind whipped over them, flushing up papers and other debris that had been hiding on the ground. He gave the older man an impressive tug, but Doug braced his feet.

"Lily's apartment is on that end of town." And

the Ashden building, too, though Doug didn't seem concerned about that. The significance didn't escape Garrett.

"I know, but, Doug, she's long gone. She was leaving before sunup. Didn't she tell you? She's safe."

Doug turned on Garrett, grabbed his arms with both hands. "I told her she couldn't go to Nashville. We had a fight.... She's always listened to me before. I won't know that she's safe until I see it with my own eyes."

Garrett's hair flew into his eyes, the force of the wind like desperate, clawing hands. The speed with which it accelerated left no doubt that the twister was heading their way. He'd hoped it would turn, that the wind would shift and carry it away from this half of town. The gray clouds above them were now nearly black, blocking out the light, yet giving an odd greenish hue to the sky.

"I spoke to her late last night. She was planning on leaving as soon as the sun was up." Garrett took both of Doug's big biceps in his hands. "She's already out of town, Doug."

A vice grip clamped on Garrett's wrists as Doug grabbed him.

"I almost lost her once, goddamn you!"

Garrett felt for the man; he really did. And for a moment, he had a flicker of panic that maybe

Lily had changed her mind and was curled up in her apartment right now, ignoring her phone because she was angry with her father.

Damn, he should have called her this morning just to be sure.

A heavy hum sounded through the air. They couldn't wait any longer. Garrett looped his arm through Doug's and pulled. They rushed inside the lobby of the jail. No one was at the security entrance. The concrete structure could withstand a whipping, but there were reinforced walls inside the jail center. That was where the employees had likely already hunkered down, and that was where he and Doug really needed to be.

He rang the buzzer once, twice, as the wind outside began to howl. A beat passed, and then another. No one responded to the buzzer. Doug caught sight of the security camera pointed at them from behind the security glass, moved as close to it as he could and waved his hands. The front door rattled with the force of the wind, drawing their attention and making Garrett's heart fall to his feet. They were going to have to ride this out in the lobby.

"Find cover or something to hang on to." There was a small coffee table and four metal-and-wood chairs, none of which were bolted down, a plastic magazine rack and a trash can. He ran a hand through his hair, suddenly remembering he'd put his handheld radio in his back pocket. Garrett grabbed it and flipped to the sheriff department's frequency.

"This is DFD Assistant Chief Mateo to Brown County, do you copy?"

There was a small chance the transmission would go over in an atmosphere like this. Remembering the static he'd experienced on the pager earlier, he didn't dare hope. But then a weak response came through.

"Copy."

"I'm inside the jail lobby with a civilian. Can you radio the warden to buzz us in for shelter?"

Before he'd finished the word *shelter,* the front door began to rattle as if it were possessed. No light could be seen through the glass. A slight dizziness went through Garrett's head, the lower channels of his ears yelping in protest to the pressure within. Garrett turned, grabbed Doug's sleeve and pulled him down.

"Get down!" He threw an arm over his head and pressed against the security door that separated them from safety. The windows on each side of the lobby exploded. Glass cubes flew through the room, pebbling down the back of Garrett's shirt, settling in his hair. Doug cursed next to him, but the sound was carried away as wind filled the small space. It swooped over them, spiraling glass around the room.

"Shit, shit, shit!" Garrett swept glass from his hair with one quick movement of his hand, glancing at Doug.

"I'm okay," Doug offered, hunkering down a little lower.

Garrett's mind filled with the aftermath of this... The town. Casualties. Fires and water main breaks and all the mess that could unfold if this tornado decided to have a raging bitch fit. He needed to be at the fire station, getting ready....

"Come on! Come on now!" The door they were leaning against buzzed and cracked open; a hunched-over deputy waved them in.

Garrett scooted back, ushering Doug ahead of him. He looked behind them, watching the front door rattle, thinking about his crew, hoping they were all safe...thinking about Lily and hoping she was on her way to her brother's by now.

Safe.

THE SOUND OF trickling water tempted Lily to fall asleep, but she knew she shouldn't. She wanted to...just close her eyes and let go. Yeah, that sounded nice. A little nap to ease the tiredness. She was so exhausted that even opening her eyes was a struggle. It was dark anyway, and cool. Perfect for sleeping.

Something poked her in the hip, hard and sharp. No matter which way she turned, the bed was uncomfortable—like sleeping on broken rocks. She shifted a little more, froze when pain seared up from her ankle to her thigh. *Damn.* What did she have on her bed that would hurt like that? Was she lying on a—

Wait. Rubble beneath her palm…cold, wet, rocky ground beneath her bottom. She wasn't in bed; there was no way she was in bed.

Lily tried to sit up, but a clamp of pain smacked her right in the forehead as another gripped her leg like talons. The dream state began to clear, but the darkness didn't. The sound of water didn't go away. The pain remained. And the scream begging to escape her throat stayed put, melting into panic. Her flight instincts kicked in, begging her to run away. Run away from the threat.

A threat she couldn't see, but she felt down to the core of her bones.

"Is your dog on crack?"

Garrett took off his firefighting helmet and ran a forearm over his sweaty face. Six hours of searching through the debris and devastation the F3 twister had left behind had brought him a lick away from exhaustion. Forty minutes after they'd taken shelter in the jail, the tornado had left. They'd stepped outside, disbelieving when they'd seen the area around them virtually untouched. A few shingles were missing and debris was strewn around like a frat house after a kegger, but for the most part, the damage was minimal.

The east side of Danbury was leveled.

Garrett had dropped Doug off at his house, which was in an unaffected area of town. Frantic over Lily and the safety of his employees, Doug made calls on the way and reached everyone but the woman who cleaned the Ashden building. And Lily.

Garrett made a wide loop to the devastated part of town, but there was no way to get to the block where Lily's apartment was because of the debris. Frustrated, he held in his anxiety, praying that she really had headed to Nashville, and went to the firehouse. The station had sustained minimal damage.

Once he'd been suited up in his turnout gear, Garrett had ridden with the department as far into the affected area of town as they could, and he'd walked the rest of the way. Lily's apartment building was missing part of the roof and had some structural damage, but it was standing. Tenants milled around, looking lost and stricken. Garrett made it safely to Lily's apartment and knocked for good measure before he kicked the door in and found her gone.

He'd already heard from another team that the Ashden building was leveled, but there wasn't a vehicle matching Lily's anywhere in the area. The relief he experienced almost buckled his knees.

Mia Smith, a member of the search-and-rescue team, narrowed her brown eyes at Garrett's blunt question. "Kiki indicated human scent inside a building down the street." She patted the search-and-rescue dog's head. The German shepherd eyed Garrett as if challenging him to refute her nose.

"That block already had a first pass hours ago. The dog didn't indicate then."

Mia's eyes became slits. "But she did *now*."

Garrett scoffed. He'd been in and out of more houses than he could count today. Had helped recover forty people—thirty-eight of whom were still alive. The remaining two had spent their last moments trapped under brick and wood. Between the cacophony of people and machines digging through the rubble, the sounds of human emotions made a disturbing cadence. That was the part he hated the most because it was the hardest to block out—the sounds of crying, the wails of disbelief and heartfelt agony. The gut-wrenching cries and sobs of grief.

Around him, people milled through what was left behind. And through every minute, in the back of his mind, he hoped Lily was tucked in nice and tight at her brother's house. He loved being a firefighter, but sometimes, like now, it twisted him up inside and made him hate the day he'd first pulled on his turnout gear. Scenes like this reminded him of why he did what he did—helping people get through the worst times. But now, since meeting Lily, they also reminded him of what he had to lose.

He hedged. He was confident the building Mia wanted him to go into was empty, considering that everyone who had reason to be inside was already accounted for.

"Look—"

"Kiki only indicates human scent. You saw her indicate—we all did. *What's* your problem?"

His problem? He'd already dealt with horrendous injuries and pulled two deceased victims from rubble today. He was running on a handful of sleep and no food. He'd never fully recovered from all the sleep he'd been lacking lately. He and every other firefighter had worked nonstop to clear roads to let emergency vehicles through and search houses, barely taking a break to hydrate. The initial surge of adrenaline that made him feel like a superhero with never-ending energy had worn off hours ago, leaving him tired, cranky and barely holding back his emotions.

Garrett wiped sweat from the side of his face and let some of the angst out with a deep sigh.

"Which building?" He'd search one more. "And

I'm in and I'm out, okay? If no one responds to my call, I'm out."

He sidled up to the rescue truck, cracked a water bottle and put another in his front jacket pocket. Garrett guzzled the water and stripped off his heavy turnout jacket and pulled the suspenders of his pants down. A breeze whipped over his soaked T-shirt, making him shudder. Damn, that felt good.

"The Ashden building."

The water bottle fell from his hand, hitting Kiki on the side of the head.

"What did you say?" Garrett spun to follow Mia's gaze down the block. They'd worked their way down the street until what was left of Lily and Doug's building was in view. But he'd been assured it was clear, so he hadn't worried another moment about it.

A huge crack sounded through the air, making them both jump.

Mia gave Garrett a hard look. "It was cracking like that when we were over there. I'm afraid we're running out of time for a search and rescue before the whole thing comes down."

The brick building was old, a historic home the Ashdens had converted into office space. Most of the upper level had collapsed. Garrett had no doubt the sound they'd just heard was the foundation cracking under the weight of all that brick and mortar.

A big hand squeezed Garrett's shoulder.

"Damn, I hate to send you in there." Dabney Grail had a smile that emphasized every tiny line in the crow's feet around his eyes. How he managed to always be smiling and laughing after eighteen years as fire chief, Garrett didn't know. "I'm sending Roan in with you. You cool?"

Garrett drained another bottle of water and kept his feelings to himself. Who else would be inside the Ashden building? Doug had said all his employees were accounted for except the cleaning lady who came early in the morning. But the odds were that she'd left long before the tornado struck.

"Which side am I going in on?"

Twenty minutes later, Garrett was back in his turnouts and helmet, a respirator secure over his face to keep dust out and oxygen in. He and Roan Stokes surveyed the building for an entrance point close to where Kiki had indicated human scent.

The building swayed and creaked, reminding them of its ability to crush them at any given second. Garrett swallowed his unease. If he could get in, he'd do a quick thermal sweep and a few callouts to see if there was any response. If not, he was gone.

Roan tapped him on the shoulder and thumbed to a split in the exterior. It was just wide enough for them to squeeze through. Two-by-fours and piles of reddish-brown brick marred their path. Dust and bits of debris clouded the air like smoke. Daylight streamed in from the breaks in the structure as they slipped inside, making the dust and tidbits sparkle like diamonds.

Garrett shone his light through the rubble. He spotted a bright orange X in a corner—the mark Mia had made when she'd been inside sweeping with Kiki earlier. He assessed what was left of the ceiling, trying to see any sign that it was going to fall on them, before easing his way to the X.

He followed the wall, holding back a bitter taste in his throat as the floor creaked and sagged against his weight. Part of the ceiling had collapsed, blocking their way into the next room. They were cramped inside a ten-by-ten space, thanks to the cave-in. The X indicated where Kiki had picked up scent, but it only gave them a vague location, not an exact pinpoint. There could be a body under the rubble or behind the wall in the next room. Worse, there was no way to know if they were looking for a living person or a dead one.

After breathing deep inside his respirator, Garrett called out, "Is anyone here?"

Tapping the wall with the butt end of his ax, he

found a hollow spot. With another glance upward and a silent prayer, he whacked the wall, slicing through weakened Sheetrock with ease. Using his hands, he carved out an opening big enough to see through. The room on the other side appeared to be completely caved in. He called out again, hoping his voice would carry through the hole and density of rubble.

No response.

Taking another look around the small space, Garrett saw scattered remnants of the business—papers, pens, file folders—tossed like leaves between bricks and drywall. Roan called out again and both men waited, listening. More debris falling around them and the squeak and slide of wood rubbed the silence.

Garrett pulled back from the hole; Roan shrugged. "We done? This house is coming down anytime. I can feel it."

Garrett bit his lower lip. He could feel it, too—that sinking, hollow sensation in the pit of his gut that told him things were about to go down.

He looked at the X. They'd only been inside a few minutes. It didn't seem like enough time when they were possibly holding life and death in their hands. But if they looked too much more, they could be the ones buried. Compelled to check it out a little more, Garrett wedged himself between the support beams inside the hole he'd made and aimed his beam to cut through the darkness.

"Anyone here?"

He managed to squeeze through the opening, finding a narrow space on the other side that wasn't filled with debris.

"Fire department!"

He took a deep breath of the oxygen coming through his mask and waited again. If anyone was trapped under all this rubble, there'd be little to no chance of getting them out without collapsing the rest of the house. A sick, heavy feeling welled in his chest. This was why he hadn't wanted to come in here. The threat of finding someone or suspecting someone was present and not being able to help was crushing.

"Garrett, let's go."

"I'm coming."

He was just about to take a sideways step when he heard it. Garrett stopped dead, holding his right hand out to signal Roan to be quiet. His chest grew tight as he tried to restrict his breathing. Each breath made his turnout coat rustle, drowning out anything quiet or faint. He was just about to blow out a huge, pent-up breath when he heard it again.

"…help."

A new surge of adrenaline flooded his body,

making his senses suddenly crisp and focused. He signaled Roan with a thumbs-up.

"Hello?" Garrett called out, moving back into the dark, rubble-filled room.

A reply came from somewhere inside, muddled and hard to pinpoint. His flashlight beam bounced off the mounds of debris and highlighted falling dust. Another sound came, pulling his attention to the far-right corner. Garrett stepped into the narrow opening between wall and cave-in, his heart racing like a derby horse. A few inches from meeting a dead end, he saw it. A hole in the floor, barely wide enough for a person to slip through.

The floor sagged as he tried to edge closer to the opening. With a grunt, Garrett pulled back and waved his light into the hole.

"Call out as loud as you can!"

The vibration of his orders bounced back at him. The floor creaked like an old spine. Garrett palmed the wall on instinct, for all the good it would do if the bottom went falling out from under him. He shuffled his feet slowly backward a couple of steps.

"Down here!" Barely audible through his headgear, the words rocked him. Someone was in the basement. Roan's hand pressed into Garrett's back.

"What's up?"

"Need rescue gear. Get me a harness and set up the rigging." Garrett threw a look over his shoulder. "I'll stay."

Walking out would mean leaving the victim alone, and he couldn't do that. He knew too well that alone and abandoned in the middle of chaos was a bad, bad place to be.

Garrett stayed close to the wall, sweeping his light down the hole while Roan left to get the gear. From this angle, he couldn't see much down the hole except for a gray refraction of his light through the inky blackness. His mind spun as his chest pulled thin strands of air into his lungs. Who was down there? *Damn.*

He called out again, waited with bated breath for a response. There was none.

Roan returned and handed the gear through the hole. Garrett eased into the harness, clipped a floodlight onto his jacket and confirmed his tank had just over half of its oxygen left.

"We're going to manually hold your line instead of hooking you to the truck," Roan said, grabbing the front of Garrett's harness and giving a huge pull.

Garrett did the same from the back. The rigging line that would keep him from crashing to his death meandered through the hole in the wall and out the way they'd come in. It was tight with tension, letting him know the men outside were set to lower him down.

"You're ready."

Roan handed over a fresh radio. Garrett put it in his pocket. The scratch of transmission went over the radio as Roan backed into the other room.

"Mateo is set to descend. Hold tight."

Garrett punched down the flutter in his gut and eased his way to the hole. Chunks of mortar crumbled from above, hitting the floor and bouncing into the opening. Bracing a hand on the wall, feeling the tension tight on his back from the rigging, he bent down to examine the opening. No way he'd fit.

He used his ax to widen the hole enough that the bulk of his turnout gear and tank would fit through. Each whack brought down more debris until the air became one giant poof of dust. He wished he could see exactly how much of the house was still standing around him, but the piles of cave-in made it impossible to gauge. One last whack of the ax made the wall behind him shudder. Garrett flinched, curling inward in reaction.

"Damn."

"What? What is it?"

The sound through the speaker connected to his shoulder made him jerk. He'd been leaning on the two-way transmission button on his radio.

He sighed to calm the butterflies in his chest. "Nothing. House just shook a little."

"Hurry the hell up, Mateo," Chief spouted through the airwaves.

Garrett scoffed. Bet Grail wasn't smiling now.

"You got it, Chief." He sat on the edge of the hole. "Descending now. Cut me slack."

The tension on the back of the harness let up some and he slid into free space. His body was immediately suspended in air, the sensation giving him a total-body chill.

He aimed his light down into the darkness. A cement floor below, piles of broken beams and junk strewn about. To the right, a cave-in had created a wall of rubble that ran the length of the room. Garrett realized this was the part of the second story that had caved, taking everything with it. A chunk of wood came flying down the hole, knocking into his helmet and bouncing off.

"What the hell!"

He pulled down the clear shield on his helmet to cover his eyes and glanced up. The jagged end of a broken two-by-four rushed toward his face. He flinched and bunched his shoulders just as the beam hit the back of his helmet.

A deep shudder rippled through the air. Heart in his throat, Garrett gripped the line tighter as it lowered him a few more inches. He pulled a couple of deep breaths from the respirator as another shudder flew through the atmosphere.

His body began to sway as if a powerful wind had caught hold of him. Before he could open his mouth to call into the radio mic on his shoulder, debris began to rain down the hole. Something hit his shoulder like an invisible monster trying to take his arm clear off. Pain ripped through him, and the mic cord was torn from his jacket.

Garrett covered his helmet with one arm and pulled his body into itself as much as he could while hanging in the air. A thundering sound burst in his ears, followed by a massive crack like a huge tree going over in a storm.

"Garrett!"

Static. He heard a pulse beating like a drum. Then the sound of rocks pouring over one another into a pile, and daylight was snuffed out as the remaining upper level crashed down.

Closing him in while he hung there helpless.

Trapping him.

A string of curse words went through his mind, but he wasn't even sure if they made it past his numb lips. Garrett uncurled slowly, his abs screaming in protest as he stretched out. He swayed gently as the floor above rumbled, deep and threatening, before all went quiet.

"Garrett, do you copy?"

He fumbled for the mic on his shoulder, found

it wasn't there. With a desperate pat, he located it hanging off his jacket, the cord frayed. He depressed the button to reply as carefully as he could with bulky gloves on.

"Yeah. I'm fine. Suspended but fine." Fire seared through his right shoulder.

Static burst through the radio. "...get you out."

He tapped the mic and pushed the button, but nothing else came through. *Damn.*

Garrett bounced in the harness, expecting it to drop some, but it didn't budge. Maybe the men had tied him off, maybe the line was trapped, but either way, he was stuck twelve feet in the air.

He followed his flashlight beam to the ground. Little piles of rubble, some boards with nails sticking up. Paint cans scattered everywhere. Not a soft landing if he had to bail.

Around him, the skeletal architecture of the basement made a creepy setting, reminiscent of a slasher film set. This wasn't the first time he'd been trapped in rubble, but it was the first time in a basement. It was dang unsettling down here.

He listened for any sound—sounds that the men were poking through for the best way to get him out, sounds to reassure him that his rescue attempt hadn't been in vain.

"Hey!" he called out, wanting, *needing,* to hear a response.

As far as he could tell, the width of the basement was cut in two by the wall of debris. Like upstairs, it would be impossible to see who or what was behind it. He swiveled in the harness, sweeping the entire perimeter with his light. Nothing.

Where had the voice come from?

"Anyone down here?" he yelled louder through the face mask, the force of his voice ringing in his ears. Damn, if he'd been imagining that voice—

"Here!"

Garrett swung back, aiming the light to the wall of debris. Pieces of brick rolled down from the center, as though they'd been poked from inside. His stomach bottomed out. Someone was under that pile. He looked up, hoping to see light peek through the opening so he knew the men were coming. Nothing.

The ceiling rumbled above his head. A muted sliding sound preceded the crack of timber. Something crashed into the floor above, making the ceiling shake again. Garrett braced his shoulders and ducked his head through the ruckus. Suddenly being suspended wasn't any safer than being on the ground. If the ceiling collapsed, he'd be caught up in the rain of debris.

The noise quieted; he swept the rafters with the light and a bead of reflection flashed back at him. His eyes narrowed at the little specks of light. Before his brain could file through what the lights could be, a huge spider scurried out from a broken beam, its eyes eerily reflective in the light.

Garrett jerked back, nearly dropping the floodlight. Easily the size of his palm, its legs arched and primed for leaping, for scurrying or even for jumping on him, the wolf spider was enough to give him a heart attack. Garrett might be six-one and built hard, and he might have one hell of a tough job to back it up, but the terrified kid inside him that hated spiders was almost wetting his pants right now.

Garrett grabbed his utility knife, wincing against the pain in his arm, and flipped it open with one hand. The spider scurried to the side, its fuzzy gray-and-brown body visible where it sprawled on the beam. Above his head. Six inches from his helmet.

Turnout gear or not, nothing would protect him from raging arachnophobia. Garrett hesitated, watching the spider with a steady eye as he brought the knife up. He could stab it…. He had the perfect angle. Grunting through the pain, he brought his arm back, ready to impale the devil's spawn when a second spider crawled out. And then a third. God, it was a spider army. Painful landing be damned. There was no way he was going to be trapped with *that*.

Garrett turned the knife on his rope, began sawing through it, never taking his eyes off the glowing-eyed beasts. He didn't look down as the rope frayed and uncoiled as he cut it down to the last tendon. Garrett pulled up his legs, closed his eyes and hoped for the best.

Goodbye, spiders.

Hello, pain.

CHAPTER THIRTEEN

THE LIGHT WAS GONE. Her chest ached with the clawing need to breathe deeper, to draw in fresh air. But there wasn't any. The air was rancid with the full-bodied taste of dirt and concrete dust and the mold of old wood.

Lily lay still, straining to hear the voices she'd thought she'd heard earlier. Her surroundings weren't silent. Slight rumbles and loud creaking sounded all around her, but nothing like a human voice. For a moment, a dim light had seeped through the debris pile next to her, giving her hope that someone knew she was there. But as it faded, like the voices, Lily suspected she'd imagined the whole thing.

She took as big a breath as she dared, and her mouth was immediately coated with dust. Coughing hurt so badly, but her lungs rejected the air, forcing it back out with deep spasms. Nausea followed, filling her throat with bile. Lily scrambled to roll onto her side, crying against the pain as she vomited into the debris. Panting through the spasms, her mind whirled with how she'd gotten here, how this had happened.

The tornado had hit so fast. She'd heard the storm sirens the first time, but the skies were clear and the radio said the winds had shifted. She'd only meant to come in to retrieve the picture of Katja from her office and the ornament Bodie had given her, which she'd hung on the side of her sister's picture frame. But she'd found herself sitting in Doug's office chair, her feet propped on his desk, lost in thought.

Thoughts of her sister, her father, the mother she barely remembered. Thoughts of the man who'd left her and the one she'd come to love.

And then the winds had slammed into the side of the house, dislodging bricks in one fatal blow. Lily had scrambled to make it down to the primitive basement, but she hadn't reached the bottom of the stairs before something had hit her on the back and sent her flying.

How much time had passed? Her head ached so badly, Lily was afraid to move. She'd slowly worked herself into a sitting position, but had had to lie back on her bed of rubble because of the pain shooting down her forehead and neck. She tried to feel her scalp for bleeding, but the ground around her was soaked, along with her hair and clothing, making it impossible to tell.

Lily rolled her head from side to side, hoping for a mouthful of clear air.

Hope? Rescue?

Rescuers were out there; she knew it. They always came as soon as the tornado rolled away. But just because they always came didn't mean they'd actually get her out. No one knew she was there. Garrett, Lincoln and her father all thought she'd left for Nashville that morning.

She wanted to sob, wanted to give in. *Garrett. Her father. Macy.* What if they'd been hit by the twister? What if they weren't okay? What if they were trapped, injured…or worse?

"Stop it!" Tears came with the words. She blinked rapidly to hold them back. She'd gotten out last time. She could do it again. The firemen would sweep the town, check the damage, look for survivors. The trickle of water that was coming from somewhere became loud in her ears, followed by the thunder of her heartbeat.

A thud and a muted grunt sounded through the fine cracks in her caved-in prison. Lily cringed and looked up, afraid the weight of the house was finally going to crash down on her. Concentrating around the sound of running water, she heard movement—maybe a curse word—coming from the other side of the debris wall. Faint light flooded the small cracks.

A rush of adrenaline gave her the courage to

try sitting again. The pain rolled down her skull like marbles, but it was more tolerable this time. Her right leg protested with agony when she scooted forward on her butt and tried to get her feet under her.

The light seemed closer this time, filtering in just enough that she could see what surrounded her for the first time. A wall of debris was in front of her, a stone foundation behind and beside her. There was no exit, no opening as far as she could tell. The light swept side to side, like a flashlight. A person. There was someone down here.

"Hey!" she croaked, her throat parched from the dirty air. Scrambling to find a bigger fissure to see through, Lily pressed her hands against the wall. A lopsided chunk of concrete popped from its home and rolled away. Light flooded the space.

"Here, I'm here!" She cried, not knowing if predeath hallucinations were messing with her brain or if it was real.

"Hang on" came the husky reply. Lily tried to pry more debris from the hole, but the material was wedged tight. She had just enough room to ease her arm through, trying to ignore the bites of pain all over her body. *Please, please, please, let this be real.*

Someone grabbed her hand.

GAME ON. THERE was someone down here. Garrett saw the small hand pop out of the wall, waving desperately. He'd grabbed hold, warmth filling him when fingers wrapped around his heavy glove.

He adjusted the floodlight, centering it on the hole and the arm that was sticking out of it. His skull seemed to freeze as the light shone on the arm, revealing a brilliant swirl of orange hibiscus and green vines. His knees weakened, making him stumble as he stepped over rubble to press against the wall. Oh, God, he'd been wrong.

"Lily! Oh, shit, Lily! Are you all right?" He hit the button on his respirator and pulled the mask down. The thick air immediately filled his mouth and throat.

"Garrett?"

Her voice was muted. He raised his light to the ceiling, looking for a sign that the air was settling, but he found only a constant stream of particulate.

Lily's fingers assumed a death grip on his glove. The urge to get to her, to get her out from behind the wall, threatened to turn him into a madman. He patted the wall with his free hand, looking for any way inside.

Deep breath. He had to stay in control.

"Answer me. Are you okay?"

He pushed down his own pain. Taking that

free fall had been a risk, and his tailbone and hips were screaming at him for it. Combined with the hit his shoulder had taken, he felt about forty years older than he was at the moment.

She coughed. "No. I mean…I don't know. I hit my head and…can't breathe very well."

He could tell by the delay in each word that she was struggling. Desperation welled higher, the primal urge to protect her, to get her out, was all consuming. Garrett pulled the broken mic and pressed the button, hoping against hope he'd get some kind of transmission. He called out to the crew, but the dead silence that echoed back at him made it clear the radio was toast.

"Why didn't you leave this morning like you were supposed to?"

She panted a little, as if she'd been running. "My father?"

Garrett tipped the brim of his helmet against the wall, getting as close to the opening as he could.

"Oh, baby, he's okay. I was with him this morning. He's fine." Filth floated into his mouth, making him spit. Garrett slid his mask back on, taking a deep draw of oxygen. God, his brain had never been so happy for fresh air, ever. "I need you to let go, Lil."

"No!"

He closed his eyes against the pain in her voice.

Why was this happening to her? Why again? She'd already been through hell once, and now...

Garrett swept the light down the length of the wall, looking for any openings he might have missed. The best he could tell, the debris was packed in tight from floor to ceiling. If he could find a space big enough, he'd pass Lily his mask and have her breathe from the oxygen tank on his back.

"I need to look for a way out. I'll be right here on the other side. I won't leave you." Her fingers relaxed, letting him go, but she didn't pull her arm back through the hole.

Forcing his heart and mind into work mode, Garrett surveyed the wall and the surrounding supports. The more he saw, the more dread filled him. The debris wall separating him from Lily was holding up the collapsed upper floor. The joists had snapped, disconnecting the floor above and angling it down like a slide into the basement. Rubble had caved in at the same time, creating a makeshift support for what was left of the floor.

If he disturbed the wall at all, it could bring the floor above down on their heads. He strode back to the opening.

"Lily, is there any light coming in at all from where you are?"

"No. It's dark unless your light is shining."

She coughed a little, her hand withdrawing into the hole. Garrett made a grab for her, but she'd already pulled back.

"Lily? Talk to me." He tried to wedge his hand through the opening, but it wouldn't fit. "Lily?"

He shut his respirator off to conserve the oxygen and pulled the mask down again.

"I know you're scared, baby. I won't leave you. I'm going to find a way inside."

Her voice was shaky and small. "Promise... you'll get me out."

Garrett held his hand against the wall. He hated promises, mostly because some you just couldn't guarantee you'd keep. Even with the best intentions, things went wrong. And there was no telling how long they had before the house decided to come down completely.

"I promise you I'll try." That was the best he could give her, or himself. "Stay right by the hole. Are you okay right there?"

A stretch of silence preceded her response, and when she spoke, her tone was dry and desperate. "Yes."

No. She wasn't fine. She needed oxygen and she needed it now. Remembering the water bottle he'd stuffed in his jacket earlier, Garrett grabbed it and pushed it through the hole. He shone the light behind it so she could see.

"Lily, here. Drink some of this to clear your

throat. Can you see it?" The bottle slid all the way out on her side. "Take little sips, okay? Maybe rinse your mouth out—get the dust out."

She moved by the opening, giving him the slightest glimpse of her face in the light. Blood crusted over the side of her face, and the eye he could see was bruised and almost swollen shut. The grogginess in her voice wasn't just the air quality. She probably had a concussion and was getting more and more fatigued by the minute.

He wasn't a medic, but he knew the basics, and letting someone with a bad head injury fall asleep wasn't good. If she did, who the hell knew what might happen? She might not wake up. He already felt the squeeze of each passing minute, but they suddenly counted a hell of a lot more. She needed a doctor.

"Lily, are you tired?"

"Mmm-hmm." Her reply was listless. He looked down the length of the wall again, wishing like hell he'd see something he hadn't seen before. Now he wasn't just looking for a way out, but he had to find a way to keep Lily conscious, too.

"Drink some of that water. Little sips. Can you do that?" When she didn't answer, he stuck his mouth to the opening and spoke louder. "Baby, can you do that for me?" He fished a small

Maglite from his pocket, twisted it on and slid it through the hole. "Here's a flashlight. Grab it."

"Okay."

The weakness of her reply made him want to hit the wall. Garrett's hands fisted, the muscles in his arms coiled and ready to unleash. Instead, he put his face mask back on and clicked the oxygen on.

He went left, searching the pile of debris for any crack that might offer an opening. There were small crevices here and there, and in a couple of places, openings big enough he could probably wedge his hand in, but nothing large enough to pass his respirator through. He turned right and surveyed the length for the same.

In the far-right corner, a pile of rubble on the floor made an incline. He scrambled up it until his head was nearly touching the ceiling. A wooden support beam lay on top of the debris wall, holding up the broken ceiling above. Just below the beam, a crevice opened up large enough for Garrett to stick his head through. Careful not to dislodge any of the rubble in the wall, Garrett popped his head through the opening and shone his light inside, seeing Lily's tomb for the first time.

Her body lay prone just beneath the arm hole, the water bottle tipped and draining from her hand. His heart lurched in his throat. He called her name twice. No response.

"No, no!"

It was happening. He'd opened his heart to Lily and now…now she was going to be taken away.

Pulling gingerly away from the hole, Garrett scanned his light around the basement for just the right thing. Going back the way he had come, he spotted a long metal pipe poking out from beneath a pile of bricks. Using both hands, he cleared the debris until the pipe was exposed.

Pebbles hit his helmet, followed by a whoosh of dust from above. He covered his head with his arm, waited to see if more would tumble down. When he glanced up, a thick haze hovered above his head. He wiped a glove over his face mask to clear it, but the haze remained. Thicker than debris dust, it swirled as if an air current was waving through it.

Another pebble hit his helmet. Garrett looked down, saw a small orange glow. He reached for it, eyes widening. An ember. He pinched the ember between his gloved fingers and moved farther down where the haze was thinner. A crack in the ceiling dripped bright orange stars like care-free raindrops.

The upper level was on fire.

Garrett stumbled to the hole in the wall by Lily.

"Lily! Lily, wake up." He whipped off his mask and shouted into the opening. "Wake. Up!"

He pulled off his glove and gathered a handful of small brick pieces. He tried to get his hand through the opening. The tightness of the cement and brick and wood ate into his flesh as he forced his hand through. Skin ripped, pain clawed over his hand until he felt free space. Breathing hard, he dropped a couple of the chunks, hoping he didn't hurt her, but needing to get her attention.

"Lily. You've got to wake up. Please!"

No response.

"Goddammit, Lily. Please!"

His mouth filled with dust and smoke, his eyes burning.

Nothing. No, no. Please, no. He'd waited years to let himself go, to find someone, and now it was burning away. He knew in that nanosecond that he was in love with her. Because it hurt. It ripped his heart out and gutted him at the same time. This was what he'd always been protecting himself from—this pain, except he'd always thought the tables would be turned, that it would be him on his way out, leaving the woman he loved behind.

He couldn't get her out. He couldn't even get to her, and she was going to die—failed by a fireman. Again.

He was about to pull his hand back when fingers entwined with his and squeezed.

"LILY...LILY?" HER name was coming from somewhere, getting clearer each time. She swore her head had become a fishbowl. Everything was swirling and unbalanced. The hand she was holding was firm and holding her up...a lifeline that she desperately needed.

Right, Garrett was here. Garrett, who'd been there the night Katja had died. Her link...the man she loved. Did he love her, too?

"You would love me if you could, right?" Lily leaned against the wall, moving her hand higher up his forearm to grip tighter. Something scratched on the other side of the wall, the sound of his body pressing against the debris with a thud. The hard material was cool against her cheek.

She knew he would have. Deep down, she knew. A few pieces fell around the hole right before Garrett's arm came through just a bit more. She clung to his arm.

"With everything inside me, Lily."

She put her cheek against his palm. She'd wasted a lot of time being angry with him when she could have allowed herself more time to love him. He was here now, risking it all for her... putting himself in danger though it would have been safer for him to stay outside. That was what they did. Every fireman on his squad had put himself on the line once or twice. Personal sacrifice was part of the job, and she'd admonished him because of it.

"I'm sorry, Garrett. You shouldn't be down here with me. You should be...out..." The words used precious breath—breath she couldn't seem to replace. Garrett's fingers squeezed hers.

"Nobody would be able to keep me from being right here, right now. Understand? I'm exactly where I want to be." He released his grip and his arm pulled back. Lily grabbed for him.

"It's okay, Lil—let go. I have a job for you." His words were heavy, and when he took a breath, she could hear it shake. "Take your flashlight and walk all the way to your left. I'll meet you down there on the other side. Point the light in the corner where the wall meets the ceiling. Can you do that?"

His arm disappeared. Lily turned in the direction he'd asked her to go, waving the small beam of light over the floor. It was littered with rubble. Tucking the flashlight between her arm and body, she kept one hand on the wall and picked her way through. Fighting the dizziness, fighting nausea, she stopped once to dry heave. Something bitter and choking filtered into her mouth...ashy and burning. It tasted a lot like smoke.

At the end, the beam of Garrett's light met her through cracks in the wall. "Lily? Shine your light up in the corner, but stand back from the wall." His voice was muted, as if he'd put his face mask back on.

Just then, a sharp beeping cut through the air, making her jerk. Garrett swore, followed by some rustling and another string of curses.

"What was that?"

"Oxygen tank is almost empty. Stand back."

There was a loud whacking sound as metal met concrete and chunks of the wall began flying out from the corner. A few pieces fell, taking more with it, until the corner of the wall began to crumble. A plume of smoke burst toward her, heavy and acrid. Garrett grunted as half his body wedged under a beam in the ceiling. When he began to wedge a pipe vertically under the beam, Lily realized if the beam collapsed, so would whatever was on top of it.

Her stomach flipped in relief at seeing him, but that feeling was quickly replaced by terror when he slumped under the weight of the beam while he tried to get the pole into position. The beam jerked, sending its weight down on his right shoulder. Garrett cried out, his body crumpling. The ceiling above shifted with a huge crack. Lily screamed, her body bracing for impact. Her chest heaved with short, tight breaths. Smoke filled the space, making it impossible to see, but the air was quiet. No crashing, no sound of the house coming in on itself.

"Garrett?"

Lily waved the beam through the smoke the best she could while covering her mouth with the crook of her elbow. A chopping sound, punctuated with pain-filled grunts.

"Garrett?"

Her airway filled with smoke. Gasping, Lily dropped the light and cupped her hand over her mouth. Her brain protested the lack of oxygen, bringing her to her knees. She was vaguely aware of the chopping sounds...things crumbling...a flash of daylight.

Lily struggled to keep her eyes open as daylight fought through the smoke. Up high, a silver beam was punctuated with rays of gold, like the flowers Garrett had first sent her. He'd found an opening when the beam shifted. Her eyelids fluttered. He'd found a way out....

"Lil? Dammit!" Her body lifted; Garrett cried out in agony. She was moving, sinking, floating. Garrett's voice was raspy against her ear.

"Get her out! Get her out now!"

Pain seemed to be ripped out of him as he lifted her high...hands grabbing her...voices. A huge cracking rumble. The cool, wet ground. Fresh air seeped into her nose and mouth, tickling her sleepy brain. Lily managed to open her eyes, saw a fireman with the name patch Cain race by—Mikey—and disappear into the pile of wreckage she'd come out of. Someone leaned over her, waved a light in her eyes. Lily fought the light, turned her head to see…to wait…

She'd been saved by her fireman, but he hadn't followed her out.

CHAPTER FOURTEEN

SOMEONE WAS GOING to get punched repeatedly. Whoever the hell was holding him down was going to get it hard.

Garrett twisted to the right, his back arching against the restraints. His arms flailed out, meeting nothing. Not pleased that he hadn't made contact with anyone, he tried to sit up, fists still clenched. He needed to get out of here. Lily was still down there…somewhere. He had to get her out, and then he was done. Never doing this again. Never letting himself get too close.… What if she was dead?

"Garrett. Settle down. Garrett…it's okay."

His eyes flew open, bright fluorescent lights glaring down at him. He froze. A cool stream of air tickled his nose, and behind it, the waft of antiseptic. Chief Grail was looking down at him, the whites of his eyes stark compared to his deep chocolate skin. "You need to settle down, son. You're going to rip your IV out."

IV? Garrett looked down at his body, realized an oxygen mask was over his face and pulled it away. His right arm was in a cast. A hospital gown covered the rest of him.

His eyes flickered around the room, his brain searching and finding the last moments he remembered. He'd shoved Lily out of the hole he'd created between the exposed foundation and the dirt. Once he'd started hitting it, the hole had opened on its own. While he'd been pushing Lily out, the soil had been falling in, settling against the beam. The pole hadn't been at a strong enough angle to support the beam and it had slid out, sending the beam down.

Mikey had come down after him. Wait…

Garrett grabbed Dabney's arm. "Mikey! Lily…"

Dabney patted his hand and sat on a stool next to the bed. "I just spoke with Lily's father. She has a concussion, some bruised ribs and lots of scrapes, but she'll be fine. Her CAT scan was clear for a more serious brain injury. They didn't have enough room here, so she was sent to Saint Mary's in Picard."

Tears filled Garrett's eyes and he didn't care. Relief was bittersweet because he wanted her safe and healthy, of course. But the absolute gratitude inside him spoke of so much more—of a love he'd never thought he'd feel, the fear that it was all going to disappear. And it almost had. He could have lost her.

The panic, the sheer terror, pulled him back to those moments his brother had taken the phone call about their father's death. He just... He couldn't do this.

He saw Brad, sickly and weak in a bed just like this one, the look of desperation on victims' faces when they found out their loved ones were dead.

He couldn't do this.

"Garrett, do you recall Mikey being inside the building with you?"

He nodded, wiping at his eyes. "Barely."

Dabney cleared his throat and put his elbows on his knees. "He took a blow to the chest. Probably from the beam that fell. He has a cardiac contusion. Basically, it's a huge bruise to his heart. He's fifty-fifty at the moment."

The tears rushed him now and Garrett didn't even try to stop them. "What? Why the hell... why the hell did he go in?"

"He pulled you out. Managed to crawl out before he collapsed. His pulse was so low, they had to shock him right there on the grass, but he's been holding his own ever since."

Garrett ran a hand over his face as he struggled to sit up. His chest ached, but with Dabney's help, he managed to get upright.

"Take me to him right now." He couldn't see Lily; she was too far away. But Mikey was right here.

"You just got out of surgery, Garrett."

He turned, ignoring the pain, and grabbed Dabney's shirt with his left hand.

"Right now, Chief. I need to see him."

Full-fledged anxiety threatened to overwhelm him. His saving grace came from knowing that Lily was safe and well. He couldn't imagine what he'd do if she were in danger, too.

Dabney pushed out of his chair, wagged a finger at Garrett, left and returned a minute later with a wheelchair.

He helped Garrett get into the chair, cracking a joke about not wanting to see his backside hanging out of the gown, and a few minutes later rolled him down the hall.

Garrett's mind was strangely numb, not allowing any one thought to really develop. But when Dabney pushed him into Mikey's dimly lit room, one thought became crystal clear: Mikey had better pull through.

"I'll be back in ten because I'm pretty sure I'm going to get in trouble for bringing you in here." Dabney parked Garrett near the bed and left. The room wore the scent of antiseptic like cologne—thick and equal parts comforting and stifling. Garrett leaned forward in his wheelchair, struggling a bit against the cast he wasn't used to.

Wires and tubes ran from Mikey's body to machines lined up next to the bed: intravenous lines, a chest tube, an oxygen mask and more that Garrett didn't know the names of. The monitors by Mikey's bed beeped and blipped, reminding him with every sound that he was in unfamiliar territory. He was helpless to do anything for his friend save for sit in this hard chair and be present.

And wait.

The pain of his own broken collarbone, dislocated shoulder and fractured arm were minimal in comparison to the ache in his heart. Mikey seemed peaceful, relaxed despite the fact he was teetering between life and death. Garrett pushed his bangs from his eyes as a burning sting prickled behind his lids.

What did a man think about when he lay there, just waiting to die? Regrets? Happy things…time lost and time well spent? Mikey was young, dedicated like the rest of them, but maybe more so. In the years Garrett had known him, Mikey had spent more time at the fire station and taking more extra shifts than anyone else. He somehow divided his time between that and taking care of his brother. He'd never married, didn't date much. Hell, there probably hadn't been time. He'd been too dedicated to his family and the job—the job that might end up killing him.

Garrett's nostrils flared as he sucked back a

thick wall of emotion. Mikey had come into the house for him. It could easily have been him on that hospital bed fighting for his life. Or Lily.

That last moment of lifting Lily out of the hole and wrenching himself out behind her could have been the end of him—if he'd been a second later. If he'd taken one more moment to consider what he was doing, he would have been crushed. All the things he was holding out for—the life he'd come to love so much—gone.

Just like that. All his fears had looked him in the face with blinding clarity. He was in love with Lily and he loved Mikey like a brother, and he'd been a hair away from losing them both. Garrett put his good hand on Mikey's arm and gave it a squeeze. God, how did people go through this emotion every day? How was this fair to Lily? There was no way to build a life with this kind of uncertainty.

Some men could do it. Some men could send their families out into the world and be satisfied with 99 percent confidence that they'd make it home safe and sound. But Garrett knew better. He knew what was out there—what was waiting to take it all away. The job was a part of him, one he couldn't give up without losing a big chunk of himself. But it came with knowing too much, fearing too much. He wasn't man enough to get over that fear.

It would consume him, every moment of every day.

He couldn't ask Lily to be part of his crazy world. Garrett reached out and stroked the back of Mikey's hand. Mikey's eyelids fluttered but didn't open as he rolled his head toward Garrett and moaned softly.

"Hey, Mikey, we've got darts on Friday. Can't play without you." It was a silly thing to say, but Garrett couldn't think of anything else that wouldn't make him start bawling like a baby.

Mikey gave a weak laugh. Even that small effort made his pallor increase. Garrett jerked as a cool, shaky hand slid into his own. He squeezed gently, lovingly, recognizing that the once-strong fingers felt fragile to his touch.

"Gonna…have to sit…this one out, buddy."

Mikey's eyes opened; their gazes caught, held. Wordlessly, Garrett nodded. He didn't stop the tear that spilled over his lower lashes and burned his cheek. When a second tear followed, and then a third, Garrett let the moisture pool beside his lip. Mikey worked in a small, shuddering inhale, the blue tinge around his mouth shocking against the gray pale of his face.

"You…you look after Bodie for me…" The urgency in Mikey's voice matched the sudden panic in his eyes. Ignoring the pain in his shoulder and neck, Garrett grasped Mikey's other hand and clung tight.

Garrett's voice shook. "Like a brother, man. Like a brother. I promise, Mikey."

"K...okay." Mikey's chest rose and fell hard as he struggled to take a breath. "Thanks."

Thanks? No way should Mikey be thanking him for anything. It was the other way around. He wanted to say something deep and meaningful, but doing so would be like admitting defeat, and he wasn't ready to give up on Mikey yet. There would never be a time he was ready for that.

"At least they didn't shave your pretty hair."

That drew a wan smile. How Mikey's face had grown so gaunt in just a few hours, Garrett had no idea. It was a sign, he supposed, that his friend's heart hadn't quite decided whether or not it was ready to admit defeat. Desperate now, Garrett squeezed Mikey's hand as hard as he dared. "Michael Cain, thank you for coming after me."

Mikey gave a tiny nod. "Lily?"

"At the hospital in Picard. She'll be just fine." He hoped. He wouldn't believe it until he saw her for himself. Seeing her... What would that do to him? To her? The memory of her prone, motionless body on the rubble sent dread over his spine.

"When's...the wedding?" Mikey's mouth moved up in a smile.

It was a joke, but it hit home. Especially coming from Mikey, who knew how Garrett felt about marriage. Everything that had just happened only reinforced why he couldn't have a family. One big sob lodged in his chest. It took him a moment to compose himself enough to speak.

"Ah, come on, man. You know I can't."

Mikey grunted. Soft footsteps sounded behind Garrett as a nurse walked in. She gave him a suspicious glance but didn't shoo him out. She quietly checked the monitors, her presence comforting in that if something went wrong, she'd know what to do.

Mikey curled a finger, indicating that Garrett come closer. He did the best he could between the wheelchair, the cast and the pain. Mikey's voice was so soft, Garrett had to listen closely.

"Bodie left a big...piece of himself on Iraqi soil. Even...if he'd left it *all* there...he'd've left the biggest piece...right here." Mikey patted his chest over his heart with a slow hand. "Can't stop bad things, Garrett, but if you leave enough good stuff behind...it evens out. You love Lily. That's damn good, brother. Damn good."

Mikey's voice trailed away, his chest rising and falling softly. The beeps of the machines became steady music.

Garrett bowed his head and let his mind go numb again. He held Mikey's hand, saying a prayer for his friend's damn fine heart and sat awhile.

LILY NEEDED TO see Garrett the way she needed to breathe. Being trapped in that hospital bed, wanting to see Garrett—needing to go to him and not being able to—was nearly as bad as being in the basement as debris rained down.

She'd tried calling his cell phone with no luck, and the hospital wouldn't put her through to his room when she'd called there. It was only because Doug had gotten through to the Danbury fire chief that Lily knew that Garrett had had surgery to repair his shoulder and collarbone. Her father had kept reassuring her that Garrett was doing well. It was the only thing that calmed her enough not to bolt out of the hospital against medical advice.

She'd almost lost him. That thought played in her mind on constant repeat. Just knowing how close Garrett had come to being seriously injured—or worse—stripped down the last of Lily's hang-ups. Whatever bad memories he might bring up could and *would* be replaced. Because she loved him, and she wasn't fool enough to keep it to herself anymore. Not after this. She'd been released this morning with steroids and an inhaler for her smoke-inflamed lungs, and was more than ready to make sure Garrett was okay. And to tell him what was in her heart.

Once again, Garrett had been by her side during a life-changing event. Only this time, he'd held her hand. And saved her life.

Hero. She'd scoffed at that term once, at the Throwing Aces when the firemen had paraded around in their department T-shirts. How her perspective had changed, and rightly so. How could she ever thank him for what he'd done?

Between Macy, Doug and her brother's constant fussing, it was hard to plan what she was going to say to Garrett. Right now, the culprit was Lincoln. She didn't want him hovering over her, but he refused to back off. He'd arrived in Picard yesterday, and while it was nice to have her twin brother around to pamper her, Lily wanted to do this alone.

The Danbury hospital was a bustle of activity even now, two days after the tornado. Lily stopped at the nurses' station on level three and inquired for Garrett's room.

"Room 302, down the hall, first on your left."

Lincoln put a hand on her back to usher her that way, but Lily stalled.

"Linc, I'd like to go alone."

Seeing Garrett for the first time since he'd rescued her seemed too personal to experience with her family around. Maybe it was silly, but she'd never been one to show much emotion in front of other people, and she had no idea how she'd react right now.

"I'll walk you to the door, and then I'll go get some coffee. You're still a bit unsteady, sis. Don't buck me on this."

He'd tried to get her into a wheelchair four times since they walked into the hospital, but she'd refused. Besides a lingering mild headache and a lot of aches and pains, she felt fine. Lily forced herself to take normal steps down the hall, even though her body was telling her to run. Each step took an eternity, but then she was there, outside the door.

Her pulse thrummed harder as she reached the handle.

"Thanks, Linc."

Her brother's tall frame and caring blue eyes had been just the comfort she'd needed. He was tired and mussed, dark hair in a spiky arrangement on his head. The smudges beneath his eyes were a testament to how well he'd handled this latest disaster. Once again, Lincoln had spent countless hours awake and by her side to pull her through turmoil.

He took a step back and nodded for her to go inside.

"Love you," Lincoln whispered with a wink right before she entered the shadowed room.

"Garrett?"

Goose bumps rose on her forearms as she spotted him sitting in the middle of the bed, his back to her while he faced the window across the room. He tried to turn to the sound of her voice, the movement jerky and stilted. Lily rushed to his side, taking in the cast and sling on his right arm and the bandage completely covering his left.

He reached for her without a word, drew her between his knees with a grunt as she fell against his chest. His arm came around her and Lily clung to him as hard as she dared without causing him pain. She held back tears, just absorbed the feel of his breathing and the sturdy, warm muscles beneath his soft T-shirt. Garrett pressed his cheek against her hair, the stubble on his jaw scratchy against her temple. She let her mind go blank as they embraced. Being alive, being here in his arms was enough.

"You're okay?" His voice was gravelly and dry.

She just nodded, not willing to pull away to look at him. She leaned closer and his legs clamped gently around her thighs.

"I was so worried about you," she whispered. "I couldn't get through on the phone."

He stroked her hair with his bandaged hand.

"I know. Me, either. But when Chief told me you were okay, I was…"

"Relieved? Same here. It had to be enough until I could get here."

Lily pulled reluctantly away as her back began to ache from the angle of their embrace. Garrett's face was shadowed, the lines and dips harder than she remembered. The deep sadness in his eyes was so foreign to his usual relaxed nature.

"I realized something." Lily cupped his face between her hands and tipped her forehead to his. "Every time I look at you, I see the man who crossed my path not once, but twice. The first time when I thought my world was ending, and the second time when I was ready to start over. I see a person who represents closure and fresh starts. I want that fresh start, with you."

A shudder went through him, and Lily rubbed his arms with her hands as if she could stop it. He said nothing, just kept his head down. Dread filled her that maybe she'd said too much too soon. He was still recovering from the trauma of being nearly buried alive. Yet holding her feelings back had seemed pointless. Especially after what they'd been through.

"Garrett, what's wrong?"

He scoffed a little and tried to look away, but she held him firm.

"What's not wrong?" His tone was bitter.

Between the entrapment and the aftermath of the storm, his surgery and probably a hefty dose of discomfort, Lily had expected some change in him. But the devastation in his expression was more than she'd imagined.

"Garrett." She tried to coax him. "I don't know how to thank you enough for what you did."

He closed his eyes and shook his head. This wasn't Garrett—the strong, sexy fireman who played bartender and swept humanity off their feet with a smile. This was a broken man.

"I failed you, Lily. Do you know that?" His eyes were stone when they met hers.

She opened her mouth to speak, but he silenced her with a tortured look.

"I should have looked for you sooner. I was at the Ashden building less than an hour after the twister hit and never even considered anyone might be inside. I was there six hours before you finally got out." She straightened and tried to touch him, but he pulled back.

"Why are you blaming yourself? It wasn't…it wasn't your fault."

His head tilted to the side as he looked at her. "I could have saved you sooner, and Mikey, too."

Lily's gut bottomed out. "What happened to Mikey?"

She racked her brain, trying to recall seeing Mikey at all. Maybe she'd gotten a glimpse of him running by, but she wasn't sure. Everything that had happened after she'd gotten out of the rubble was a blur reduced to the paramedics giving her oxygen and checking her over. She'd fallen into a tailspin of memories in that moment about the last time she'd looked up into the faces of nameless paramedics and the thought that she'd had enough disaster for two lifetimes.

"He got hit in the chest by a beam and he's fighting for his life." Garrett slid off the bed with a grimace and a deep, low groan. Lily stepped in to help him somehow, but he waved her off.

"See, this is the thing, Lily. This is the thing I've been avoiding all these years—the bad stuff that happens to the people you love. I didn't want to take on anything more…didn't want to add to the worry. But I did."

A hot tear rolled down her cheek. The finality in his tone spoke for him; he didn't need to say any more. They'd chased each other in their own ways, and came together with a passion that was more than physical. But it wasn't enough… maybe it was too much. Either way, she knew the outcome.

"What are you saying?"

His cheeks flushed red. "That I can't do this, Lily! I can't worry about you…and Mikey and Brad and everyone else in this goddamn town. I can't. *I won't!* God, I almost lost you. Don't you see? It's my biggest fear—the woman I love being taken away, and there it was, right in front of me."

He sank back onto the bed and tried to run his left hand through his hair; he cursed when his bandaged fingers couldn't do anything.

After Katja's death, Lily had realized she'd run purely on emotion. The high kind of emotion that could easily make a person drive into a brick wall if it wasn't controlled, or drink a six-pack of Red Bull to avoid falling asleep. Nothing good ever came from that kind of emotion. She recognized this same emotion in Garrett now because she'd been there, just a year ago.

She stepped into him, taking his shoulders and pressing in with her fingers so he couldn't shrug her off.

"I love you."

His shoulders moved in a helpless shrug. "No… we got caught up in each other, Lily. It was the joy of the chase. That's all."

"Garrett…"

"I've never had a woman walk away from me, Lily. I chased you until I got you. That's all. I never lose, remember?"

Another tear raced down her cheek, followed by a constant stream of its friends. He was hurting. So was she, but it was clear he wanted to break free. Her head knew he was lying and acting out because of stress, but her heart didn't want to look at it that way.

"Please, just go. Now that I know you're all right...please."

The repetition of the word *please* did it—sent Lily over the edge from quiet tears into full-blown crying. She grabbed a tissue from the table next to him, not caring how badly her hand shook.

Garrett's head was down, his shoulders tight. She placed a soft, simple kiss on his head and hurried to the door. She paused before she turned the handle. His body was a shadowy figure once again, but she soaked it up, committed it to memory.

"Garrett," she said just loudly enough for him to hear. "When your glass gets too heavy to hold, don't forget to put it down." And she walked out.

Lincoln was there, waiting, his face displaying that he'd heard every word. Lily wanted to be angry that he hadn't backed off the way she'd asked him to, but couldn't. Because when he gathered her up, his comfort was exactly what she needed as her world refused to stop falling apart.

CHAPTER FIFTEEN

IT HURT GARRETT to move, to breathe and to think. But mostly it hurt to remember what he'd said to Lily. In his mind, he'd been doing the right thing by pushing her away. It was for her own protection. It was too risky to be with a firefighter; hadn't he just proved that by nearly getting buried alive? The problem was that the old arguments weren't as convincing as they'd once been.

He didn't believe his old standby reasons for keeping his heart to himself. Not after facing his fears head-on and coming out alive. Lily was fine. He was fine. They'd come through what had been thrown at them and they were okay. And really, what was the alternative? To deny that he'd ever felt anything for her? That he didn't love her?

That was a cop-out. He just didn't know if he could make it up to her after what he'd said.

Garrett ran a hand through his hair and groaned as he rose from the edge of the bed. A sound by the door made him hope that the nurse had arrived with his discharge papers. Roan should be

here soon to drive him home. But when he looked
up, Garrett saw a tall man standing in the doorway. The serious look on his face was familiar—
it was the same one Doug Ashden wore.

"Garrett?" the man inquired, coming forward
with an outstretched hand. "Lincoln Ashden."

Great. Lily's brother.

They shook hands, the simple movement sending a sharp pain through Garrett's side. The
similarities between the siblings were painfully
apparent. They had the same hair, the same blue
eyes. A sudden lick of panic hit him.

"Is Lily okay?"

Maybe her concussion had been worse than
they'd thought. What if something had happened
after she'd gone home?

Lincoln's eyes narrowed, and, though the foot
of the bed was between them, Garrett had the
sensation that the other man was towering over
him. He wasn't easily intimidated, but the whole
pissed-off-brother thing was getting the job done.

"Okay is relative. Physically, she's fine. Emotionally, she's holding her own."

Thank goodness. Garrett had the feeling that
saying the wrong thing might cause further damage to his health, so he waited. Lincoln tapped
his thumb against his lips, giving Garrett a blatant once-over.

"This town is going to need Ashden Construction when it comes time to rebuild," Lincoln said. "My father and Lily are needed here, in this community where they have roots. Yet she still insists on going to Nashville with me. Any idea why she might do that?"

The thought of Lily leaving before he had a chance to talk to her gutted Garrett.

"I have a pretty good guess."

Lincoln nodded. "I was here the other day. I heard every word you said to her. That was a cowardly way out."

Garrett looked away, the pain in his chest making it hard to breathe. "I deserve that."

"No, you deserve more than that. Frankly, I'm tired of the people in Lily's life hiding their feelings from her. She's gone through hell with our father and with her ex-fiancé. Now you." Lincoln stopped inches from Garrett, his big arms crossed. "Tell me—are you in love with my sister?"

He couldn't answer that quickly enough. "Yes. Hell, yes."

Lincoln glared at him a moment longer before a rush of relief went over his face. A small smile tugged at his lips.

"Then you need to help me figure out a way to make her stay. I have a plan, but I need to know that you're in. All in. For Lily."

Garrett had been all in firefighting and taking

care of his uncle, running the bar and watching out for his friends and family. And as much as he held all of that close to his heart, he'd never been as committed to anything, to anyone, as he was to Lily. He knew that now.

Garrett grabbed Lincoln's wrist, his heart pounding. "Whatever we have to do. I can't lose her now."

"GOT IT, GIRLIE?"

"Yeah."

Lily held a box and reached for the handle of a fabric bag at her feet. She wobbled a little, the movement sending a dizzy streak through her. Doug was at her side immediately, a hand on her back, the concern he'd worn since she'd been hurt deeper than ever.

She'd been surrounded by everyone she cared about both in the hospital and her new residence at Doug's place. Everyone but Garrett. Lincoln was staying a few more days, having handed off management of the Nashville office to his assistant, and Macy made frequent stops to fuss over her. Doug had been a constant, which was almost as irritating as it was touching.

And Garrett—she felt him with her, in a strange way, though she hadn't heard from him or seen him since leaving his hospital room a week ago. The way they'd parted was like a knife constantly twisting in her gut. Lincoln and Macy encouraged her to give it time, and there seemed to be a lot of that lately.

Lincoln had heard around town that Mikey was recovering, another thing to add to her relief pile. All the good things aside, trying not to be depressed about the town was hard.

The east end of Danbury was devastated. Homes were nothing but piles of tinder and brick, traffic lights lay like matchsticks, vehicles were crushed and tipped. The roads had mostly been cleared, allowing people the chance to get to what was left of their homes and look for treasures that had been left behind. Seeing the Ashden building was surreal. They'd found her car upside down a block away, slammed into what was left of the hair salon.

With the business destroyed and a third of the town in rubble, time seemed to go at a molasses pace in Danbury. The Red Cross had come in to offer aid. The disaster tent was set up on the edge of the Throwing Aces parking lot. Lily had made Doug drive her past, but Garrett's truck wasn't there. She didn't bother going by the fire station, because torturing herself with the bar had been enough.

Maybe he truly didn't want her and what he'd said was true—he'd chased her because he wasn't going to lose. Maybe he was lying because of stress. Regardless, she had to work on herself, just like she had the last time. If she didn't stay on top of her emotions and her reactions to the world, to life, she'd shut down again. She'd do anything to keep that from happening.

Lily could barely recall her time underneath the destroyed building—realized the concussion she'd had had kept her in a dreamlike state for much of it. The only thing she remembered with clarity was Garrett reaching his bleeding hand through the hole to grab her own, and how tightly he'd grabbed on when she'd pressed her palm to his.

Garrett had saved her, but he'd done so much more. In his own way, he'd brought all the things she'd needed to move on with her life. She'd give him everything she had if he'd let her. Facing his rejection after everything they'd been through…

She caught Doug's concerned look out of the corner of her eyes. "I'm okay, Dad. Let's go inside."

She waited for him to unlock the door of the office space he'd rented in a strip mall on the west side of town. For blocks and blocks, this end of Danbury was exactly the way it had been before the tornado touched down. Save for some litter and trees down, everything was the same here.

Knowing that homes and businesses would need help rebuilding, Doug had found this space for them to set up shop until they could find a new building. Luckily, their computer records were hosted by a third party, so all their documents could be recovered. They'd made a trip back to Picard that morning to purchase a couple of laptops and some office supplies.

Despite the devastation, life and business had to go on. As Doug always said, work over emotions. She'd spent the past few days on her father's couch in his tornado-untouched apartment. Despite the minor headaches she had and the soreness in every muscle, Lily was ready to get to work. Her mind needed something to do until life could resume a sense of normalcy.

Doug and Lincoln had left her in the new office yesterday while they'd met with a client, the first to call them up since the devastation. She'd spent the day setting up what few office supplies they'd had and finding things to do to keep her mind off Garrett. Knowing more work would be coming in so she could continue to do just that was a blessing.

She and Doug made a couple more trips to the truck until everything was unloaded. He sighed and glowered at the new pile of things they now had to unpack and set up.

"Where's Lincoln, exactly?" Lily inquired with a laugh, toeing a box with a file cabinet inside. "We could use him about now."

Doug put his hands on his hips. "Yes, we could."

They got to work unpacking the computers, and Doug rearranged the desks and chairs she'd so carefully arranged yesterday. Lily shook her head when she realized the desks were now set so they'd be facing each other when sitting down.

"No way am I looking at your ugly mug all day, Doug."

He stopped pulling a rolling chair across the room to look at her. "How about Dad?"

"What?"

Doug gave the chair a shove in the direction of his desk and put a hand on her shoulder. His black-framed glasses slid down his nose, but he didn't push them up like he always did. Instead, he smiled. The first real smile she'd seen out of him in years.

"I'd like it better if you'd call me Dad."

Lily gripped his arm to steady herself. He'd never requested that before, not even when she was a teenager and he could have put his foot down about the first-name thing. She wanted to respond, but she couldn't. So she nodded instead.

He chucked her under the chin. "What do you say to a walk, Lily? I could use the air."

"Sounds good."

The recent tumultuous weather had smoothed out, leaving behind sunshine and clear skies. Lily put a few odds and ends away while her dad rummaged around. They stepped out into the sun, started down the sidewalk. She glanced at the small bag Doug had over his shoulder.

"What's in there?"

"Water," he replied quickly. "You know, that boy of yours has called me a couple times. I can't figure out why he won't just call you. Want to tell me about it?"

This was new, Doug caring. And though it shouldn't matter, because Garrett had turned her away, she had to ask.

"He's not my boy, Dad. Just a friend." Heck, she didn't even know if that was true. "What did he want?"

Doug looked up at the sky. "To know how you're doing."

Lily slowed her pace. "Oh. Well…how is he doing?"

Doug pulled her to a stop on the sidewalk. "Okay, look, your *friend* bailed me out of jail right before the tornado hit."

She whipped him a look. "What?"

"See, when Rob left you, I just figured if I stayed out of it, you'd…get over it faster. You never wanted my advice when you were younger, so I didn't figure you would have wanted it when Rob walked out, either. The thing is, I should have given it to you anyway, because then maybe you would have known how much I do love you.

And maybe it would have helped you to see that Garrett is an outstanding young man with a lot going on in his head right now."

Lily paused on the sidewalk. "Dad..."

Doug looped his left arm through her right and hugged her.

"I'm sorry, Lily. I'm sorry for not being there when you were younger, for shutting you out after Katja died. I didn't know how... I should have done better. I know that. God, I almost lost you twice and I can't be that man anymore."

They embraced as traffic and people went by, and the sun warmed Lily's back while Doug warmed her heart. She finally pulled away before the waterworks started. It took two accidents to finally get true feelings out of the man, but here it was.

"Thank you. I've waited years for you to open up to me."

Lily narrowed her eyes in thought. This was it, the final closure. All the things that had been left open-ended after Katja's death were now re-solved: Rob, her father's indifference, her own ability to deal with losing her sister. A clean slate—was that what this was?

They resumed walking, her soul so light she could have floated away. Except for one little weight. The one Garrett had planted inside her, because there was no closure there. Not yet.

"So…you didn't say why you were in jail."

Doug led her across the street and around a corner. "Got arrested for knocking Rob in the face when he came to get the ring."

Lily's mouth fell open. "You did not!"

"Should have done it a year ago."

Lily laughed and leaned her head on her dad's shoulder, walking in step with him for another block until she realized where they were.

Businesses faded away into a quiet stretch of street. Concrete turned to grass as they approached the old shoe factory. Nestled on an off-street half-acre plot, the historic redbrick building was flanked by trees and a small creek along the north side. Doug led her up the cobblestone walk, where she noticed the Frasier for-sale sign near the entrance had a red bow tied to it.

The door opened and Garrett came out onto the walk with Lincoln right behind. His hair shone in fractured gold tones; the fullness of his mouth curved into a smile. His right arm was in a sling. The end of a tan-colored cast covered his hand and up over what she could see of his shoulder. Lily stopped in the middle of the walk as his gaze landed on her and a tiny smile lifted his lips.

Doug met Garrett with a handshake. He

reached into the small bag and produced a beer and a white envelope. "I figured I owed you a beer for your bail money. I'll take them inside for you."

They shook again, and then Doug and Lincoln disappeared inside the shoe factory. Leaving her alone, staring at Garrett and not knowing what to say. What to feel.

"Hey," he said, coming down the walk to meet her, his body language betraying that he was feeling as unsure as she was. "How are you, Lil?"

His eyes raked over her. He stopped close enough to touch her...close enough to reach out and pull her against him, but he didn't.

"Confused," she admitted. She glanced around. "What's going on?"

He looked good, considering. The hardness on his face was gone, replaced with the boyish good looks that got him anything he set his sights on. Including her heart.

"Planning." He turned back toward the building. "Lots and lots of planning that won't mean a damn thing without you."

Garrett stepped into her then, his left arm looping around her and bringing her against him. Lily let out the breath she didn't know she'd been holding as a weightless sensation claimed her legs. His lips pressed against her temple, her cheek.

"I panicked, Lily. I don't want it to sound like a cop-out, but that's what it was. Pure panic."

She swallowed hard, conflicted. She'd known, of course, that what they'd gone through had influenced the harsh things he'd said. But it didn't take the sting away.

His lips brushed her ear. "I've never said this to another woman, and I never want to say it to anyone but you, so listen close. I love you."

Lily squeezed her eyes shut, wondering if her brain had slipped into some kind of postconcussion delirium. His lips found hers, and she was willing, though her better judgment warned her to take it slow. Her lips parted to allow the sweep and tangle of his tongue with hers. His taste and warmth and the familiar feel of his body pressed against hers was real. It was all so real.

"I thought you said you couldn't...you won't." The stubble on his jaw scratched her fingers when she touched his cheek.

"You're a very stubborn, persuasive woman. And I want to. I want this, all of it. In the basement, all I could think of was that I'd been given this opportunity, this one perfect woman, and I was going to lose her. It was the first time in my life I'd been terrified to let go. Yes, I'm scared, but I want you too much to let it rule me."

Lily turned her cheek to his chest and held him tightly. "I love you, too."

Garrett ran his fingers over the tattoo on her arm. The sensation of his touch lit a fire on her skin and in her soul, making her act on the sweeter side of pure emotion and throw her arms around his neck. He groaned, maybe from pain, but it was hard to tell. The loving way he held her said he didn't care. He fit her so well—how his body complemented hers as they embraced, the way his humor and charm offset her stubbornness. And he was hers.

They could have a clean slate, together.

Garrett ran a hand between her shoulder blades and over her back. "So the shoe factory was for sale, as you know. Your brother came to see me in the hospital. Gave me a pep talk, you could say." He winked as Lily pulled back, stunned.

"He did?"

"Yeah, after what I said to you when you came to see me... Let's just say I deserved every bit of what Lincoln had to say. I needed to hear it, Lily. After that, we just started talking and out came his ideas for this place. It became very apparent that the acreage and the square footage of the building would make both our dreams possible. There's enough space for Ashden Construction offices and an architectural showroom with a minibar and snack kitchen, provided by the Throwing Aces. Win-win."

She looked at the bow on the for-sale sign, the emotion in her chest full and glorious. "But Sylvia owns this!"

Garrett ran his fingers through her hair. "Mmm, seems your father is a very good negotiator. In fact, I think they might be going out on a date."

"Shut up!" She gave him a gentle slap on the chest.

Garrett shrugged and kissed her again. Longer. Pulling her against him tighter until they both winced from their injuries and collective bruises. She laughed as she leaned back, the sun warming them both.

He ran a finger down her cheek before leading her down the walk toward the front door. "Is this what you want, Lily?"

Oh, hell yes, it is. "I still want to go to Nashville. Spend some time at Lincoln's and see the sights."

Garrett draped his good arm over her shoulders and led her toward the front door.

"I'll follow you anywhere that makes you happy."

She stopped and plucked the bow off the for-sale sign and stuck it to Garrett's chest. "In that case, I think Hawaii sounds good, too."

He opened the door, urging her toward the beginning of a whole new life.

"Only if you promise to bring my favorite coconut bra." His eyes raked over her chest right before he shook his head with a wicked gleam in his eyes. "On second thought, that corset would work...."

* * * * *

LARGER-PRINT BOOKS!

GET 2 FREE LARGER-PRINT NOVELS PLUS
2 FREE GIFTS!

🜚 HARLEQUIN®

Romance

From the Heart, For the Heart

LARGER-PRINT BOOKS!

LARGER-PRINT BOOKS!
GET 2 FREE LARGER-PRINT NOVELS PLUS
2 FREE GIFTS!

⬧ HARLEQUIN®

INTRIGUE®

BREATHTAKING ROMANTIC SUSPENSE

YES! Please send me 2 FREE LARGER-PRINT Harlequin Intrigue® novels and my 2 FREE gifts (gifts are worth about $10). After receiving them, if I don't wish to receive any more books, I can return the shipping statement marked "cancel." If I don't cancel, I will receive 6 brand-new novels every month and be billed just $5.49 per book in the U.S. or $5.99 per book in Canada. That's a saving of at least 13% off the cover price! It's quite a bargain! Shipping and handling is just 50¢ per book in the U.S. and 75¢ per book in Canada.* I understand that accepting the 2 free books and gifts places me under no obligation to buy anything. I can always return a shipment and cancel at any time. Even if I never buy another book, the two free books and gifts are mine to keep forever.

199/399 HDN F42Y

Name	(PLEASE PRINT)
Address	Apt. #
City	State/Prov. Zip/Postal Code

Signature (if under 18, a parent or guardian must sign)

Mail to the Harlequin® Reader Service:
IN U.S.A.: P.O. Box 1867, Buffalo, NY 14240-1867
IN CANADA: P.O. Box 609, Fort Erie, Ontario L2A 5X3

**Are you a subscriber to Harlequin Intrigue books
and want to receive the larger-print edition?
Call 1-800-873-8635 today or visit www.ReaderService.com.**

* Terms and prices subject to change without notice. Prices do not include applicable taxes. Sales tax applicable in N.Y. Canadian residents will be charged applicable taxes. Offer not valid in Quebec. This offer is limited to one order per household. Not valid for current subscribers to Harlequin Intrigue Larger-Print books. All orders subject to credit approval. Credit or debit balances in a customer's account(s) may be offset by any other outstanding balance owed by or to the customer. Please allow 4 to 6 weeks for delivery. Offer available while quantities last.

Your Privacy—The Harlequin® Reader Service is committed to protecting your privacy. Our Privacy Policy is available online at www.ReaderService.com or upon request from the Harlequin Reader Service.

We make a portion of our mailing list available to reputable third parties that offer products we believe may interest you. If you prefer that we not exchange your name with third parties, or if you wish to clarify or modify your communication preferences, please visit us at www.ReaderService.com/consumerchoice or write to us at Harlequin Reader Service Preference Service, P.O. Box 9062, Buffalo, NY 14269. Include your complete name and address.

HILP13R